W9-ACU-115

WELCOME

Praise for *When I Meet You*

"Readers are in for a top-notch mystery in *When I Meet You*. Using a stepping-stone trail of documents, photographs, and letters to bridge past and present, Olivia Newport delivers a dual time line tale of intrigue. From the timeless setting of a mystery bound by train journey, to the involvement of Pinkerton agents and passengers of questionable identity, this well-researched story is sure to carry readers away!"

–Amanda Dykes, author of *Whose Waves These Are*

"Olivia Newport has penned both a lively and cozy story in *When I Meet You*. Fans of family origins and faith will love this dual time line exploration of history. An element of mystery and romance (not to mention mouthwateringly scrumptious foods!) add to this delightful read. Truly a pleasant story with a fantastic setting readers are sure to enjoy!"

–Heidi Chiavaroli, award-winning author of *The Tea Chest*

"An ancestral mystery told in split-time format, *When I Meet You* is a charming book that will leave readers fascinated and intrigued to discover the prologues of their own stories."

–Sarah Monzon, award-winning author of the
Carrington Family time-slip series

WHEN I MEET YOU

Olivia Newport

SHILOH RUN PRESS

An Imprint of Barbour Publishing, Inc.

© 2020 by Olivia Newport

Print ISBN 978-1-68322-996-4

eBook Editions:
Adobe Digital Edition (.epub) 978-1-64352-585-3
Kindle and MobiPocket Edition (.prc) 978-1-64352-586-0

All rights reserved. No part of this publication may be reproduced or transmitted for commercial purposes, except for brief quotations in printed reviews, without written permission of the publisher.

All scripture quotations are taken from the King James Version of the Bible.

This book is a work of fiction. Names, characters, places, and incidents are either products of the author's imagination or used fictitiously. Any similarity to actual people, organizations, and/or events is purely coincidental.

Cover design: Faceout Studio, www.faceoutstudio.com

Published by Shiloh Run Press, an imprint of Barbour Publishing, Inc., 1810 Barbour Drive, Uhrichsville, Ohio 44683, www.shilohrunpress.com

Our mission is to inspire the world with the life-changing message of the Bible.

 Member of the
Evangelical Christian
Publishers Association

Printed in Canada.

DEDICATION

*For Kara, an unflagging cheerleader for my writing
who will drop everything for a trip to Canyon Mines.
When I met you was a happy day. I love you.*

CHAPTER ONE

J illian supposed she should be grateful he hadn't gagged and blindfolded her when he intruded into her home office, snatched her, and stuffed her in the truck. She'd already been out for a morning run and wasn't planning to spend all of Saturday afternoon working. Tidying up was all she had in mind. And then he burst in, and now she was strapped into the front seat without her phone as the truck rolled out of town.

She gripped the passenger door armrest. He clicked the power button to lock all the doors.

"Dad. You can tell me where we're going." Jillian side-eyed her father. "I'm hardly going to leap out of a moving vehicle on the highway."

"Why do you demand to know every detail about everything?"

From behind the steering wheel of his pickup, which he'd been driving so long he talked about it like an old friend, Nolan grinned at Jillian with green eyes that mirrored hers. Spring mountain sunlight bounced off his pupils, and he reached in the console for his dark glasses and set them on his face. In his midfifties, he still cut a fit, youthful figure. Rediscovering skiing over the winter, after a long hiatus, had suited him.

"And why do you insist on doing everything by the seat of your pants?" Jillian raised both hands to draw her long, dark waves under control behind her neck. He hadn't given her a chance to grab a band or clip before leaving the house, a circumstance she was likely to regret if there was any wind once they were out of the truck at their mystery destination.

Her retort was halfhearted. Who could complain about a Saturday afternoon drive on a day like this? The rainy mid-April week was behind them, the bounty from the sky having nourished the earth and coaxed forth undulating, ripe, burgeoning greens of the season. They were barely out of Canyon Mines, so the mountains still cradled them, and a mammoth burning flare of sunlight radiated across the landscape. Immaculate snow lingered on the shoulders of the Rockies. The views, as they did on so many days when she paused from her work to raise her eyes to the dazzling Colorado terrain, tugged at her spirit.

"I promise you'll like it," Nolan said. "You have to admit I know you well."

"The people stipulate to that point, Your Honor."

"Someday I might give up lawyering and become a judge and you'll really have to use that title with me."

"And I would do so proudly," Jillian said. "Now let's see. Heading east. Probably downtown Denver." Unless they would turn north to her Duffy grandparents' home once they got to I-25.

"Maybe, maybe not."

"So it is Denver."

"You think you're so smart."

"I am smart."

"The court stipulates to that point."

"What's going on in Denver that we need to go today?"

"A museum. You like museums. And you've never been to this one."

"Why not? Did I have a deprived childhood?"

"Hardly. I always let you bring home souvenirs, and you'll get a doozy today."

"Okay, you've got me curious."

"Good. You need to get out more."

"We're both going to St. Louis in a few weeks for Tucker and Laurie Beth's wedding," she pointed out. Jillian had already started on the complex genealogy project Tucker hired her for—which would likely take years for the number of individuals involved. In addition to the nuptials, visiting St. Louis meant she would see where the story of Tucker's family history first tangled in the baby snatching that had nearly undone him when he found out.

"And we'll have a spectacular time," Nolan said, "but we have our own great city right here with history and culture and all the good stuff. You liked it when you went to college."

"I still do. I just haven't had a lot of reason to come down lately."

"Well, today you do." Nolan merged into a faster lane and accelerated.

"I have a feeling there's a story here," Jillian said.

With her dad, there was always a story. People liked to talk to Nolan.

He was one of those people who made friends wherever he went and stuck in people's minds. In his work as a family law attorney and legal mediator, he met a variety of people other than his clients, but he could still drop into a random coffee shop or a hardware store and come out having met four new people—and probably would talk with them long enough to find a common connection with at least one. Shops, parties, sporting events, business meetings. People remembered Nolan Duffy. He thrived on it. Not Jillian. She inherited some sort of recessive introvert gene—and another one for preferring a well-ordered life.

"The curator called me," Nolan said.

"And how do you know a museum curator?"

He shrugged. "We had coffee once."

That meant Nolan had chatted with the curator in the line ordering coffee or something else equally ordinary and forgettable to most people.

"And?" Jillian said.

"And he has a situation he thinks may require legal attention. Or at least he'd like to probe a legal opinion about the advisability of legal representation around matters of liability and financial consequence."

"Now that's legal speak if ever I've heard it."

"Do not mock my profession, young lady."

"Never!" Jillian laughed. "What does this have to do with me? Or a souvenir? Is this all just an excuse to get me out of the house?"

"What if it is? It's a fine day for a drive, and I enjoy your company."

"You don't have to charm me. I already love you."

"Oh, right."

"It's Saturday. And you'll be in Denver on Monday. Why the special trip?"

"Because I wanted to bring you along, obviously."

"Dad."

Nolan checked his mirrors and changed lanes again. Clearly they were headed to Denver now.

"Here's what I know," he said. "It's not much. Years ago—decades, I think—the museum received a trunk that was abandoned at Union Station."

"Decades?"

He nodded. "The curator is relatively recent, but the museum is about fifty years old. He's not at all sure of the story, but from what he can tell, the trunk arrived at Union Station over a hundred years ago and somehow was separated from its owner."

"Surely the railroad would have had a procedure for unclaimed luggage."

"We don't know what happened, Jilly."

"How did the museum get the trunk?"

"I don't know that either. He didn't say. I'm not sure he knows. It's not a large museum. It's one of those places where a historic home in a notable neighborhood has been converted to a museum and gradually they collect pieces that might have been authentic to the period. My guess is that they ended up with the trunk that way."

"Union Station wouldn't just give away lost luggage."

"Not at the time, no. Perhaps never, officially. But at some point, someone took possession of it. Maybe someone just thought it was in the way of a renovation project. Rich—the curator—discovered it just a few days ago while he was overseeing an effort to clean out and organize overcrowded storage space in the house's basement. There's no record of the item being logged into the collection of the museum, yet there it is."

"Very irregular."

"Yep."

"Somebody must have had it in between. Whoever's hands it ended up in after Union Station got tired of it and dumped it on the museum because the thrift store didn't want it. It's probably been painted and full of junk while somebody used it as a coffee table after finding it at a flea market."

"Nope. It's the real deal. Rich brought in a locksmith to pick the locks as carefully as possible to preserve the integrity of the trunk," Nolan said.

Jillian's jaw dropped. "You mean it hadn't been opened before this? In a hundred years?"

"As I understand it, that seems to be the case."

"They didn't find a body, did they?"

Nolan chortled. "I'm pretty sure Rich would have recognized that as a legal matter without requiring my opinion."

"Then?"

"The usual personal items," Nolan said, "along with a considerable stack of business records from a company in Ohio. Financial records."

"Enter the legal questions."

"Maybe or maybe not."

"It is a curious question why someone travels from Ohio to Colorado with a trunk full of business financial records and then abandons them."

Nolan wiggled one eyebrow. "See? Isn't this better than cleaning your office?"

"Just tidying." Jillian turned her palms up. "But my piles can wait."

"As a historian, Rich is intrigued. But he's concerned both for the matter of the museum having custody of these records and whether there might be legal liability without due provenance of the alleged donation if there should prove to be any value connected to it because of the records. He's also worried about the issue of the financial documents and what they might mean for who could have benefited by how the matters they represent were—or were not—resolved."

"But you said it was over a hundred years ago," Jillian said. "Can you really figure that out now?"

Nolan nodded. "These are all questions I'd have to look into. My instinct is that Rich merely wants to dot every *i* and cross every *t* but that there won't be any legality to pursue."

"But you don't know for sure."

"Not until we see what he has."

They weren't far from Denver now. In a few minutes, Nolan exited the highway and began a series of turns along surface streets taking them through downtown.

"What's this place called?" Jillian asked.

"Owens House Museum."

"Never heard of it."

"Me neither, until I met Rich. From what I understand, it's just a turn-of-the-century house."

"Denver has a lot of those."

"That we do."

Nolan pulled up in front of a house and put the truck in PARK. Jillian considered the structure as they got out.

"Considering what this neighborhood was like a hundred years ago," she said, "this house is fairly modest."

"I agree," Nolan said. "No wonder I couldn't place it. It must have been an ordinary family's home, not the mansion of a silver mine millionaire."

"I wonder how it came to be a museum then."

"I'm sure Rich will tell you if you want to ask."

Jillian pivoted in a circle. "And how did it survive all the demolition and modernizing in the immediate neighborhood?"

"You have an inquisitive mind," Nolan said. "Now let's go see a man about a trunk."

Side by side, they proceeded past the sign that welcomed visitors to the Owens House Museum and up the wide walk at a pace that allowed them to absorb the details. The sandstone house, built in the Queen Anne style popular in the last two decades of the nineteenth century, was a simple two-story home in contrast to some of the three- and four-story homes of the era popular among Denver's most wealthy. With a downtown location, it likely never had much of a lawn, but the carriage house set back from the street suggested that it supported at least one pair of horses with space for a full-size carriage, a service cart, and living quarters for liverymen above. The house itself boasted the requisite rounded tower, steeply pitched roof, twin chimneys, and generous windows of Queen Anne architecture.

"This house could be in Canyon Mines," Jillian said.

"It's certainly the right era." They went up the front steps, and Nolan pushed the door open. A young man at a welcome desk looked up expectantly, and Nolan asked for the curator.

"They've done an amazing job with the restoration," Jillian said while they waited. "The woodwork is gorgeous. Nia and Leo would love to see this. Even Veronica and Luke." The Dunstons had undertaken an ambitious renovation of a sprawling Victorian home and opened a bed-and-breakfast in Canyon Mines, and the O'Reillys ran the Victorium Emporium because Veronica was enthralled with all things Victorian.

"I'm sure they have some brochures you could take home," Nolan said. "Here's Rich now."

"Thank you for coming." Rich offered a handshake.

"This is my daughter, Jillian Parisi-Duffy."

"I'm glad to meet you," Jillian said. "Your museum is very inviting."

"We have the standard drawing room, music room, dining room, and kitchen on the ground floor," Rich said, "and offices in the back. Bedrooms and attic upstairs. And of course the basement, which is what has brought you here today."

"Are we going downstairs?" Nolan asked.

Rich shook his head. "I have the piece in my office. We've taken the liberty of cleaning it up a little bit."

Nolan rubbed his palms together. "Then let's have a look at it."

They followed Rich through the house, bypassing a tour in progress and slipping past a red-lettered No ENTRANCE sign to an area behind the kitchen that originally might have been a back porch, enclosed at a later stage. Rich opened the door to his unassuming office. Centered in the space between the door and his desk stood a steamer trunk. Its sonorous presence beckoned to the most profound calling of Jillian's work. Her breath stopped, and the pulse at her temples audibly magnified.

"Can I touch it?" she blurted out.

Nolan smiled.

Rich nodded. "The gloves are on the desk."

"Of course." Jillian donned the pair of white gloves that would keep her oils off the antique piece and ran her hands around the upright form of the wardrobe-style steamer. "Did my dad tell you what I do for a living?"

"Genealogist. I can imagine you have special appreciation for what you're looking at and the story it might tell in the hands of the family."

"I don't usually get to look at the past quite so directly," Jillian said. "It's stunning."

The stenciled blue beryl and muted gold canvas was far more captivating than the brown or green metal trunk Jillian had mentally prepared for. This was sheer enchantment, artistry created and selected with care. And monogrammed. Someone's story.

"It doesn't have many stickers," Jillian observed.

"I noticed that too," Rich said. "It might have been used for regional rail travel, but it was a steamer trunk only in name. This trunk was never on the water. I would stake my reputation on it."

"But my dad said you think it came from Ohio. Colorado is not regional to Ohio."

Rich shrugged. "A single exception."

"Perhaps we should have a look at the papers you mentioned," Nolan said. "Are they still in the trunk?"

"Yes," Rich said. "It seemed the safest place to leave them."

"May I?" Jillian couldn't help herself. Although the steamer had been opened at least once—and occasioned Rich's call to her father—*she* hadn't opened it. The moment would be exquisite, a first look not just at census records or overlooked birth certificates or a chain of addresses tracking an individual's movements from fifty years ago, but at abandoned personal possessions that had been shut and locked for over a century until a locksmith's delicate touch two days ago.

But why?

CHAPTER TWO

Jillian flipped the latches one at a time, delicately. They sprang open just as they were designed to do, most likely before 1900.

"Phenomenal," she whispered.

"It's a very well made trunk," Rich said. "There can be no doubt of that."

Like all wardrobe trunks, this one stood upright, functioning as a portable closet and drawers. Jillian eased the two halves apart on hinges that squeaked slightly but operated appropriately.

"Wow."

On the left hung three lined silk suits, with coordinated blouses tucked under the jackets, in stately neutral tones—gray, taupe, and a dark green subtle stripe. Tasteful pins and necklaces hung with suits, most likely high-end paste but convincingly made. Above the clothes, on a small shelf, sat a handheld mirror and hairbrush with pewter handles and a small toiletries case. The right side of the trunk held a set of drawers and space for a hatbox.

"Is there a hat in there?" Jillian glanced at Rich.

He nodded. "We looked but then left it alone."

"And the drawers?"

"You're wearing the gloves. Feel free."

Jillian opened the first and saw an oversize Bible, a leather notebook, and a fountain pen. She lifted the Bible reverently and opened the cover. "The family record. It's full of names going back before the Civil War. A lot of birth dates, some death dates. Even some places."

"A genealogist's treasure," Nolan said.

The next drawer held a handful of photos, assorted images of three generations, but the largest was a young couple with two small boys set in an oval porcelain frame ready to display on a flat surface.

"This doesn't seem like something a person would leave behind willingly," Jillian said. "Is this the woman who owned the trunk?"

"It's all very strange," Rich said. "I'm sorry to say it, but a mugging would be the least suspicious explanation."

Jillian pulled open three more drawers, all stuffed with papers. "That's a lot of documents."

Nolan stepped toward the trunk now. "Clearly the documents were a primary purpose of the journey."

"There are some letters," Rich said. "Of course, we only have one side of the correspondence, but there is one salient, very curious feature. The third drawer."

Jillian found the pages, moving through nine fragile sheets. "Dad."

"What is it?"

"Pinkerton correspondence."

"Pinkerton?"

"Letters from James McParland."

"The manager of the western division of the Pinkerton's Agency?"

"The very same."

"That's a very famous, very colorful character for a female traveler from Ohio to be corresponding with."

"My thought exactly." The letters were addressed to "Miss" Bendeure. The correspondent was unlikely to be the young mother in the photo. One of the other women in the photos, then. The older one was not likely to be traveling alone, nor to be unmarried, since the photos also included an older man.

Nolan turned to Rich. "My friend, this does indeed bear some looking into. It might still be nothing, but I understand why you have questions."

"So you'll help?" Rich asked.

"I'll try."

"I'm not qualified to analyze the financial documents," Rich said, "and for now, I've been careful not to handle them too much—though they seem to be in good condition since they haven't been exposed to light or air all these years. The trunk may never have been on the water, but it was constructed to protect the contents."

"It's a lot of papers," Jillian observed.

"More than someone would have carried in a small valise during a train ride," Rich said, "especially if a woman had other personal items to keep track of during a journey of some distance."

"That makes sense," Nolan said. "Even a hundred years ago, documents from a bank could have been verified or replaced in some manner, I would think, but someone went to a great deal of trouble to assemble these records specifically for this journey."

"The Pinkerton letters," Jillian said.

"I'm not sure what I'm wandering into," Rich said. "I just felt I should get a legal opinion before simply disposing of any contents. Even if I transferred everything to another museum, I don't want to simply transfer any sort of liability or wrongdoing as well. What if there was foul play that could still be righted if a knowledgeable person looked at the available information? And that person is not me."

"A valid question," Nolan said. "I'm not sure it's me either, but I will do my best to find someone qualified to render an opinion about what financial narrative emerges and, depending on those results, investigate from there what the legal ramifications might be. After more than a century, the law may be limited unless we uncover violations that directly affect rights of property or inheritance with criminal intent, especially if interstate commerce is involved. The applicable laws at the time may be very different than we would expect now, but we can certainly take a close look at all those questions."

"I would be very grateful." Relief flushed through Rich's face.

"I will need the papers," Nolan said. "On the phone you mentioned you might be happy for us to take custody of the entire trunk—considering there is no official record of the museum's possession of it."

"I did say that—if it would be helpful to you in any way to have the entire trunk."

Yes! Jillian's mind screamed. *Please!*

Aloud she said, "I would be happy to do what I can to help as well. Sometimes when I stare at things long enough, the connections start to click." The silk suits nearly had voices of their own, calling out in chorus for their lost form to fill them again.

"She speaks truth," Nolan said. "Having the trunk will help."

"Then by all means you should take it," Rich said. "We can wrap it and crate it for proper transport."

"My truck is right out front," Nolan said. "I got lucky with a parking spot."

The men disappeared in search of suitable supplies to protect the treasure, leaving Jillian to close up the steamer trunk and fasten the latches. She double-checked them—and then triple-checked them, even though she knew Rich would return with protective blankets and straps. The elegant trunk would be nestled and cushioned within a crate for its journey to Canyon Mines.

It was so dissimilar to the other trunk in the home she shared with her father, one she hadn't examined for years, one that disclosed an incomplete story and whose bequest was a yawning void in her life. A better genealogist would have filled the chasm by now with revelatory understanding.

That wasn't true. She was a very good genealogist. Some tasks were imposing.

And poignant. And painful.

Nolan and Rich returned, each with his own intended method for accomplishing the job. As they set about negotiating a compromise, Jillian excused herself in favor of fresh air. She was only in the way. Wandering back through the museum rooms, she found brochures to take to Nia Dunston and Veronica O'Reilly before returning to the sunshine, waning now in the late afternoon with wisps of clouds stretching like spun cotton candy across a setting sky readying for nightfall. When the sun began to descend, orange and golden hues would diffuse in shifting aspects fading into gray and then midnight blue, yielding the day one more breathtaking moment.

And when Jillian woke in the morning, the stenciled canvas trunk would be in her house, awaiting her explorations of its holdings and her part in finding its story.

She'd had fourteen years to incline her ear to the story of the trunk at home. Nevertheless, it perplexed her—even distressed her at times. Why had its voice been so stubborn? She was too close to it. Every failure of discovery stabbed her, making her bleed all over again.

Nolan and Rich, with the help of the young man from the welcome desk, now eased a dolly, with the crate securely strapped to it, down the front steps of the Owens House Museum. Once it was on the flat sidewalk, Nolan strode ahead to unlock the tailgate of the truck.

"You all right, Silly Jilly?" he said.

She nodded.

"I promised you a good souvenir."

"And you delivered, Dad. You always do."

The men unstrapped the crate from the dolly and eased it into the bed of the pickup.

"You'll go straight home?" Rich said.

"Directly," Nolan said. "This early on a Saturday evening, it shouldn't take more than half an hour. I'll send you a text to let you know the steamer trunk arrived safely."

"I would appreciate that."

Nolan made the turns to get them back on the highway and pointed west toward Canyon Mines.

"You're quiet," he said.

Jillian shrugged.

"That trunk behind us is not the only one you're thinking about, is it?"

She looked at him and shook her head.

"How long has it been since you opened it?"

"A long time." It was Nolan who first urged her toward an interest in genealogy after her mother died when she was fourteen, and he used her mother's trunk to do it. But the contents, while they seized her curiosity, did not produce answers. Nolan was there the last time Jillian opened the trunk. He witnessed the vexed mass of mud she morphed into that day.

"I should have asked more questions about the Parisis when Mom was alive," Jillian said. "Why didn't I?"

"You were a child, Jilly."

"They're half of me. I should have been more interested in my mother's family while she was still here."

"Jillian, you couldn't have known we were going to lose her. None of us did. We all thought there was plenty of time."

Jillian sighed. "Sometimes she tried to talk to me about the Parisis. I didn't listen as well as I should have."

"There were so many Duffys around you all the time," Nolan said. "Cousins everywhere. Big family gatherings just an hour away. How could one pair of grandparents compete on their own all the way from Arizona?"

"Tell me again why Mom came back to Denver after her parents moved?"

"She was halfway through high school when Grandpa Steve decided to take that job in Phoenix. She never felt connected there. Coming back to Colorado for college was her way of coming home, so she stayed after graduation."

"Then she met you."

"No turning back after that." Nolan flashed a grin. "Besides, the Duffys would have given up custody of me before they would have relinquished Bella once I brought her home to a family dinner."

Jillian laughed. "That sounds like Nana and Big Seamus."

"I know your mom would have wanted you to have that trunk—with whatever clues it contains about the Parisis. That's one of the reasons I thought you might want to explore your Italian roots after she was gone."

"But I didn't find many answers, did I? Grandma Marta and Grandpa Steve were lost in their own grief and didn't have much patience for my questions, and then they were gone before we knew it too. There wasn't anyone else to even give me reliable names to work with." No family Bible. No scrapbook. Just vague stories about brothers and Sicily, and the trunk that dared her to make sense of what she did not know.

"Everything in that trunk is still there, Jilly," Nolan said. "When you're ready, you'll go at it again."

Jillian stared out the window. She wasn't so sure.

CHAPTER THREE

Denver, Colorado
March 18, 1909

Dear Miss Bendeure,

The matter you raised in your recent correspondence
is of course of grave concern. We at our agency are well
acquainted with these manipulations and do not take them
lightly. Without more complete information I hesitate to
render an authoritative conclusion upon which you should
take action, and I do not wish for you to be unduly alarmed
in a premature manner. Nevertheless, what you have described bears some similarity to patterns identified by our
New York and Chicago offices, with whom we are in frequent
communication. So you are not without cause to be framing
the questions which you have put to me in a confidential
manner. I can give you every assurance that we are well
qualified and well staffed to act on your behalf. We would
be pleased to receive more details of the events and transactions that have suggested concerns in the minds of you
and your father so that we may undertake specific investigation and reply with particular recommendations on an
expeditious course of action to protect your business
interests and put your minds at ease. I am enclosing
information on a private courier. Due to the sensitive
nature of the information, you may prefer this method to
ordinary mail. I am at your service.

Yours sincerely,
James McParland
Manager, Western Division
Pinkerton's National Detective Agency

The steamer had been her mother's, selected for its manageable size suitable for trips of short duration and gently used because her mother was not given to unnecessary travel and never left Cleveland at all once illness set in ten years ago. The trunk had never crossed the ocean, though Lynnelle had no doubt it would have stood up well. Without such a voyage, and only the occasional short excursion, it still looked brand-new. When her mother passed, Lynnelle appropriated the stenciled canvas trunk. The EPB monogram was not her initials, but no other woman would remember her mother with the same fondness Lynnelle guarded.

The steamer was packed now, roomy enough for the stylish hat in its box, mementos to keep her heart close to those she loved, her clothing, and all the records she would need for her meetings without crushing anything. In miles the journey was long—to Denver and back—but Lynnelle hoped to accomplish its purpose swiftly. For the train she would carry a wicker case with several changes of fresh shirtwaists and nightwear. A simple hat and practical shoes would do for transit, but once she reached Denver, she must look the part of her father's qualified emissary with silk suits in colors and accessories that would assure any man she meant business. She wouldn't travel with expensive jewels but rather carefully selected pieces that added elegance to each ensemble without drawing attention to themselves.

She closed the trunk, fastened the latches, inserted the key to secure them, and tucked the key deep into the Moroccan leather satchel her father had given her especially for this journey. Its long strap would make it easy to keep on her person while she used her hands for the tasks of being in transit for three days. This too would lock at any point she felt necessary, with its tiny brass key pinned inside the waistband of her navy shepherd's plaid skirt.

"May I take the trunk?" The young man in the doorway proffered both arms. "The driver is here."

"An automobile? Not a carriage?" Lynnelle checked the contents of her satchel.

"Yes, miss."

"Thank you." If Lynnelle had made the arrangements herself, she would have chosen a carriage. "Please tell the driver I will say goodbye to my father and be right out."

"Yes, miss."

He hefted the steamer and carried it into the hall, where his footsteps shuffled slightly under its mass. Listening as he reached the transition from the wide wood floor of the hall to the carpeted stairs, Lynnelle scanned the room. She'd be back in a week, but she liked to leave a tidy space.

Downstairs, her father was in his study.

"I'm going now, Papa."

He raised his haggard features with the increasingly gray complexion.

"I do wish I didn't have to send you," he said.

"We've talked about this. The doctor has told you more than once that it would not be good for your health to travel—especially not to a stressful situation."

"It was my decisions that brought this upon us."

"You have always been a shrewd businessman. You've done well for our family and well for Bendeure & Company."

He peered over the rims of his spectacles. "This circumstance may be an exception to the general rule, or you would not be making the journey."

"I'm quite up to it, I assure you."

"You're sure about this McParland fellow? I read the newspapers, you know. He has rather a colorful reputation with all that business with the mines and the unions. Whether he is forthcoming in all matters is questionable."

"But whether he gets results is not questionable." Lynnelle smoothed one hand across the satchel. "You've seen his correspondence for yourself. It's reasonable in every regard, and if he blusters when he confronts criminals, isn't that exactly what we need?"

"So you are persuaded?"

"I want to be prepared."

"You understand the documents?"

"We've been over them three times, and I've been corresponding with Mr. McParland for weeks. I am well versed in the entire matter." Nevertheless, she would continue to review the details as she traversed the miles.

He ran his right index finger along the edge of the massive walnut desk. "I would have sent your brother. If only."

Lynnelle moistened her lips. If only he hadn't loved that stallion's speed so much and taken such risks. "We've lost him, Papa. But I'm here, and it's best to have someone from the family take matters in hand. So I will go and I will do a good job."

"I'm sure you will. But are you certain you shouldn't take a maid as companion for propriety's sake?"

"There's no one to take. Joan's mother only fell ill three days ago, and I will not cheat her of what might be her last weeks with her." Lynnelle knew what it was like to sit at the bedside of a dying mother. When the news came that her maid's mother had a consumptive illness, Lynnelle dispatched her immediately. There was no one else she trusted for a journey of such delicate nature. "Besides, these are modern times, Papa. You know what women are capable of or you would not have trusted me with this."

"I only want you to come home safely to me."

"There is no reason I won't."

"You're wearing your mother's brooch."

"It makes me feel close to her." Lynnelle fingered the porcelain piece at her neck. Ever since she was a little girl, she had admired the hand-painted florals with tiny sapphires and amethysts at their centers. The gold filigree around the oval had been the height of fancy to a dreaming child.

"Your mother would like that," her father said, "but is it wise?"

"I would never part with it, even for a week. Not even for a day."

He sighed. "Very well. You have all your tickets?"

"Right here. You really did not have to book compartments for every leg. I'm hardly going to need them during the portions that are not overnight."

"You might like to rest or wish some privacy. Considering what you are undertaking on my behalf, the least I can do is ensure you are comfortable."

Lynnelle had urged her father more than once to release himself from the guilt that had morphed his posture from shoulders held straight to a chronic discouraged slump. Certainly she did not blame him. She had grown up in a well-to-do household, attended some of the best schools in Cleveland, and wanted for nothing throughout her childhood because of her father's business acumen. Not every endeavor had met equal success, yet this one—and his inability to untangle the circumstances—personally distressed him to a degree she'd never witnessed. Perhaps he'd protected her more than she'd known. Perhaps the loss of her older brother made him see her differently. Perhaps the withdrawal of his brother's wife from the family—with the grandchildren—bound them in a new way.

"Cousin Marabel is looking forward to seeing you." Her father brightened. "It's thoughtful of you to take the time to visit in Chesterton."

"It's only a few stops from Chicago. An extra day before resuming the trip is no trouble. Besides, I've always enjoyed Marabel."

"Your mother would appreciate the effort to stay in touch with her family."

"I should go. The driver is waiting." Lynnelle circled the desk to kiss her father's cheek. "I will send a telegram from Denver as soon as I have news. See you in a week or so."

She held on to her unpretentious gray hat with its single yellow feather during the ride to the train station. The driver her father used was respectful enough with the speed of an automobile, but Lynnelle grew up with horses and carriages. Although automobiles had joined the traffic of Cleveland years ago, she never felt at ease with the way her stomach moved out of position going around corners, and drivers squeezing the bulbs of their horns in impatience with people still using carriages never sat well with her. One hand on her hat and one hand gripping the side of the car was her standard posture.

Cleveland to Chicago, with a brief respite in nearby Chesterton, Indiana. Then Chicago to Omaha. Finally Omaha to Denver on the Colorado Special of the Union Pacific. Traveling in mid-May should avoid snow, and spring rains shouldn't slow the trains. Lynnelle was well versed in rail travel around Ohio, Pennsylvania, and New York and to some degree a few Southern cities along the Eastern seaboard. She'd even been to the World's Columbian Exposition in Chicago as a child in 1893, though of course she traveled with her entire family on that excursion. Nothing about the travel itself rattled her nerves. Only the possibility of reporting an unsatisfactory outcome to her father discomforted her, but she had long hours on the rails to review the documents in her satchel yet again. She could be twice as confident as she was now that she could answer any question Mr. McParland raised in connection with the investigation he had been undertaking already for some time now.

"Here we are." The driver pulled up in front of Union Depot and set the brake on the car. "I'll get your trunk and find a porter."

The massive brick building, with its arched tunnels and long narrow windows, had stood since the Civil War era and showed its age. For the last twenty years, authorities had debated how to fund the necessary replacement, but for now, it still served the network of railroads in and out of Cleveland. Lynnelle would see a string of stations in the next several days. Denver's Union Station had been remodeled more recently. Photographs of the new Welcome Arch from only three years ago had been in all the newspapers. She would breathe relief when she walked beneath it.

Lynnelle opened the Moroccan satchel and extracted the first set of tickets she required, the first-class ticket to board and the second ticket to her private compartment. Perhaps her father was right and she would appreciate a quiet space to continue mental preparations for what was ahead once she reached Colorado. She stared at the ticket that bore her name and the descriptions the agent would punch before long to verify her identity.

Slim. Medium. Stout.

Tall. Medium. Short.

Hair: Light. Gray. Dark. Red.

Beard: Mustache. Side. Chin. Full. None.

No beard, certainly. If she pulled herself to her full height, she might pass as medium at best. And she wasn't stout. Light hair. She could be one of any number of women on the trains she would board, even any number carrying first-class tickets.

"I've found a porter, miss," the driver said. "He'll help you with your trunk and make sure it gets aboard and ticketed all the way to Denver, just the way you asked."

"Thank you. I'm sure I can manage the smaller case from here." Lynnelle showed the porter her ticket, and he nodded and led the way. She was tempted to inquire whether she could simply take the trunk with her to the compartment rather than the baggage car. Though the most important papers were in her satchel, having the trunk out of sight disquieted her. Yet even a private compartment hardly had space for the trunk, and squeezing it down the aisle of the train during boarding seemed an unreasonable request. She tipped the porter generously and watched carefully as he loaded the trunk and handed her a claim check before turning to find her way to her Pullman compartment.

A porter aboard the train guided her, opened the compartment, and handed her the key. Alone, she stepped inside and pulled the door closed. Without Joan's companionship there would be no need to open the upper berth that swung down from the ceiling on any leg of the journey. Even the lower berth, made by converting two facing seats, would be narrow and short enough to make her glad she did not qualify for a *Tall* punch on her ticket. The private sink would be nice if she wanted to splash water on her face, and she could check her face in the mirror before venturing out to the dining car. Otherwise she hardly had space to do more than make herself comfortable on one of the high-backed benches.

"Well, Mr. McParland," Lynnelle said aloud, "when I meet you, we will straighten this out once and for all."

CHAPTER FOUR

I'm going to grab Luke before he heads out for his Sunday afternoon date with ESPN." Nolan wedged past Jillian in the church pew.

"I suspect you won't be far behind him for that engagement," she said.

He wagged a finger at her. "You don't know that."

"Don't I?"

"I don't have time to argue the point. Luke has a banking background. He might be able to help us."

"Go for it."

Nolan eyed Luke across the sanctuary, anticipated his exit path, and calculated an intercept trajectory.

"Now, Nolan," Luke said, "you know there's a game I want to watch this afternoon, and it starts in less than thirty minutes."

"Softball? High school soccer? Maybe a ping-pong tournament?"

"Very funny. Major League Baseball is well underway. Tell me again what people find so likable about you?"

"Everything you do and more," Nolan said. "I'll pay your cable bill for a month if you give me five minutes."

"I think you're making a symbolic gesture with all the teeth of your pathetic golf swing." Luke tilted his head. "But I'm listening."

"You worked in banking in a past career, correct?"

Luke nodded. "Until I saw the charms of making far less money running a shop in a small mountain town."

"That's what the love of a good woman will do for you," Nolan said. "But in that fine-tuned noggin of yours, I'm pretty sure there are still residual numbers smarts, and I have some papers I'd love for you to take a look at."

"Made a bad investment, did you?"

"Way more interesting than that. A hundred-year-old mystery."

Luke scratched his nose. "Isn't that up Jillian's alley?"

"She's part of the team."

"There's a team? I'm being recruited?"

"Yes! A sports metaphor! Why didn't I think of that sooner?"

Luke tapped his watch.

"Right," Nolan said. "I'll get to the point. Jillian and I haven't had a chance to digest all the documents yet, but we're trying to help someone interpret financial records in a trunk from 1909. I was hoping you could assist."

"What is the nature of these records, if I may ask?"

"If I had to guess, records of bank transfers and payments by check, some of them across state lines. But I could use help determining the picture the patterns make. And considering how old the records are, you might have ideas for how to proceed."

"Maybe," Luke said, "but doesn't your firm have a division for things like this?"

"I will be consulting a wide swath of experts." Nolan winked.

"Flattery, huh?" Luke said. "A desperate move. Well, without seeing the papers, I can't speculate. But because you're my friend, and because I want to get home to my game—which is neither softball, nor high school soccer, nor ping-pong—I'll be happy to look at the papers. If I saw them, I could probably decipher enough of the old transactions to point you in the right direction."

"Then the recruitment effort has been successful!"

"Bring the papers by the Emporium this week, and I'll have a look." Luke raised his glance to catch Veronica's eye six pews back, where she was chatting with Nia Dunston, and headed toward her.

Nolan joined the general exodus from the church building and found Jillian waiting for him in her small SUV. At home he tossed his own keys in the copper bowl on the granite kitchen counter, as usual, and stared down the hallway running through the center of the house.

"Shall we uncrate your souvenir today?" Nolan said.

"I can't get attached to it," Jillian said. "Rich is not going to let me keep it."

"You don't know that. His primary interest seems to be liability and legality. We don't know that he wants the piece itself for the museum."

"He'd be a fool not to. It cleaned up beautifully, and the personal items inside are gorgeous."

"Be that as it may," Nolan said, "we do have to unwrap it if either of us is going to be able to help him."

"Then I'll get a crowbar."

"Scissors will do the trick. We only used museum-grade duct tape to secure the crate closed."

"Museum-grade duct tape? You're making that up."

She may have doubted him, but Jillian pulled open a kitchen drawer to extract a pair of scissors while Nolan began loosening the clasps on the straps holding a blanket around the crate. Within a few minutes they had the straps unhitched, the blanket spread on the floor, the tape cut, and the crate open.

"You hold the crate, and I'll slide the trunk out," Nolan said.

Jillian complied, and in another few moments, they had cleared away the debris and relocated the trunk near the piano at the end of the elongated room that served as a cozy TV space. Jillian slid her hands into the gloves Rich made sure to send along in the crate and unfastened the latches for the second time in two days.

"You've spoiled me, Dad," Jillian said. "I thought I knew what projects I was going to work on this week, and you plopped this in my lap. How am I supposed to walk past this and not want to spend every moment solving this mystery?"

He cocked his head and grinned. "You're not. I want you to have some fun with it. However, I'm certain I heard your tummy rumbling, and I feel obliged to feed you."

Jillian nodded absently as he wheeled on one heel and left the room. He could rustle up some leftovers for lunch without too much trouble, perhaps revive the seasoning in the butternut squash soup he'd made a couple of days ago and throw together a plate of fresh vegetables. At the doorway to the kitchen, Nolan turned and looked back at Jillian. She squatted in front of the trunk, careful not to handle the contents frivolously but lost in curiosity. Nolan would have to borrow those gloves at some point to have a close look at the papers and figure out where to start on the financial questions. Those were his marching orders. But between the information on the correspondence and the entries in the family Bible, Jillian would soon theorize who the traveler might have been and what trail she left behind.

The landline rang, an unusual occurrence in a household with two cell phones, and Nolan picked it up in the kitchen.

"Nolan, it's Marilyn."

"Good afternoon!"

"I'm calling around to remind everyone about the organizing meeting tomorrow evening."

"At the Heritage Society," he said.

"Seven o'clock sharp. And make sure Jillian comes too. I need you both."

Nolan reported the reminder to Jillian and let his mind drift to his schedule. Mondays often were long and busy days in his Denver office, especially in anticipation of more peaceful atmosphere of working from home on Tuesdays. This week was no different. He'd have to find several corners to trim the edges out of to ensure being back in Canyon Mines on time for an evening meeting. If he worked through lunch, delegated his four o'clock meeting to an associate, and pulled his five o'clock mediation session to the earlier slot, it might just work.

On Monday, by the time Nolan and Jillian slid into their seats in the community room at the Heritage Society, he'd barely had time to stop by the house to drop off his briefcase and trade his navy suit and tie for a pair of khakis and a comfortable gray knit pullover. The chicken Jillian had roasted would have to wait while a small paper plate of cheese cubes and green olives speared by toothpicks with multicolored paper flags staved off his appetite.

Jillian handed him a cup of black coffee. "Maybe we'll be able to scoot out early." She wiggled her fingers across the room at the Dunstons from the Inn, Luke's wife Veronica, and Jillian's friend Kris Bryant, who ran Ore the Mountain Ice Cream Parlor.

Now Nolan wanted ice cream, not cheese and olives.

Nolan shook his head at the notion of an early exit. "Marilyn has been working on this for months. If the idea works, the Legacy Jubilee can raise enough money to get all the new windows she needs."

At the front of the room Marilyn clapped her hands to call everyone to attention. The group wasn't large, mostly comprising downtown business owners, a representative from the chamber of commerce, and a few other individuals who had committed to donate supplies or time.

"Thank you all for coming," Marilyn said. "Our Legacy Jubilee is less than three weeks away now, so I'm afraid you will find me cheerily pestering you a bit more often as we nail down the details we've discussed in previous planning meetings and circulated by email. I am grateful for everyone's willingness to undertake this effort to raise funds in a way that celebrates not only our little museum but also gives us a chance to show off our jewel of a town to people from the surrounding area. We've had some good press, with articles and listings of special events in various regional newspapers and small magazines. Reservations for some of our events are already quite encouraging."

Banners to hang.

The stage to erect for the schedule of regional bands that would play beginning Thursday evening and continuing through Sunday afternoon.

Extended evening hours for many of the Main Street shops.

Children's activities under tents at Thunder Way Park behind the elementary school.

Docent orientation for the extra visitors they expected at the Heritage Society building and the special displays still in process.

Additional vendor stations around town to feature ice cream from Ore the Mountain, hand-tempered candy from Digger's Delight, pastries from Ben's Bakery, and other food options to keep people circulating and spending money, a portion of which would go to the Legacy Jubilee fund.

Schedules.

Lists of volunteers.

Follow-up phone calls to make.

"She does have help, doesn't she?" Nolan whispered to Jillian.

"Theoretically there's a committee," Jillian whispered back. "She's had trouble letting go of the details."

"And then of course," Marilyn said, "we are thrilled to be showing off our most delicious talent in one of our spectacular local venues. Nia and Leo have agreed to open the Inn at Hidden Run to dinner on Saturday evening. Veronica O'Reilly is handling the decorations. Nolan Duffy will prepare the food, and if you've ever tasted any of his menus, you know it will be utterly scrumptious. As the meal comes to a close, Jillian will favor us with a presentation in her area of expertise. I can't wait to hear how she weaves genealogy into the theme of the weekend."

A spattering of applause made Nolan wink at his daughter.

"And what will you be preparing, Nolan?" Marilyn said. "Perhaps we should whet the appetites of everyone here and boost our reservations!"

Jillian elbowed him.

"You flatter me," Nolan said. "I have a few things in mind, but I'm still finalizing the details."

It wasn't the answer Marilyn wanted—the slight narrowing of her eyes told him that—but it was the best Nolan could do. She answered several questions, distributed a handout of FAQs, issued several more reminders, and dismissed the group.

Nolan stacked his empty coffee cup on the remains of the snack plate and pictured sliced roasted chicken on a real plate beside colorful vegetables and wondered if Jillian had made rice or potatoes. And was there any ice cream in the freezer? He couldn't remember if he'd eaten the last of the pralines and cream from Ore the Mountain.

"A word, please, Nolan."

He turned toward the event organizer. "Hello, Marilyn. It's going to be a grand weekend."

"I do hope so," Marilyn said. "Should I be concerned that you don't have a menu yet?"

"Not at all. I promise to pin that down soon."

"We're planning to print menus for the place settings."

"Yes, I remember."

"We can't wait until the last minute to do that."

"Right."

"The designer will need some time to lay it out first, and then the printer will require time."

"Of course. I'm just trying to make sure I can be efficient with food preparation on the night of the meal."

"I'm sure you're up to the challenge and it will be delicious," Marilyn said. "Let me know if there's any way I can help."

Marilyn pivoted away to chase after another victim, and Jillian snorted a laugh.

"You don't have any idea what you're cooking, do you?" she said.

"Have you got your talk prepared?" Nolan shot back.

"Not the same. I give genealogy talks all the time. I get *paid* to do it.

I can do it in my sleep."

"I have one or two details to iron out," Nolan said. "Then I can decide between littleneck clams in a delicate Italian sauce or barbecued rabbit."

Jillian laughed. "I would see how that would be a tough choice when you're cooking for a hundred and twenty."

"A hundred and twenty!" Nolan's response was louder than he intended. "But Nia's dining room doesn't hold more than about twenty."

"Dad, this is a fundraiser. Nia will have extra tables all over the Inn, and remember, you already agreed to jump from two seatings to three."

In fact, he remembered no such thing.

CHAPTER FIVE

Jillian craned her neck to the left to confirm her suspicion. The large taupe mug with a maroon swirl around the lower portion—her favorite for the last six months—was empty. She would have to do something about that soon if she expected to maintain productivity on this family tree. It wasn't complicated, as far as genealogies went. She'd met the client at a conference for amateur genealogists where she spoke a couple of months ago, and the woman had made a valiant effort on her own based on family stories, memorabilia, spotty documents, and public records. Several simplifications to name spellings of ancestors who came from Eastern Europe to the United States had slowed her progress, however, and after chatting with Jillian over a conference meal, she asked to hire her to finish the job. Ultimately she hoped to produce a book for the extended family, and she wanted to be as sure of the information as possible. Jillian had only had two cups of coffee that morning—the *size* of the cup was irrelevant in her thinking, and she would never apologize for a mug that required both hands to hold properly—and three was the magic number for her brain's maximum efficiency.

Fortunately, on the gray-speckled granite kitchen counter a coffee preparation system gleamed in a way that would stoke any barista's passion. None of her father's black coffee nonsense. That's what the single-serving brewer machine was for. Jillian would maximize the potential of the machine that could produce the latte worthy of the mug her mother had loved. Jillian reached for the mug she had set a safe distance from her keyboard and rolled her chair back from her desk.

The kitchen was only a dozen steps from her office in the old Victorian house that had once been a duplex of mirroring two-story residences, but Jillian didn't make it to her destination. When the doorbell rang she angled her stocking feet toward the wide door on one side of the living room that served as the home's main entrance.

"Hey, Veronica," Jillian said when she pulled the door open.

"Well, hello, my favorite secret keeper."

"Huh?" Jillian stepped aside for Veronica to enter.

"On occasion it takes awhile for my husband to get around to telling me things, but eventually he remembers. Why didn't you mention the trunk yourself?"

Jillian snickered. "Veronica, would you like to see this really cool, really old trunk my dad arranged for me to bring home from a museum?"

"Why yes. Yes, I would. Thank you for offering." Veronica tucked her dishwater blond hair behind her ears. "As you know, I have a lifelong interest in really cool, really old things."

"I was going to tell you last night after the meeting, but you disappeared."

"Luke and I hadn't seen each other all day, and he made me promise not to dillydally." Veronica gasped and took several long strides across the room toward the steamer trunk, which stood open. "It's gorgeous!"

"Slow down. Strict instructions from the museum curator." Jillian set down her empty coffee mug and handed the white gloves to Veronica.

Her hands covered, Veronica circled the trunk, gently touching several of its features. "This dates at least to 1900."

Jillian nodded. "It contains correspondence from 1909."

"E. P. B." Veronica touched the monogram. "The owner?"

Jillian shook her head. "We don't think so—at least not the person who was traveling with the correspondence. I have to carve out some time to dig into it."

"Luke said there are some financial questions."

"Right." Jillian pointed to a drawer for Veronica to slide open.

Veronica's eyes widened at the papers.

"Three drawers like that," Jillian said. "My dad hasn't had time to go through it all yet either, but he's enlisting help."

"Like Luke." Veronica gently fingered each of the three suits. "The clothes are to die for!"

"The 'delicates' are in the back," Jillian said. "Hat. Shoes. Everything's there."

"I can tell you right now that these are not off-the-rack clothes." Veronica closed the drawer and removed the gloves. "It's probably in the best condition of any trunk I've seen for its age."

"That's saying something," Jillian said.

At the Victorium Emporium, Veronica catered to tourists looking for souvenirs. Many of the items she stocked were replicas and priced for rapid turnover to keep the shop's cash flow in the black. Luke insisted on some practicality to the business model. But Veronica also scoured estate sales and auctions for authentic period pieces to put on careful display in one corner of the store for more discerning shoppers.

"Don't hate me," Jillian said, "but I have another trunk I've never showed you. It's at least as old as this one—probably older."

Veronica's eyes narrowed. "Jillian Parisi-Duffy, what are you saying?"

Jillian wasn't sure why those unpremeditated words gurgled up her throat and out of her mouth, but she couldn't wash them down now. Ever since she and her dad brought Lynnelle's trunk home on Saturday, Jillian's own trunk had been a specter lurking behind every thought. "It was my mother's. It came from her mother's side, but it also has things in it from the Parisi side."

"Oh Jillian." Veronica softened. "I didn't mean to make light. Your mom's things—I understand you would want to be private about that."

Jillian exhaled. "I suppose that was it in the beginning. I was only fourteen. It used to make me cry to look inside. Then I would be frustrated that I didn't understand the family history better, even though I tried to research it. Now I haven't looked at it in years."

"I've never noticed a trunk any time I've been in your house, not even in your bedroom."

"It's in the attic. Under some blankets to help keep the dust out."

"Well," Veronica said, "if you're ever ready to share it, I'd love to see it."

Jillian shrugged. "No time like the present." *Never* would be a better time, but in the last three days, she couldn't think about one trunk without the other swelling to fill the space as well. It was only a matter of time before she'd have to face it. Maybe the rock in her gut would not burn quite so hot if she had a friend with her.

"Are you sure?" Veronica said.

"No. But let's do it. Be quiet, though. My dad is working at home today."

Jillian reminded herself to breathe evenly as they climbed the stairs that went up through the center of the house, and then she opened a door to stairs leading to the attic. She found the light switch, and they ascended the second set of steps, steeper and narrower and rough and wooden.

"Watch your head," Jillian said. "The eaves are fairly low except in the middle of the attic." She wiped her hands on her jeans and swallowed against the stark dry sensation in her mouth, trying to force saliva from lost corners of her mouth. Veronica was behind her, so she couldn't turn around and run from her choice.

Neither she nor her father had reason to come up to the attic often. For just the two of them—and there had been only three when her mother was alive—the house had ample storage in two floors of living space, and there was a basement as well. Jillian stored several crates of mementos from high school and college, and Nolan kept a few pieces of small furniture that had belonged to his parents during his childhood with the notion that someday he would restore them to beauty and usefulness. Assorted, more modern but still dated luggage lined one wall. Jillian led the way to one corner where her mother's trunk sat on top of one old blanket and under the protection of two more.

"It's dark in this spot," Jillian said, "and we'll bump our heads if we're not careful. But we can drag it out under the light." She eased out her breath, ignoring the pounding rise in her heart rate echoing in her ears.

They gripped the corners of the blanket beneath the trunk and shifted it to a better position under a bare bulb before pulling the blankets off. The trunk's blond wood finish had darkened with age and use—another project Nolan talked about restoring, but Jillian hadn't wanted him to—and its two leather belts were well worn and brass buckles heavily tarnished. Both ends featured a light tan leather binding with some slight irregular stains from use.

Veronica gave a low whistle. "When you collect trunks, you don't mess around. Another beauty."

"Thanks." Jillian unbuckled the straps and dislodged the primary latch, which hadn't locked at any point in her lifetime, to lift the lid. Inside, the trunk was lined in a green cotton print fabric with white piping. The fragility of both lining and piping attested to their authenticity. "We can lift out this tray. Everything is underneath." She hadn't done this for six years, but she knew just what she'd see and in what arrangement.

"Your mom's things?" Veronica asked. "You don't have to show me her private belongings."

"That's not really what it is." She'd come this far and managed to steel her nerves. Jillian knelt to move the tray and carefully set it aside. Chuckling, Jillian lifted out a sealed gray plastic tube. "My mother's main contribution is a time capsule she put in the month I was born."

Veronica laughed. "I love that! When are you going to open it?"

Jillian shrugged. "I don't know. Maybe I'll leave it for a child I have someday."

"Even better. Did she tell you what's in it?"

"No clue. Even my dad doesn't know." Jillian set the tube aside. "Everything else is older—some of it quite a bit, as far as I can tell."

"What do you know about the Parisis?"

"Not as much as I wish. They came from Sicily to New Orleans in the late nineteenth century, and my particular branch of the family ended up in Denver. I'm sure there were other brothers—at least that's what I was always told—but I've never been able to get solid ties to what happened to them." Family stories called them by American-sounding monikers Jillian never believed were the names the brothers left Italy with.

"These dishes are lovely." Veronica squatted to pick up a plate. "Early twentieth century, but not all of them are original. Somebody was trying to collect them by matching the pattern."

"How can you tell that?" Jillian asked. "They look like an Italian pattern, don't they?"

"It's an incomplete set, which you would expect if they were someone's original dishes and this old, but I don't think they were manufactured together." Veronica picked up a couple more pieces and pointed out slight variations. "The pattern was likely in production over a span of time, but these small differences mean these pieces didn't come out the same year."

Jillian peered at the swirls and strokes and saw what she'd never seen before. "Grandma Marta must have been collecting. My mom's mom. I wish I'd thought to ask before she died."

"What do you know about this wool coat?" Veronica asked.

"Mom said she used to like to wear it for dress-up when she was little." Jillian said. "That's why Grandma Marta kept it. Mom too, I guess. Just sentimental."

"It's a sturdy piece, that's for sure." Veronica stood up and let the black coat drape its full length. "Not much of a fashion statement."

"Nope." Mannish and boxy, the panels showed decades of wear.

Veronica opened the coat and ran her fingers around in the seams. "Here's a label."

"Probably the brand," Jillian said.

"No, not that one. That's in the collar. This one's more hidden."

Jillian stood now as well. "What are you talking about?"

Between them, they gently pressed the old label in a side seam near the hem as flat as they dared directly under the light. The lettering was faint, some kind of script or handwriting.

"*A, d*," Veronica said, "no, *A, l, d*."

"*A, l, d, o*?" Jillian asked.

"Yes, that could be it, though most of the *o* is gone."

"My great-grandfather's name."

"Did your mother know she was playing dress-up with her grandfather's coat?"

Jillian blanched. "I'm not sure." She should know. Had her mother ever said and she hadn't paid attention? Aldo Parisi was Grandpa Steve's father, not Grandma Marta's. Grandpa Steve had never struck Jillian as interested in the details of family history—perhaps because he never knew much about them to begin with. Perhaps he felt as unmoored from the Parisis as Jillian did. Her breath hitched.

Veronica unfolded a cloth packet to reveal a christening gown. "Jillian, this is a treasure!"

"I know. My mother wore it, Grandma Marta, and her mother. By the time I came along, it was too fragile."

"So it's not a Parisi item?"

Jillian shook her head. "The trunk is a mishmash. I'm not sure who it belonged to originally."

"Well, it's yours now, and they are all part of you."

Jillian folded the coat and set it aside before kneeling again and lifting the last item out of the trunk, a cardboard box. "This is some odds and ends." She set it on the floor between them and removed the lid.

Stamps from Italy on crumbling envelopes gave clues of where the Parisis hailed from. She'd had the letters the envelopes originally contained translated years ago, but their newsy nature gave few real clues about family roots. Even after she became more skilled in her profession, she could read between the lines well enough to draw credible conclusions. A couple other letters came from New Orleans. Both addressed to Sal, even in translation they were distinct from each other, one flowery, trying hard, with a request to be welcomed in Denver and signed simply *Lou*. The second was far shorter, straight to the point, a plea to *At least take Geppetto. Save him. Think of Joe.* Sal. Lou. Joe. In some versions of distant family lore, these were brothers, but in others the names were different. And Geppetto? Jillian didn't know.

A map of Denver's streetcar system from the early 1900s threatened to fall apart if she unfolded it, as she had so many times as a teenager, so she didn't.

Fuzzy photos of New Orleans—fruit stands, docks along the water, a grocery sign with the Parisi name on the canopy, a trio of children standing and squinting into the lens.

Veronica chortled. "That's your hair!"

"You are not wrong." What was the point of trying to dispute that the mass of uncontrolled black curls on the little girl's head was a near-perfect match for Jillian's? In all the ways that her father's large Irish family had dominated her upbringing, they could do nothing about that Parisi gene.

She heard steps on the stairs. "Dad?"

Nolan's head poked out of the top of the staircase. "What's this ruckus I hear?"

"We didn't mean to disturb you," Veronica said.

"Imagine my surprise when I went in the kitchen and found my personal barista missing," Nolan said.

"Very funny, Dad." Jillian began to repack the trunk.

"I came over to have a look at one trunk and discovered two gems," Veronica said. "And look at all that gorgeous mid-twentieth century luggage over there."

"That's my inheritance, which I shall someday bequeath to my daughter," Nolan said.

Veronica jumped up. "Oh. I almost forgot. Nia called me even before I swallowed my breakfast at the crack of dawn. I'm supposed to tell you both that she'd like us all to come over after supper and talk about decor and room arrangements for the big night."

Jillian eyed her dad. "As long as no one wants to know what the menu is, right, Dad?"

"Hush," Nolan said.

"I have to scoot," Veronica said. "Luke will start wondering what happened to me. He doesn't have any help at the store right now. See you tonight."

Despite their steepness, Veronica tapped down the wooden attic steps with admirable speed.

Jillian replaced the tray in the trunk, lowered the lid, and buckled the leather straps. She let her fingers linger.

"Your mother loved that trunk too," Nolan said, "and she didn't know everything about it either. From the day you were born, she hoped someday you would value it. And you do."

Jillian nodded. *I should have valued it better when she was here to know that I do.* There was no changing that regret.

CHAPTER SIX

Denver, Colorado
March 26, 1909

Dear Miss Bendeure,

I am in receipt of the additional documentation you
provided by courier. You've chosen wisely what information
was significant, and a brooding picture does indeed emerge.
With the name and credentials of the agent your father has
authorized to act on his behalf in Denver, and the several
financial institutions involved in the transactions, I
believe we will be able to get to the bottom of things.
Please relay to your father that he is right to have suspicions and to take no further actions at this point in time
that will shift the balance of matters in the midst of the
investigation. I will assign my best operatives. Although
Pinkerton's has made inroads into these sorts of activities
of late, we have multiple details yet to pin down in order
to move forward persuasively on the legal front with this
particular group of associates. I am hopeful that you have
given us just what we need. As long as you take no action
on your end, I do not believe you are in immediate danger.
I will send further reports as they materialize.

Yours sincerely,
James McParland
Manager, Western Division
Pinkerton's National Detective Agency

The compartment was private. The compartment was quiet. The compartment swayed in its stillness. Other than the mechanical sounds of the train propelling its massive weight along the track as a backdrop to her own breath, Lynnelle heard very little from outside the privacy her father had ensured. Even turning her head occasionally to the scenery rolling by outside did not make the compartment feel larger. If Lynnelle had Joan with her, as originally planned, they might have had something to chat about in their facing seats. Instead of Joan, her mute wicker case, with its leather corners and handle, sat on the opposite seat. It held nothing of value, just personal items for travel and what she might need for a couple of nights before she was reunited with her trunk. The thought of not having the steamer in her possession even for the night at Marabel's was unsettling, but Lynnelle and her father had spent two entire dinners discussing the impracticalities of claiming the trunk repeatedly with every transition when the railroads were well qualified to make the transfers and assure it arrived in Denver, and some of the transfers were very brief in time. Especially after it was clear she would be traveling alone, practicality won out.

She would like to have kept her mother's Bible with her, but it was bulky. Given the size of her wicker case, Lynnelle might have been willing to do with fewer fresh blouses on the journey, but the weight of the large, ceremonial tome would have added enough to the case to make it unwieldy as she navigated the aisles of passenger cars, hotel lobbies, and cavernous train stations.

Denver was more than thirteen hundred miles from Cleveland. Lynnelle had looked it up in one of her old school geography textbooks when she and her father first discussed this journey. That was too many miles to sit alone in a compartment, no matter how well intentioned her father was in arranging these accommodations.

No harm would come from going out to the main seating area. At least she could sit comfortably without having to twist her neck to look out the window to avoid having her gaze jolting into the barricade of a wall. Better yet, a cup of coffee in the dining car would perk her up, or she could read in the library car. The numbers were running together on the pages Lynnelle had in her lap. She scooped them up, evened out the edges, and returned them to the satchel—making sure to fasten and check both the latch and the strap. Locking the compartment door behind her, she turned in the direction of the dining car and progressed forward along the aisle. A few people caught her eye, and she nodded and smiled. A porter opened the doors between the cars to ease the transition across the porches, and she continued through the next car and two more after that. In the dining car, she aimed for a tiny table. Sitting alone with a cup of coffee wouldn't require much space.

"Hello there!"

The cheery voice made Lynnelle glance toward its owner, and to her surprise the words were aimed at her. A young woman, perhaps three or four years her junior, waved her over. Lustrous blue eyes were irresistible above a skirt and printed shirtwaist in a color nearly matching them.

"We have plenty of room at our table," the woman said. "I never like to see people alone at a table on a train. Why not use the journey to make new friends? That's my philosophy."

Lynnelle shifted her satchel. The papers could wait a few more minutes. "I was only going to have coffee."

"We were just about to order coffee ourselves, weren't we, Henry?"

"As a matter of fact, we were." The man's tone matched the woman's, though his gray pin-striped suit was more muted garb than hers. "Henry Hollis here. My wife, Clarice."

"Lynnelle Bendeure. I'm pleased to meet you."

Henry pulled out a chair, and Lynnelle arranged herself in it as he signaled a waiter. "Bring us a pot of the best coffee you have. One does get sleepy with all this chug-chug-chugging."

Lynnelle couldn't help smiling. A pot. She was only planning on a cup. "What brings you aboard the chug-chug express?"

Henry laughed. "I like you already."

"We're going to a wedding!" Clarice said. "We've only been married ourselves for a few months. Somehow the Ohio family thought that made us the best ambassadors to represent everyone who couldn't make the trip. We have a trunk full of glittering gifts in the baggage car."

"Which I'm sure you will deliver with aplomb," Lynnelle said.

"The aunts would be impressed with your vocabulary." Henry winked at his wife.

"The aunts?" Lynnelle said.

"Three of them, if you can believe it." Clarice leaned toward Lynnelle. "Ivy, Ida, and Iola. Great-aunts, actually, all of them on my mother's side. They favor the fancy comforts of life and don't believe anyone can get married without racks and racks of silver this and that."

"At the very least silver plate." The coffee arrived, and Henry took the pot from the waiter and poured.

"But of course." Lynnelle entered the banter.

Clarice spooned sugar. "We tried to point out that since the cousin to whose nuptials we have been dispatched lives in Colorado, the land of mines, there is a bit of irony about carting a trunk load of silver wedding gifts halfway across the country, but I'm afraid the humor was lost on the aunts."

Lynnelle chuckled. "Colorado?"

"Denver. Gateway to the wild west."

"I rather think it's not as wild as it once was."

"But wouldn't it be fun if it were? I've never been. Have you?"

"No, actually," Lynnelle said. "I'm also heading to Denver for the first time."

"Don't tell me you have a cousin getting married. That would be too much coincidence."

"No, nothing like that."

"Clarice, dear," Henry said, "give our new friend some room to breathe."

Clarice tilted her flowered hat conspiratorially. "My husband thinks I can be a bit much at times. You can tell me to be quiet at any point. You don't even have to be polite about it."

"No, no wedding." Lynnelle tested the coffee. "But your aunts do remind me of my mother's elderly cousin, Marabel. I'm stopping off to see her near Chicago for a day. She's a precious soul, and I don't get to see her often. Like your aunts, she doesn't travel any longer."

"I wouldn't trade my aunts for all George Pullman's wealth," Clarice said.

"Then we have that in common."

"I told you, Henry." Clarice wagged a finger. "I knew it the moment I saw her."

Lynnelle enjoyed two cups of coffee with the Hollises before excusing herself. She'd gotten out of the compartment, and they'd taken her mind off her dilemma briefly, but the satchel in her lap seemed to gain poundage by the minute, and eventually she asked a porter where the library car was and made her way there. Two older gentlemen sat in opposite corners reading newspapers, but otherwise Lynnelle had the space to herself. She chose a table between facing seats, unlatched the satchel, and slid out the slim stack of carefully curated papers. Two dozen sheets of the most provocative financial information from among the files in her mother's steamer. Numbers. Telegrams. Transactions. Together they told a story. If only her father had been wrong.

Mr. McParland did not think so, but when they met in a few days he could ask his questions, she could ask hers, and they would find out for sure.

Lynnelle folded a blank sheet of paper in half to guide her reading. She'd been over the pages—and dozens of others—so many times, but when she met Mr. McParland she must have no hesitation about any detail. Questions of interpretation, yes, but no hesitation about the content of what she held in her hands. If he, or anyone he introduced her to, began talking rapidly about the columns and lines on the pages, her mind must immediately know what the type or handwriting said, even if she did not have the particular page in front of her. She would murmur these lines under her breath as many times as necessary to be able to repeat them back flawlessly. If in the process some new perspective or inconsistency leaped out, she would point it out to Mr. McParland and see if he thought it significant. He himself was not a banker, but he did say the agency was well versed in matters of this sort.

Whatever this sort was.

Lynnelle blew out her breath and readjusted a crucial hairpin holding her hair up on the back of her head under her gray hat.

The door at the back of the car opened, and a pair entered. The man, in a dark blue blazer and subtly striped trousers, gently guided the elbow of the woman, who wore a deep burgundy traveling suit. Lynnelle offered a vague smile.

"Are there any more newspapers?" the woman asked.

"I'm not sure." Lynnelle gestured at her own pages. She hadn't paid attention to what the racks offered.

One of the men in a corner grunted. "Over there."

"Thank you." The young man took a couple of papers from the rack and handed one to his companion. "Let's sit here."

Other than the isolated men in the corners, the car was empty, yet the pair sat in chairs directly across from Lynnelle's table.

"Oh look." The woman snapped her paper open. "This one's from Memphis. The *Commercial Appeal*. I didn't expect that."

"You never know what you're going to get on a train," the man said. "I once ran across a journalistic account of the yellow fever outbreaks in Memphis in the 1870s."

"Of course you did," she said. "What paper did you get?"

"Newark." He smoothed the paper down on the table.

"Newark?" The woman looked up. "Not New York?"

"Not New York. Newark."

"I would think people would prefer to read a New York paper rather than a Newark rag."

"Now, Willie, behave yourself," the man said. "For all we know this nice gentlewoman is from Newark."

Willie looked at Lynnelle, her gray eyes wide beneath hair the color of Lynnelle's. "Are you? From Newark?"

Lynnelle shook her head. "Cleveland."

"That's a relief. I should mind my tongue. I'm sure the Newark paper is a perfectly fine publication."

"No doubt."

"I'm Willie Meade. This is Carey."

"Also Meade," he said. His eyes were a darker shade of gray, and the long and deep dimple in his right cheek was a smile of its own.

"Lynnelle Bendeure. Nice to meet you." Lynnelle had never met a female Willie before. Perhaps her name was Wilma. She didn't seem like a Wilma. Willa, then. Lynnelle had once known a girl in school called Willeen. In any case, Willie suited this sassy woman. Lynnelle slipped her papers under her satchel. "Where are you headed?"

"We're not sure." Carey's dark hair, on the long side compared to the men Lynnelle knew, had a wave she found attractive.

What was she thinking? A strange man she'd just met. A *married* man. Lynnelle pursed her lips and immediately drew them back in, trying not to look rude.

"We really don't," Willie said. "We're taking a few weeks to ride the rails, see the country."

"That sounds like an adventure," Lynnelle said. "No destination at all?"

"We want to see the West. We might ride all the way to San Francisco," Carey said. "Or maybe we'll find someplace along the way that appeals and stay there."

"No one is expecting you back wherever you came from?"

They both shrugged.

"Not really," Willie said. "We're looking for a place to put down roots. If we find a place we love, we'll stay. If not, we'll go back to Buffalo."

"I for one have had enough of the snow in Buffalo winters," Carey said.

Lynnelle laughed. "I suppose by comparison we have it easy in Cleveland, but I have an idea how you feel."

"What about you?" Willie said. "Where are you going? Chicago?"

"Nearby, for a stop. Eventually Denver for a few days. And then home again. No grand adventure for me."

"Somebody waiting for you?"

"My father. I could never leave him."

Willie met her eyes. "I'm sure he's lucky to have you."

CHAPTER SEVEN

At least you're going out to another meeting properly fortified this time." Jillian pulled the front door shut behind her, gave it a second tug to be sure it was locked, and fell in step beside her father going down the porch steps.

"Thanks to your leftover roast chicken, stretched into dinner two nights in a row," he said.

"When you offered to make the biscuits and gravy to go with it, what could I say?" Jillian tried to do her share of the cooking, but she was no fool. Her father's food was delectable. Whatever she knew about cooking she'd learned from him, but she didn't have the finesse or spontaneous repertoire he mustered. No one would ever suggest she should prepare a sit-down meal for a fundraiser dinner.

"I still wish we had Kris's ice cream," Nolan said. "Now that would be fortification."

The walk to the Inn at Hidden Run would take ten minutes at most on a mild spring evening. They made it often, Jillian more than Nolan. When her former babysitter had returned to Canyon Mines, husband in tow, and bought a rambling, neglected Victorian more than twice the size of Jillian and Nolan's home and set about renovating it to open a bed-and-breakfast, Jillian giggled with delight at the thought of having Nia just down the street.

"I didn't mean to upset you with the trunk," Nolan said. "I thought you would enjoy it. I didn't think about what it might stir up in you. I'm sorry."

"Dad, no. You can't protect me from myself forever."

"As much as I'd like to."

"I *do* like having the trunk in the house, even if it's only on loan while we—mostly you—figure out if there's anything to be worried about. I'm going to try to clear some time to dig into it myself soon."

"Now you sound like yourself. But you surprised me when I found you in the attic."

"You're the one who said when I was ready I'd go at it again."

"Are you ready?"

"Trying to be." It seemed like she should be. What would being ready feel like? At least this time she'd managed to put everything away herself rather than storm out of the attic in tears, leaving Nolan to store everything, slide the trunk out of the way, and cover it with blankets as she had six years ago. "I'll be all right. Let's focus on what Nia needs."

"If this is about decor, I don't know what she needs me for," Nolan said.

"It's about the dinner as a whole." Jillian made a large circle with her hands. "Besides, we've both learned not to argue with Nia unnecessarily, haven't we?"

They went in through the front door of the Inn. Nia recently had changed the round table in the large entry area, buying one that Veronica had come across at an estate sale and assured her came directly from the only other home it ever had. Some elbow grease and wax was all it took to make the table shine, and with a large vase of flowers it was the perfect welcome to visitors. A couple of midweek guests sat in the parlor enjoying the evening fire, where Leo leaned against the mantel. Nolan crossed the room to shake Leo's hand, while Jillian went through the dining room in search of Nia. She found her in the kitchen with Veronica.

"Where's your father?" Nia asked.

"In the parlor with Leo."

"Oh no, no, no. That is not what he's here for."

"He's just saying hello."

"Jillian, don't be naive." Nia tossed the dish towel in her hand on the counter and her dark single braid over her shoulder. "You know those two can jaw on half the night about nothing. I'll be right back."

Nia left the room, and Jillian and Veronica burst out laughing.

"She means business," Jillian said.

"You know she's right," Veronica said. "The only thing that would make it worse is if Luke was here."

"You won't hear me arguing," Jillian said. "Do you have a theme in mind for the decorating?"

"I have some ideas, but it's Nia's inn, so ultimately I'll defer to whether she thinks they'll work."

They wandered into the dining room, where the table was already set for the next day's breakfast.

"Wednesday," Jillian said. "Usually a small crowd except in the summer. She'll do an egg casserole of some sort and homemade scones."

"Makes me want to happen by before work."

Nia returned with Nolan, who looked not one bit sheepish, and they sat at the end of the table with no place settings.

"Nolan," Nia said, "I know you've been in my kitchen a thousand times, but before you leave tonight, we should pull open the drawers and cabinets so you know what's there and available to work with. We don't need any surprises on the night of the dinner."

"Can't he just bring everything he needs?" Jillian suggested. "Cook with the pots he's used to?"

"He might forget something," Nia said, "and he should have some idea of what is available to improvise with. Slotted spoons, extra pots, and whatnot."

Good point.

A choke of air announced the front door had been breached, and Nia cocked her head toward the hall. In another minute, Leo ushered Marilyn in.

"Oh good," Marilyn said. "You're all here. I thought I was just dropping in on Nia."

"What's up?" Nolan asked.

"Good news, I think," Marilyn said, "but it will take some reconsidering. We're still a couple of weeks out, and at the pace of ticket requests we already have, we could have quite a few more reservations than the seats we were planning even with adding the third seating. The dinner is turning out to be a smashing success—perhaps the best event of the weekend. Of course, we can always start saying we're sold out, but I wonder how many more we could accommodate."

"How many are we talking about?" Nolan said.

Jillian watched the color in his face fluctuate through several shades, each paler than the other. Not much flapped her dad, but apparently cooking for an increasingly large crowd did.

Marilyn turned to Nia. "I know you said you could easily find space for between forty and fifty at each seating. I wonder if we can push that to seventy. I can rent additional tables and chairs if you think you have a place to put them. The expense will be well worth the extra ticket sales."

"Seventy! Goodness. Let's see." Nia stepped out of the dining room, and the others trailed after her. "On occasion I've put as many as twenty-five in the dining room, and maybe I can squeeze in four more. I was planning to use the parlor and part of the lobby. We can use more of the lobby, I suppose, and make a quiet space in the library for eight or ten."

"We have to think about where Jillian will present from," Marilyn said. "Everyone must be able to see her."

"Agreed," Nia said.

Jillian continued to watch Nolan's face while this virtual reconfiguring went on in the minds of Marilyn and Nia. His eyes roamed between the two of them and the spaces they pointed to as his usual affable expression dimmed.

"Perhaps we can have the high school students who will be the wait staff assist guests in turning and carrying chairs." Marilyn pointed to the wide staircase. "If Jillian stands there, and we wait until after dessert to bring people in from the outer areas, they should be able to see her. I think I can find more students to help."

"Well, there you have it," Nia said. "I think that could work, though I suggest keeping the seatings at no more than sixty-five."

That was still almost two hundred meals for Nolan to prepare—more than two hundred if he was expected to feed the volunteer high school students, which only seemed fair, since they would be spending their entire evening at the Inn.

"Very well," Marilyn said. "I will make the arrangements. Thank you for being flexible. It would have seemed a shame to walk away from the additional ticket money this will raise."

No one had asked the chef.

"Dad?" Jillian said. "How does that sound? Do you need more help?"

"I'm sure I can find it," he said. "It's all for a great cause."

Marilyn said good night, and Nia turned to the others. "Nolan, it looks like we may need both your pots and mine."

"We'll figure it out." Nolan's complexion had recovered.

"Now about the decorating?" Nia turned back toward the dining room. "Veronica, you said you had an idea?"

"Trunks!" Veronica said.

Jillian blinked at her.

The front door opened again, and Kris Bryant entered. "A little birdie told me you'd all be here. I have ice cream."

Jillian tilted her gaze at Nolan. "Did you text Kris?"

"I plead the fifth," he said, "but I hope she brought cherry chocolate chip chunk."

Jillian avoided speaking the name of that flavor aloud because too often she tripped on the repetitive sounds, but it was one of Nolan's favorites.

"Also butter pecan." Kris raised her sack.

"Then we're moving this meeting to the kitchen," Nia said. "I'm not having ice cream dribbled on my table set for breakfast."

In the kitchen, Nolan dished out ice cream, and the decorating discussion resumed.

"I was inspired by a conversation Jillian and I had," Veronica said. "Steamer trunks used on ocean liners and railroads represent heritage for a lot of families because they represent how families got from one country to another or from one part of the country to another."

"I was thinking in terms of table decorations," Nia said.

"I'm still working on that," Veronica said, "but steamer trunks or other vintage-looking luggage could establish some ambiance, and we'll work off of that for the rest."

"We just gave away valuable space to Marilyn for extra seating," Jillian pointed out.

"True," Veronica said, "but we don't need a lot of pieces. They just need to be elegantly and strategically placed. I'll bet we'll have people telling stories around the tables in no time about what luggage reminds them of in their family histories. It could be the perfect setup for your talk."

"I think she's right." Nolan licked his spoon. "It might even help with getting people to sign on as Friends of the Society with regular donations."

Jillian smiled. Nolan had lost his stunned expression. The ice cream helped.

"I've got some we could use," Veronica said.

"I have one." Kris peered into a now-empty ice cream carton.

"So do I," Nia said. "Several. I'll pull them from the guest rooms temporarily."

Jillian ran her tongue over her bottom teeth, not ready to volunteer her trunk—as much as she loved the decorating theme.

"I'll make some calls for a few more," Veronica said. "What about dishes?"

"Leave that to me," Nia said. "I'm not having any disposable nonsense in my Inn. It would completely undercut the effort of the evening. We'll have to wash and reset quickly between seatings, but I think I can come up with the china."

"Agreed."

"I have my grandmother's china," Kris said. "Sixteen place settings."

Nia nodded. "I've seen it, and it will do nicely."

"I'll make centerpieces from knickknacks at the store," Veronica said.

"The classy ones." Nia pointed a stern finger.

"Absolutely. With candles and low lighting."

Nia stood. "Thank you, everyone. You may now return to your regularly scheduled programming."

Back at home, Jillian and Nolan sprawled in the living room, Nolan on the navy couch surrounded by cookbooks and Jillian on the favorite purple chair and matching ottoman with her laptop and a yellow legal pad.

"Okra soup," he said.

"Too unfamiliar."

"Creamy pumpkin."

"Out of season."

Nolan alternated flipping pages in three cookbooks. Jillian opened the 1910 census. The correspondence in the unclaimed trunk was addressed to Miss Lynnelle Bendeure in Cleveland in the spring of 1909. If she returned to Cleveland, for some reason without her luggage, and was present there in April 1910 at the address on the letters, she would show in the census. Having a fixed address removed the guesswork from the initial search.

Not there.

Nobody by the name of Bendeure at that address, in fact. Nobody living at that address at all on the dates of the census.

"Herbed monkey bread," Nolan said.

Jillian laughed. "Marilyn would love printing that on her menus."

"Blanquette of veal."

"Ew to all things veal. People have principles about baby cows, Dad."

He flipped more pages.

Jillian widened her census search to all the counties of Ohio. No Lynnelle. No Bendeure.

"Spinach venison quiche," he said.

"People won't eat Bambi either."

"It's not actually Bambi."

"Doesn't matter."

"Coq au vin."

" 'What is that?' people will say."

"Chicken."

"Maybe you could just say chicken."

"And have people think this is another rubber chicken fundraiser? No thanks."

He flipped more pages.

Jillian moved her census search to Colorado. Lynnelle Bendeure's trunk arrived in Denver. But did she? She might have arrived but never gone home, or she might never have arrived at all.

Jillian clicked through one Colorado county after another while Nolan turned pages.

"Lamb brochettes."

"Getting closer," she said—though *she* was getting no closer.

"Yorkshire pudding."

"Don't ruin it now." Jillian moved her computer off her lap and crossed the room to the trunk. With the gloves on, she pulled out the family Bible and returned to her chair.

"What's going on, Silly Jilly?"

"I just want to write down some of these names." The family section on the opening pages listed multiple Bendeures. Not all of them had death dates entered prior to 1909. They should have been in the Ohio census. It was unlikely the entire family had left the state—and a family business—in the months between Lynnelle's journey and the census. It was less than a year.

Her trunk was abandoned.

She was not in the census in either state.

The family disappeared.

This was going to take some digging. Jillian jotted down names from the family tree on her legal pad, not yet ready to tell Nolan her primary suspicion was a preinternet version of identity theft.

Or worse. Get what you need and then do away with the identity—and the person you stole it from—altogether.

"Well, if you won't let me serve monkey bread or Yorkshire pudding," Nolan said, "I'm going to bed."

"You'll come up with the right thing," Jillian murmured.

As Nolan checked the locks before going upstairs, Jillian moved to her office. The family tree had yielded Lynnelle's middle name, which could be a useful piece of information.

Lynnelle Elaine Bendeure.

On a large whiteboard hanging on the wall of her office, behind her desk, Jillian began to scribble.

Lynn E. Bendeure.

Elaine Bendeure.

Lynne Bendeure.

Lynnette Bendeur.

Lyn Bender.

Lynnette Bender.

Elaine Bender.

Ellen Bender.

Jillian started plugging these variations and dozens more into the search bars of archived Colorado public records—births, marriages, and deaths. She started in the counties around Denver and moved out from there. As fast as she could think of a variant, she recorded it, typed it in search bars, and checked it off as attempted. Her eyes drooped, her handwriting deteriorated, and still she kept going into the yawning hours of the night.

When she finally got a hit, she was so blurred with fatigue she nearly cleared the search bar without acknowledging the result. Rubbing her eyes, she looked again.

It was an ordinary enough name for 1909. It could be anybody.

Yet the thought niggled.

CHAPTER EIGHT

Nolan had to be in his Denver law office on Wednesday but not until midmorning. He showered, dressed in the dark suit—the one his daughter said made him look like a shark attorney when he first bought it—and took his briefcase down the rear stairs that would deliver him to the space between the doorways to Jillian's office and the kitchen. Judging from the aroma that greeted him, she was already at work, which would have been true on many days no matter what time he descended.

He looked into her office. Not only was she working, but she wore the same jeans and soft plaid flannel shirt she'd had on yesterday.

"Jilly."

She looked up. "Good morning."

"You didn't go to bed, did you?"

The shake of her head sent her curls, free from any restraint, rattling in several directions.

"How much coffee?" he asked.

"Don't go there."

Nolan moved into the office and set his briefcase in one of the chairs Jillian kept opposite her desk for infrequent visitors and more frequent overflow research piles. "Thinking of redecorating?"

In addition to her whiteboard full of scribbles and lines and arrows and circles in five different dry-erase colors, another wall served as a make-shift bulletin board featuring the Pinkerton's correspondence and select financial documents. On a third wall, Jillian had removed the artwork above the bookcases and taped up sheets of easel paper. The whiteboard often was a temporary tool. The rest of this was wholly uncharacteristic of the way Jillian worked.

"What's going on, Jillian?"

"I have to be able to see these letters, Dad." Jillian opened her fingers and let a pen drop to her habitual yellow narrow-lined legal pad. "Something is niggling, and the information is there. It has to be. So I took the liberty of making some photocopies."

"The approach is not without merit." Nolan faced the display of letters. "But shouldn't you sleep?"

"I need to figure this out."

"We're not on a deadline, Jillian. There's no real client and no rush. I'm just doing Rich a favor. Whatever happened was over a hundred years ago. No one is in imminent danger. We haven't begun to sort out if there would be any legal recourse." In fact, he doubted there would be. They didn't have much to work on that would lead to true evidence, and even if they did, statutes of limitation would work against them. All Rich wanted was peace of mind for the museum.

"I know what I'm doing," Jillian said. "Obviously we only have one side of the conversation, but if we deduce the right things, the narrative will crack right open. That's not so different from genealogy research. And the family Bible will be a big help there."

"I'm not doubting your skills, Jilly. Just whether the urgency was worth losing a night's sleep."

She shrugged. "I was going to think about it all night anyway."

"You have a theory, don't you?"

"I can't prove anything. I copied a few of the financials because they are mentioned in the letters. But it's hard to guess which ones they were talking about. I'll probably need all of them eventually."

"You don't have enough wall space for that. You're not planning to wallpaper the dining room, are you?"

"Hey, that's an idea!"

"Veto!"

"In any event, I think there are gaps."

"What do you mean?"

"The records are not all there. Missing dates. Missing lists. Missing reports. Like somebody deliberately removed certain documents."

This wasn't like Jillian. The thoroughness of her approach to the data was characteristic, but losing sleep and papering over her office because of a long shot that had no pressing consequence made little sense. And Jillian was one of the most sensible people Nolan knew. Her theory about the trunk's owner wasn't the only thing niggling at her. It was just all she was prepared to admit to—and she was hedging around even that.

"I'll make you a deal," Nolan said. "I was planning to make some copies of my own. I need a set for Luke, and I want to take a set with me to Denver. I have a colleague I think could help. If I also make you a complete set, while I'm doing that, will you go in the kitchen and have a proper breakfast? Yogurt and fruit?"

"I could be persuaded."

"Have you got space in your schedule today for a nap?"

"Not in preschool, Dad."

He'd pushed too far.

"Whatever you do," Jillian said, "don't put the sheets through the automatic feeder on your cranky copier."

"I've handled a few important papers in my time." He went to the living room to retrieve documents from the trunk's three drawers, listening to Jillian's movements to be sure she held up her end of the bargain. Occasionally she liked to remind him that if they didn't share a home, he wouldn't know whether she slept or when she ate or how much coffee she consumed or that she never switched to decaf. But so far it was an idle threat. After attending college in Denver, she'd moved back home and never once talked seriously about moving out. Still, a father was entitled to recognize the old undercurrents of behavior in his own child.

At least when he left the house, Nolan knew Jillian had eaten and even showered. He left one set of the financial documents with her and took two with him. His first stop was the Victorium Emporium. The shop wasn't open for daily business yet, but a text message brought Luke to the door.

Inside, Nolan set a stack of papers on the counter. "I tried to get the best quality I could, but the old typewriter ink is faded in places."

"Or gloppy in the wrong places." Luke put his finger on a number. "Is that an eight or a three with extra ink smudged in it?"

Nolan peered. "Hard to be sure."

"Well, I'll have a look," Luke said. "This is quite a pile."

"There's no time frame."

"I still have some connections in the banks, depending on what I find. Can I share these?"

"Just keep me posted who has eyes on them," Nolan said.

From there Nolan went to Denver. He had just enough time before his first meeting to stop in a colleague's office and watch his eyes grow large at the sight of the historical documents.

"You drop something like this in front of a history nerd and then stand there with one of your silly grins on your face?" Pete said.

"I need somebody to help me understand what they mean." Nolan leaned over the desk.

"How many billable hours are there in this?"

"Exactly zero."

"One of your pro bono projects?"

"More or less."

"You dog. Where did you get this?" Pete turned sheets over from one neat pile to another.

Nolan gave him the short version of the story as Pete continued to scan documents.

"On the surface of things," Pete said, "given the timing, I'd wager this Bendeure & Company's interest in Colorado was to expand financial investments into the revitalized Colorado mining and financial markets after the mining industry recovered following the 1893 recession. The recession was nationwide, but by about 1906, downtown Denver was back on track. Certainly by 1909 many people would have considered it safe to invest again."

"But is there any funny business going on?"

"You want an opinion based on a four-minute audit of two hundred pages of numbers?"

"You can have the full five minutes," Nolan said.

The speaker on Pete's desk buzzed, and he pushed a button. "Yes?"

"The McCormicks have arrived," a voice said. "I put them in the conference room."

"Thank you. I'll be right out." To Nolan, Pete said, "I'll get back to you."

At the end of the day, Nolan shot Jillian a text message to let her know when he was leaving the office. When she didn't acknowledge at least with a thumb-up emoji, he dared to hope she was napping before dinner, though he recognized the foolishness of the thought. Even when Jillian was a preschooler, Bella couldn't get her to stay down for a decent nap. Other mothers talked about everything they got accomplished while their kids napped—even if it was simply enjoying two hours of quiet in the house—but Bella knew not to plan on doing more than reading the mail and loading the dishwasher. Some days it was one or the other, she used to say, before Silly Jilly would pop up, afraid she was missing something. Bella was the first one to use that nickname. Jillian was twenty-eight and far from silly now. Nolan suspected she tolerated his use of the nickname because it reminded both of them of Bella and made it feel like she was still part of them.

Of course she would always be part of them.

Traffic was on the heavy side, but Nolan finally made it out of downtown and headed west on I-70 toward Canyon Mines. On congested days, the commute could take closer to forty-five minutes than thirty, but once he was headed west and the views of the Rockies saturated his eyes, the day's pressures sloughed off his shoulders. He had arranged to take the next two days off, only touching base at work on essential issues, so he could face reality on the commitment to cook for Marilyn, which had snowballed into two hundred meals.

Nolan approached the house through the back door, which stood open, and immediately knew something was wrong. Every window in the kitchen and dining room was also open.

"Jillian!"

No answer. He tossed his briefcase and keys on the breakfast bar.

Glass crunched beneath a shoe, and he drew back his foot. Mingled with food remains, shards of glass strewed a path across the kitchen. And blood. That was blood. He was sure of it. The oven door was wide open.

"Jillian!"

Her office was empty. Nolan took the back stairs two at a time, letting out his breath only when his daughter's bedroom door cracked, and he saw her head wrapped in a towel, her body snug in a bathrobe. He exhaled relief.

"I'm all right, Dad. I'll be right down to clean up the mess."

"What happened, Jilly?" He didn't care about the mess.

"I took a break to get supper in the oven. An unstuffed cabbage casserole. You know I never could make actual stuffed cabbage rolls. They would just fall apart. But I forgot to set the timer, and the smoke alarm went off. It wouldn't stop. I had to open all the windows. The casserole had burned to a crisp, of course, and I dropped it getting it out of the oven. Then I stepped in it with no shoes."

"How bad is the cut?"

"It's all right now. I finally got the bleeding stopped. I won't be taking any morning runs for a few days."

"Did you burn your hands?" She turned her palms to his inspection. "I let go too fast for any real damage."

"I will clean up the kitchen," Nolan said. "And I'll call for Chinese food."

"Sorry. Guess I could have used a nap after all. I might have had better judgment on a few decisions."

"Don't worry about it. Come down when you're ready."

Nolan stopped in his own bedroom long enough to get out of his suit and into clothing more appropriate for restoring order to the kitchen. By the time Jillian finished cleaning herself up and limped down the stairs, beef and snow peas and cashew chicken were on the way. Nolan settled Jillian in the purple chair, the only place she ever wanted to sit in the living room, helped her prop up her bandaged foot, and brought her a large glass of cold water.

"No more coffee for you," he said. "Tonight you sleep."

"No argument from me there," she said.

"Before this disaster, how was your day?"

"Reasonable. I got a few things checked off my list, and in between read the Pinkerton's letters about six more times."

"And?"

The doorbell rang, and Nolan pivoted toward it, returning a minute later with the aromatic brown bag. "I'll get plates."

They shared the fried rice and both entrees, and he prodded Jillian to resume her report of her day. If she got some of this out of her system, maybe it would help her let go and sleep tonight. And he might garner some clue about why it had become so urgent to her.

"It's pretty easy to see what they were discussing," she said. "People were representing themselves as financial agents to get access to other people's money. This Lynnelle Bendeure seemed determined to come to Denver and sort out whatever her father had gotten involved in."

"Foul play?" Nolan scooped up a forkful of the chicken, seasoned just the way he liked it.

Jillian nodded. "I've been looking for Lynnelle Bendeure on and off all night and all day. But she seems to have done a disappearing act."

"You only started looking last night," Nolan said. "Perhaps it's too soon to conclude anything."

"I'm telling you, Dad, something happened to her that shouldn't have."

Nolan nodded, placating, and swallowed a chunk of pineapple. "I had Pete look at the papers today. The time frame is such that people were investing in gold mines again after the bottom fell out of silver. The records are buried in general business records of the company."

"That's all he came up with?"

"He did observe that the pattern of influx of cash in this case seems irregular."

"Irregular how?"

"Apparently that will take a closer look. We'll have to get the right people on it—just to set Rich's mind at ease."

"If we follow the money, it will tell us what foul play happened to Lynnelle."

"Maybe," Nolan said. "But when I took you with me to the Owens House Museum, I just thought you'd like the trunk. No one is expecting you to find a missing person from so long ago. That's not Rich's question."

"But it's mine. I'm going to find her, Dad."

CHAPTER NINE

Denver, Colorado
April 2, 1909

Dear Miss Bendeure,

Your questions are astute, and I will endeavor to address them based both on my own observations and the wider experience of the Pinkerton's Agency across the nation. The operations we investigate most similar to the one that Bendeure & Company may be caught up in come in a variety of forms. The commonalities, however, are convincing duplicity, gaining trust, and acting swiftly when the moment is ripe. In some cases, the individuals we apprehend have operated under multiple identities, whether invented or appropriated wrongfully. They may have participated in lesser roles before becoming more daring. They may be young or old, male or female. Financial institutions are rarely intentionally culpable. We work closely with them and find them fully cooperative nearly one hundred percent of the time. For some time now, we have annually reported the details of our work to the American Bankers Association. All it takes is an eye for finding a weak spot. I am not suggesting your father has been weak. To the contrary, he has asked more questions than most I have known in these circumstances, and this speaks well of him. I have had several fruitful conversations in recent days that seem to point in the same direction, and while I cannot give you complete answers on this date, it is my hope that neither of us will be waiting much longer.

Yours sincerely,
James McParland
Manager, Western Division
Pinkerton's National Detective Agency

"Were you able to find it?" Lynnelle took the claim check from the porter's hand outside her compartment on the second leg of her travels.

"Yes, miss. Your trunk made the transfer safely and is aboard this train now headed for Omaha."

Lynnelle leaned back in the seat outside her compartment. "Oh good. Thank you so much for indulging me and putting my mind at ease by checking."

"It was no trouble."

Another Pullman car also on a line operated by the New York Central, the compartment was nearly identical to the one in which Lynnelle departed Cleveland the day before yesterday. This time her wicker case sat on a bench across from the sink.

According to the schedule, this day's journey would be nearly fourteen hours after the train left Chicago before the final leg from Omaha to Denver began in the middle of the night. After leaving Cousin Marabel late last evening, boarding the Lake Shore and Michigan Southern line out of Chesterton to Chicago to connect to the Union Pacific line, she'd slept a few hours in a downtown hotel before breakfasting heartily in Chicago. Now, reassured that her trunk was making the trip as well, she was tempted to nap in her compartment at the back of the car. She wouldn't ask the porter to make the bed in the middle of the day, but she could at least remove her hat and shoes to doze without anyone staring at her.

She tipped the porter. "Thank you again."

"Lynnelle!"

The iridescent eyes of two days earlier sparkled at Lynnelle once again.

"Hello, you two," she said.

"Good morning, Miss Bendeure." Henry Hollis rose from the bench outside Lynnelle's compartment, gesturing for her to join them.

"Please call me Lynnelle." A nap could wait a few more minutes.

"Such a lovely name," Clarice said. "Like a song."

Lynnelle laughed as she sat down. "No one's ever said that before."

"Where does it come from?"

"My mother always said it was Welsh. How was your day in Chicago?"

"Utterly fabulous. We went to gawk at all the mansions on Prairie Avenue, where all the obscenely rich people live."

"Clarice." Henry patted his wife's hand. "You might have pointed out that we went to the art museum."

"That too."

"We are not completely without culture," Henry said. "And a springtime walk along Lake Michigan."

"So romantic." Clarice's gaze briefly lost its focus in wistfulness.

"It sounds as if you made a full and satisfying day of it," Lynnelle said.

"Perhaps we'll never have another opportunity," Clarice said. "Back to Cleveland and the aunts after the wedding."

"When is the ceremony?"

"Sunday evening." Clarice elbowed her husband. "But this one couldn't get another week away from his office, so we'll have to get back on a train the very next morning."

"That's too bad."

"Did you enjoy your visit with your cousin?"

"Immensely," Lynnelle said. "She sent me off with a picnic basket of biscuits and cookies and jams and apples, as if she doesn't trust railroad dining cars. Even a jar of green olives."

"The aunts would say one never knows," Henry said.

"That's just what Marabel said!"

The whistle blew. Henry looked at his watch. "Departing right on time."

A shudder coursed through the car, and passengers up the aisle reflexively gripped armrests as the locomotive coaxed its massive load into motion. A few still stowing their belongings found their balance slightly challenged as speed picked up and the train advanced out of the Dearborn Station and across Chicago neighborhoods.

"Are these your seats?" Lynnelle asked.

"We're in the next car, actually," Clarice said. "But we were stretching our legs, and then I spotted you with the porter and wanted to be sure we said hello. Imagine finding each other again."

"It is a bright bit of fun, indeed."

They'd had coffee together on the leg from Cleveland, and when the Hollises later spotted her walking past their seats headed for a simple meal, they decided they could do with a bite as well. Exchanging stories of the aunts and Cousin Marabel had them all chortling so hard they could hardly chew. More than a few heads turned toward the ruckus of Clarice's imitation of the aunts. It wasn't like Lynnelle at all, but the breach in decorum produced a soothing release of stress in her shoulders, and she'd been grateful.

A porter approached. "Excuse me, sir, but it seems that you are in the seats that this couple have specifically arranged for."

Henry popped up and tugged Clarice with him. "My apologies."

"Mr. Meade!" Lynnelle said.

"You know these folks?" Clarice said.

"I met them on the same train where I met you," Lynnelle said. "This is Carey and Willie Meade, of Rochester or thereabout. This is Henry and Clarice Hollis, from Cleveland. It seems we're all headed to Denver."

"What a great big beautiful country," Willie said.

"We'll leave you to your seats," Henry said. "We staked our claim in the proper car, but we would do well to be sure we haven't been displaced."

"Now you know where I am." Lynnelle pointed over her shoulder. "My compartment is just there."

"We could have a meal together again," Clarice said.

Willie spread her hands. "Why not all of us?"

"Why not?" Carey said. "We're probably all changing trains in Omaha. We're going to be together for a couple of days. Might as well have some friendly faces."

"Lynnelle?" Clarice said.

Lynnelle nodded. Once her large breakfast wore off, she'd want to eat. Willie and Clarice, with their lively temperaments, were similar enough to surely get on well.

"A fashionably late lunch it is!" Willie said.

"Or a quirkishly early dinner, in deference to the aunts." Clarice grinned.

Lynnelle blinked. The conversation had progressed swiftly from the theoretical meal to the specific. The men checked their watches and agreed on a time to meet in the dining car, the wives consented, and Lynnelle was nodding agreement all in the space of one minute. The Hollises left, and the Meades settled into their seats.

"What a pleasant coincidence that we are all back on the same train." Lynnelle settled her hands on the satchel on her lap. "What are the odds?"

"Well," Carey said, "let's see. How many cars were there on the previous train? A predictable fraction of passengers would be terminating in Chicago and others continuing westward, and I suppose it's not uncommon to take a day to enjoy the city if one has the time and opportunity, and the means for the overnight stay and a fresh start on a morning train rather than enduring overnight travel if not necessary. The railroads could probably supply the numbers. It's a matter of simple mathematics."

Willie slapped his forearm. "Silly. She doesn't actually want you to calculate the odds."

Lynnelle's smile was plaintive. "My brother used to tease like that. He would make quite a show of it in front of guests, to my mother's consternation."

"I might have to meet this brother of yours," Carey said.

"I'm afraid he has departed this life. My mother as well."

"See what you've done, Carey," Willie said. "You've made Lynnelle sad."

"Quite the opposite," Lynnelle said. "It was a lovely memory."

"I'm sorry about your other new friends," Willie said, "but I'm secretly very glad that we're lucky enough to have seats right outside your compartment."

"It will be handy, won't it?" Lynnelle said. "I had the oddest experience yesterday while I was visiting my cousin in Chesterton. I thought I saw you."

"Us?" Carey said.

"Only Willie," Lynnelle said. "It was a fleeting thing. A woman ducking into a shop in a small town in Indiana while we were out to lunch, and for a moment I persuaded myself it was someone I'd met on the train. Wishful thinking, I suppose."

"I'm flattered." Willie grinned. "If I could have been in two places at once, I'm sure one of them would have been Chesterton."

"The same thing happened last night when I arrived at my hotel in Chicago. Just a glimpse of someone across the lobby. The back of a woman walking away."

"Oh how odd," Willie said. "But now we have all the way to Denver, and at least until Omaha we are next-door neighbors."

"I'm afraid we disturbed you the other day in the library car," Carey said. "We were frivolously passing the time, and you looked far more industrious when we stormed in."

"You hardly stormed in," Lynnelle said. "The distraction was not unwelcome."

"You seem to have more purpose in going to Denver than we do."

"A sort of business errand on behalf of my father and perhaps some pleasure as well. I hope to learn more of the West. I've traveled in the East, and the South to a lesser degree, but never past the Mississippi."

"Then you are having an adventure as well, at least for a few days."

"I hope so." Lynnelle's travel history was accurate even if she had embellished her reasons for going to Denver.

Several hours later, after resting and freshening up in her compartment, Lynnelle sat shoulder to shoulder between Willie and Clarice, while the men sat opposite. A fashionably late lunch—or a quirkishly early dinner—seemed to be a popular idea—at nearly four in the afternoon. When they arrived in the dining car, the only open table was meant for four, but Willie and Clarice were intent on making the arrangement work, and they had, with cooperation of the waiter who relaid the table according to their instructions.

"It's a bit cozy, but it will do just fine," Clarice pronounced.

"The aunts would be proud of your resourcefulness," Henry said.

"The aunts?" Willie said.

Lynnelle and Clarice chuckled in tandem. Clarice launched into imitations of Ivy, Ida, and Iola. Arranging place cards at the dinner table. Discussing which book might be most appropriate for a thirteen-year-old neighbor girl. Expounding their opinions on changing fashions and the loosened ways women wore corsets these days. Scowling at the growing acceptance of automobiles.

They perused the menus, which offered three kinds of soup, half a dozen hot sandwiches, a Cobb salad, and three full-course entree options, including broiled mutton chops, breaded veal cutlets, and roast goose with apples. Even diners with high-end palates and budgets would find delectable experiences. The waiter had just brought warm bread to the table and topped off their water goblets when the train lurched.

"What happened?" Spilled water soaked through the linen tablecloth as Lynnelle scrambled to right a couple of glasses.

Behind them, an elderly woman gasped. "Not another robbery."

"What does she mean?" Lynnelle said.

"Let's all stay calm," Carey said.

The train listed and slowed.

The elderly woman reached for her cane and pushed herself up out of her seat. Lynnelle and Clarice exchanged glances. It was hard not to think of Cousin Marabel, and Clarice must be thinking of the aunts.

"I've been robbed once before," the woman said. "They probably killed the engineer. They'll shoot out the mail car and then come looking for jewelry."

Carey stood and raised his hands, palms out. "Easy now. Would you like to sit at our table while I go see what I can find out?"

"Does anyone have a gun?"

"Surely it won't come to that." Lynnelle caught Carey's eye. "Come sit with us. I'm Lynnelle. Mrs.—?"

"Sweeney."

Carey delivered the woman to the table before leaving the dining car, as a couple of other men had done before him.

"Perhaps I should go as well," Henry said.

"Perhaps you shouldn't," Mrs. Sweeney said. "If I wanted to be at a table with no man, I could have stayed where I was sitting alone."

"You're very welcome to stay with us." Lynnelle raised the bread basket. "Did you have a chance to eat anything yet?"

Mrs. Sweeney took a brown roll. "I do love these."

"Butter?"

"Thank you." Mrs. Sweeney picked up an unused knife.

"What is your destination today, Mrs. Sweeney?"

Willie nodded at Lynnelle's efforts to keep Mrs. Sweeney calm and occupied.

"I wish it were Council Bluffs. I have happy memories of visiting there years ago with my husband. But my daughter insists I come to Denver and stay with them for the summer. She doesn't like me being on my own."

"I'm sure you'll have a lovely visit."

"My grandchildren are rather noisier than I would prefer, and the house is not overly large."

"They'll play outside. Children do as soon as the weather warms."

"And they might have matured since you saw them last," Henry said.

"We're all heading to Denver," Lynnelle said. "At least you won't be alone on the train."

Waiters were making their way around the dining car replacing tablecloths and dishes and even removing plates of upended food. None of them seemed to know what caused the train to slow and eventually stop. Clearly, though, their instructions were to resume service as seamlessly as possible, and food began flowing again while Lynnelle, Clarice, and Henry kept Mrs. Sweeney chatting. They ordered, with Willie choosing on Carey's behalf and Clarice once again asking the waiter to rearrange the snug table to include Mrs. Sweeney.

Carey returned and leaned in. "The news is not good. They'll have something official to say soon enough, but I wrangled information out of one of the conductors. A piston rod threatens to eject from a cylinder on the engine. They think they can position it well enough to slowly get to the nearest depot—Luzerne—and telephone to arrange help. But it would be a great danger to resume full speed."

"Goodness," Lynnelle said. "How long will the delay be?"

"They haven't said."

"My guess is at least overnight," Henry said. "It will be dark in a few hours, and a piston is not a minor repair. They'll have to send a crew out from somewhere to assess. If they can't fix it, they'll have to get another locomotive out here, and they'll still have to clear the damaged one from the track somehow."

"You've done this before," Lynnelle said.

"Unfortunately, yes," Henry said. "We're past Cedar Rapids, which is much larger than Luzerne, and there's no turning around a train this size. The best we can hope for is moving forward at all."

"People will be worried about late arrivals and missing connections." Lynnelle would have to rearrange her own appointment with Mr. McParland. Her chest clenched at the thought, but she framed her features evenly.

"The railroad will have to make new bookings, obviously," Carey said. "A small depot won't want their telephone line tied up with everyone on the train trying to make calls, but I imagine they will handle telegrams."

"Mrs. Sweeney, let's see about letting your daughter know you're all right." Lynnelle also began mentally composing her own message to the Pinkerton's office in the fewest words possible.

CHAPTER TEN

English cucumbers
Mint
Fresh dill
Chinese eggplant
Shallots
Tarragon
Heavy cream
Prosciutto
Baby Swiss
Chickens, two
Tenderloin roast (from butcher, not grocery)
Leg of lamb, four (also butcher)
Barley
Long grain wild rice
Fresh rosemary
Mushrooms, half pound
Portobello mushrooms, six large
Chervil

No doubt he was forgetting something, but for now Nolan set down the pen, slid the half sheet across the granite breakfast bar so that it touched Jillian's place mat, and opened the refrigerator to double-check available resources.

"Dad, what is this?" Sitting on a stool at the breakfast bar, Jillian stirred her oatmeal and tapped the sheet of paper.

"We're having a dinner party tonight. One of us needs to go shopping. You are incapacitated, but I felt you should still be fully informed." Nolan pulled his head out of the refrigerator, arms full of bounty. "The good news is we have plenty of celery and onions and a couple of ordinary cucumbers that will do. And we always have garlic."

"Excuse me?" Jillian's spoon clinked against the bowl. "Dinner party?"

"Yes. I also need you to invite the guests to try out some recipes. Luke and Veronica will do nicely. And Kris, if she's free."

Jillian tilted her head. "When did this idea strike?"

"Two hundred meals, Jillian." Nolan unloaded his arms and braced himself on the counter. "Two hundred people are plunking down good money—overpriced if you ask me—and expecting a fancy meal at the Inn."

Jillian tapped the list. "Three meats? Wait, prosciutto makes four."

"The menu is not final."

"I can't exactly sort out what the menu is."

"The list is not complete. Obviously we're going to need some vegetables, and a salad that makes an impression. I haven't decided whether to have a fish course. Perhaps herb-crusted red snapper? I don't need to experiment with breads, and desserts will be a variety tray. I'll just make a little bit of everything in advance."

"Dad."

"You're using that tone." Nolan reached into a lower cabinet for a large pot, deciding to pull out two. His daughter had a vocal way of warning him she was about to give some advice. She claimed she learned it from him, but he refused to accept responsibility.

"I just wonder if you couldn't put on a very nice meal with not quite so many moving parts."

"It needs to be classy, Jillian. I can't serve an Irish stew on Nia's Victorian china."

Jillian scooped oatmeal into her mouth. He was right on that point, and she knew it.

"If these dishes don't work out," Nolan said, "I have some other ideas. But we'll start with these, and you'll get some hungry people here who will be honest."

Jillian lifted the list. "Chinese eggplant?"

"I might have to go to that store that sells all the organic food."

"The one halfway to Denver?"

"Is that where it is?"

"Perhaps we could allow for some substitutions."

Nolan hesitated. "If absolutely necessary. But we have a butcher's shop in town, don't we?"

"Surprisingly, yes. A vestige of another era."

"Then I'll go there."

"What is chervil, anyway?"

"In the parsley family. I'm sure I've seen it somewhere."

"A dubious claim, since you don't actually shop," Jillian said. "Why not just get parsley?"

"I need that too. I'll try the new health food store for the chervil." Nolan pulled three knives from a drawer. "The tourists love that place."

"This is a lot of running around, Dad."

"I know you don't believe I can buy groceries, but I'm sure I can manage."

"Do you know where the butcher whose meat you like so much is located?"

"Canyon Mines is a small town. I'm sure if I drive around I'll see it."

"And the health food store that might or might not have the fancy parsley?"

Nolan wiggled his fingers. "It's over down by Cutter Creek, near the bridge."

"Eastbridge or Westbridge?"

"Does it matter?"

Jillian scraped the last of her breakfast from the bowl. "I'll go upstairs and put some shoes on."

"What about your bad foot? Are you sure you can drive?"

"It's been two days. It's not so bad if I don't walk fast, and I'll drive carefully. You make sure there's nothing else you need. But try to keep it to something the regular grocery store will have. Deal?"

"Deal."

Nolan picked up his pen.

Parsley

Eggs

Carrots, three pounds

Almonds

While Jillian shopped, Nolan checked his office email and answered a couple of phone messages. Then he set out soup pots, roasting pans, saucepans, cutting boards, knives, and ladles. On a series of sheets of paper, he recorded every item of equipment he arranged in his kitchen and began a tentative time line for food preparation that would result in a complete meal with all dishes ready at the same time. Experimenting with a menu for five people would be a far cry from cooking for the Legacy Jubilee, but he had to start somewhere.

In the mood for cooking, he couldn't help singing as he worked. Donizetti's "L'elisir D'Amore" comic opera.

Una furtiva lagrima negli occhi suoi spuntò:
Quelle festose giovani invidiar sembrò.
Che più cercando io vo?
Che più cercando io vo?
M'ama! Sì, m'ama, lo vedo. Lo vedo.
Un solo instante i palpiti del suo bel cor sentir!

What was a good opera about if not a dream of love? A love potion—even if it was fake—and a comedy of errors made the happy ending all the sweeter. *Ah Bella*, Nolan thought, *we had our love where our hearts beat as one. Perhaps one day our girl will find hers—without first suffering the indifference poor Adina had from Nemorino.*

By the time Jillian returned with canvas bags stuffed with his requests—everything but the chervil—he'd prepped as much as he could and was ready to get to work with the array of fresh ingredients while she took refuge in her office. He hummed, occasionally breaking out with the words playing through his mind.

I miei sospir, confondere
per poco a' suoi sospir!
I palpiti, i palpiti sentir,
confondere i miei coi suoi sospir
Cielo! Si può morir!
Di più non chiedo, non chiedo.
Ah, cielo! Si può! Si, può morir!
Di più non chiedo, non chiedo.
Si può morire! Si può morir d'amor.

Ah, love. That feeling that love is heaven, and you could ask for nothing more than love. When Jillian was younger, Nolan told himself he was not ready to love again, as he had loved Bella. It would only confuse his daughter. It would have confused him as well. But Jillian was older now, and she was the one he hoped would find love that made her heart quicken. Someday. Perhaps soon.

Nolan stuffed the chicken breasts with prosciutto and baby Swiss for his own version of chicken Kiev and simmered the rest of the birds to create stock for soups. The beef, after he browned it, would be wrapped in a flaky bread dough for beef Wellington to roast later and served with a mushroom-laden sauce that would cook quickly. The lamb was stuffed with garlic slivers and rosemary sprigs to roast medium rare. Nolan hadn't decided what to stuff the portobellos with yet, but he would need a vegetarian option for the jubilee dinner, so he might as well try something tonight.

At lunchtime, surrounded by enough food to feed at least two dozen people, Nolan nevertheless shooed Jillian out of the kitchen, dispatching her down the street for sandwiches from the Canary Cage coffee shop. She disappeared into her office with hers. He barely touched his. The chicken stock was ready to begin making soups.

The rolling pin got away from Nolan as he flattened the dough, to a thin casing to go around the roast, and clattered to the floor and then bounced between cabinets.

"Hey, hold it down out there!" Jillian's admonishment came from her office.

Nolan dropped the rolling pin in the sink—with another clangor—before taking a small bowl out of a cupboard and ladling a bit of warm liquid into it.

"A peace offering," he said to Jillian as he proffered the bowl at her desk.

"What is it?"

"Nourishment."

"Specifically?"

"Taste it."

She did. "It's terrific, Dad. Onion soup, but creamy. Delicate."

"See? Elegant." Nolan examined Jillian's whiteboard, which still bore the evidence of her late-night—or all-night—brainstorming from a couple of days ago. "Any progress on the foul play theory?"

"You're supposed to be helping with that."

"Two hundred meals, Jillian. It's a bit of a distraction." Whatever happened a hundred and ten years ago would be unchanged if it wasn't solved until after the Legacy Jubilee. He scanned the board, looking for shifts in her thinking, something she might be focusing on too much. "Besides, I delegated. Luke may come up with something."

"What you really need help with is the two hundred meals."

"Are you volunteering?"

She made a face. "There must be somebody in town more qualified to help in the kitchen. Have you even thought about who you could ask?"

"First I have to figure out what I'm cooking." His eyes returned to the whiteboard with its names and arrows and color codes. "So you're tracking name variants."

She nodded.

He put his finger on one at the bottom of the list. "And you think this one means something."

"I'm not sure it is the same person, but I'm not sure it's not either. Genealogically speaking."

Nolan considered his daughter's hedging expression. If he were a betting man, he'd bet she felt more sure than she was admitting.

Jillian scrunched her nose. "What do I smell?"

"I'm cooking half a dozen things."

"I think one of them is burning."

Nolan pivoted and loped back to the kitchen with Jillian right behind him. The brown sauce. He'd left it on the stove when he started rolling out the dough, and it had boiled over. What was left of it was seared to the bottom of the pan. Grabbing a pot holder, he transferred the pan to the sink. As soon as he turned on the faucet, sizzling steam rose toward his face.

"I'll have to start over." First he'd have to wait for the stove to cool down enough to clean it up.

"Or do something simpler," Jillian said.

"I've already browned the roast, sliced the mushrooms, and rolled out the dough. I'm not giving up on beef Wellington now."

"You could always save that for another night. We have the chicken and the lamb chops—and the soup."

Nolan waved her off. "A slight setback. Just a brown sauce. I'll make another. Go back to whatever you were doing."

"Looking for a long-lost sibling who is legally entitled to a share of his mother's estate, even though they haven't spoken in twenty years, he doesn't know she died, and the rest of the children are not too thrilled about him."

"Yes, that. The magical stuff you do. What time are the O'Reillys coming?"

"Six o'clock."

"Kris?"

"Yes."

"See you then." Nolan squirted dish soap in his burned saucepan and grabbed a scrubbing pad. "Two hundred meals."

By the time Jillian opened the front door to welcome Luke, Veronica, and Kris, Nolan had laid out a buffet on the dining room table. The pearl onion soup and the cucumber soup. The beef Wellington, chicken Kiev, and lamb chops à la Béarnaise with eggplant and peppers were perfectly warmed and sauced. The portobellos held spinach, goat cheese, and marinara sauce. Baked barley and wild rice would complement any of the entrees.

"Pralines and cream." Kris handed Nolan a half gallon and settled her eyes on the open trunk in the living room. "This is the famous museum souvenir."

"That it is," he said. "Jillian can give you gloves if you want to touch. Thanks for the ice cream."

He turned to take the dessert to the freezer.

Veronica tossed her purse on the couch and followed him to inspect the table. "Nolan Duffy, what have you done?"

"I threw a few things together." Nolan straightened the beef Wellington platter on his way past. "Please sit."

When he returned from the kitchen with the final dish, the buttered carrots with almonds to add both color and a note of familiarity, Jillian had wrangled everyone into seats. Nolan took his place. "Jillian, would you like to say our family's traditional blessing?"

"May you always find nourishment for your body at the table," Jillian said. "May sustenance for your spirit rise and fill you with each dawn. And may life always feed you with the light of joy along the way."

"This is quite a bit of nourishment for the body," Veronica said.

"The rules," Nolan said, "are that you taste everything and you tell the truth."

"We can do that," Kris said.

"Are we allowed to talk about other things while we eat?" Luke asked.

"Please." Nolan gestured acquiescence.

"I haven't had a chance to consult my people yet," Luke said, "but my instinct is the person doing the bookkeeping in your papers was simply doing just that—bookkeeping. Entering transactions in the right columns without interpretation. There's no nefarious effort to hide the fact that what went out was not balanced by adequate income or offset by assets. But the bigger issue is that despite the number of pages you gave me, the records are incomplete."

"I told you!" Jillian said. "I saw the gaps. I think Lynnelle Bendeure kept some papers with her on the train, and those might have been the ones that mattered most—and could explain what happened to her."

"But we're never going to find those," Nolan said, "are we?"

Luke shook his head. "Unlikely. Even if the company was still in business, there would be no reason for them to keep those old records."

"But we still have one side of the correspondence," Jillian said, "and those letters give us every reason to suggest Lynnelle Bendeure was traveling with documents that would authorize her to act on her father's behalf once she arrived in Denver. Suppose someone knew that. That would be motive for something."

"So what do you think happened to Lynnelle?" Veronica asked.

"That's what I intend to find out," Jillian said, glancing at Nolan.

"Jillian thinks she found Lynnelle," Nolan said.

"Or at least how her identity morphed in the hands of the person who stole it," Jillian said. "I need to dig more into some public records, but digitization can be spotty. Everything I need is so old."

"Oh nuts," Veronica said, "I meant to bring you something."

"For me?" Jillian said.

"The envelope on the counter?" Luke asked.

Veronica nodded. "I was choosing some luggage we might use for the decor at the dinner. I had Luke get down a small case we've been using purely for display purposes at the Emporium for a long time. I got it at a lot auction years ago. I'd forgotten it had anything in it."

"What did you find?" Jillian asked.

"Somebody's old dissertation about the history of Italian immigrants. And the Mafia! I thought maybe you'd like to read it."

"Absolutely!"

"Let's meet at the Cage tomorrow. Coffee in the morning."

"I'll be there."

Veronica closed her eyes and savored a mouthful of lamb. "Delicious. As fine as any restaurant I've ever been in."

"It's the Irish way." Nolan basked in her culinary pleasure.

"Are you going to serve all of these choices?" Luke asked.

"No, he is not." Jillian's words darted at Nolan. "Two hundred meals."

"Which one are you suggesting I drop?" Nolan said. Every dish had seemed a winner.

"The lamb," Veronica said.

Nolan set down his fork and knife. "Ten seconds ago you loved it."

"I still do." Veronica forked another bite of the lamb. "But it may be too sophisticated for many people's palates when they are not placing individual orders. Cute little lambs?"

"Jillian made the same objection about veal and venison," Nolan said. "What am I left with?"

"Chicken and beef."

"Boring."

"Two hundred meals, Dad." Jillian spooned more baked barley and wild rice onto her plate. "But in my book, this stuff is a keeper no matter what."

"And you might want to steer clear of any nuts," Luke said as he slid an almond into his mouth. "Even the thought of cross contamination can make people nervous if allergies are an issue."

"Do you really need two soups?" Veronica said.

"Two hundred meals," Jillian muttered.

"Kris," Nolan said, "I notice you didn't try the onion soup."

Kris shrugged and scrunched her face. "It's not really my thing.

Honestly, I don't think it will be popular. Maybe don't make it?"

No Irish lamb. No nuts. No onion soup. And that hateful number was going to drive every decision. He'd asked for honesty. He couldn't complain that his guests had delivered it.

"Jillian," Luke said, "what's next in your search for this person who may or may not be Lynnelle?"

"Finding something more solid than conjecture, right?" Nolan said.

She eyed Nolan, considering whether she wanted to answer, just as she had when she was little and thought he was being nosy about her guilt. He eyed her in return. She was keeping something from him. Weren't they in this together?

"Property records," she finally said. "I'll have some more of the lamb, please."

Nolan couldn't remember the last time Jillian kept a secret from him. But she had one now.

CHAPTER ELEVEN

Nolan was at it again, pots and mixing bowls and utensils taking over every square inch of the kitchen. A couple of sacks told Jillian he'd managed to find his own way to the grocery store today while she was hunkered down in her office with a client phone call. No telling what he'd bought. Her father was subject to whimsy in a grocery store more than anyone else she knew. The Brussels sprouts in the colander were new, as were four kinds of apples, lettuce she had no name for, and meat.

More meat. At least he hadn't paid the butcher's prices this time—probably because he couldn't find the shop.

"London broil, Dad?"

"I haven't decided which kind of apples to use with it."

"So you bought them all."

"Apples are always useful."

"A bit pricey for—"

"No need to say it. I've already told Marilyn I would underwrite the cost of the food for the dinner as my contribution to the fund-raising effort, so what does it matter what I spend?"

"Dad, London broil for two hundred people? Are you planning to cash in your 401(k)?"

"I asked you not to say that."

"Sorry." At least the pork cutlets option, also laid out on the breakfast bar, wouldn't ravage his bank account so viciously.

"Pork cutlet Parisienne," he said. "I know you're wondering. Although apples also go nicely with pork in the right sauce."

She didn't ask what it meant to cook something *Parisienne*.

"How's Raúl?" Nolan asked.

Since Raúl represented an insurance company that gave Jillian steady paying work, she didn't often put off his messages.

"Three new projects," she said.

"A glut of missing heirs?"

She laughed. "Something like that. One quarrel within the family about how to respond to a secret daughter no one knew their dear mother had."

"Surely that's a simple matter of a DNA test."

"Probably. Raúl just wants me to cover the genealogical bases for why the woman would even want to reveal her secret now, after her death." Jillian picked up her phone. "I'm going now to meet Veronica at the Cage. Luke is going to be there. Want to come?"

"Who's minding the store?"

"They do have employees, Dad."

"You're sure you're okay to walk on your bad foot?"

"I would accept a ride."

"I'll get the truck." Nolan untied his apron. "Give me a minute to figure out where to put this meat."

Good luck with that.

Nolan crammed the morning purchases into the refrigerator somehow, and they drove the few blocks down Main Street to Canary Cage. The day was mild enough that Jillian wore only a zipper hoodie over one of the long-sleeve T-shirts she favored when she worked and didn't have any video calls scheduled.

Behind the counter at the Cage, Clark Addison dipped his head at their arrival and moved to the coffee machines.

"He thinks just because he used to be a hippie," Nolan said, "and has a gray braid and an earring, he knows what I want."

Jillian snickered. "Have you ever *not* ordered black coffee in here? And Clark knows I'll drink anything as long as it's the opposite of plain black coffee."

Clark pointed at Nolan. "She speaks truth."

"Maybe I want something to go with my coffee," Nolan said.

"You want a jelly-filled doughnut," Clark said. "You think I don't know? Now go sit down. They're waiting."

Jillian grinned at Clark and limped behind her dad as he sauntered toward Luke and Veronica.

"What's the word, Luke?" Nolan said.

"I had some news on the bank situation and thought I might as well tag along. Veronica promised it wasn't going to turn into one of those girlfriend coffee klatches with Kris and Nia."

"Actually we're overdue for one of those." Veronica pulled out her phone. Luke snatched it from her.

Nolan and Jillian settled into seats across from Veronica and Luke.

"The bank where most of those transfers were going," Luke said, "managed to survive the 1893 recession that put a lot of Denver financial institutions under. I thought it sounded familiar. It had some backing from New York."

"That might explain why a Cleveland business would choose it," Nolan said.

Luke nodded. "But twenty years after these transactions, Black Tuesday happened."

"The Great Depression started," Jillian said.

"Any banks that survived the earlier recession were now swallowed up by bigger banks, sometimes for pennies on the dollar. This one was gone before the end of 1929. And that was the biggest of the bunch. The others that show up in the records probably closed within a week of the crash, gone for good."

"So there really would be no way to track the records," Nolan said.

"Or hold anyone accountable."

Clark arrived with coffee and pastries. "You all have what you need?"

Nolan winked. "Maybe you should tell us."

"Maybe I should." Clark withdrew.

"It was a long shot to think we'd find anything," Nolan said.

"I've put out some other feelers," Luke said. "I have a friend who is a forensic accountant, and he would know much better than I the depth of any funny business. We just have to wait. It won't be at the top of his list."

"No hurry," Nolan said. "It's extremely unlikely there is any legal action to pursue, and that's the main concern."

"Is it?" Jillian said.

"The mystery of the trunk itself, of course, is intriguing in its own right," Nolan said. "But if we put Rich's mind at ease about the legal questions, we can all enjoy the trunk for a while."

Jillian shifted her weight. "Am I really the only one who wants to know what happened to Lynnelle Bendeure?"

"I know you're working on that." Nolan sipped his coffee. "If you come up with something solid, I'm sure we'll all be interested."

Jillian pushed her chair back, irritated. "It was her trunk after all. We owe it to her to find out what happened to *her*."

"Do you really think somebody stole her identity?" Veronica said. "What can we really do about it now?"

"Not give up so easily, to begin with. There are people living on property near Pueblo right now who probably have no right to that land."

Veronica's violet eyes widened. "Related to Lynnelle?"

"Or *not* related to her but related to her money."

"Jillian, we'll have to let the various lines of investigation play out," Nolan said. "There's no hurry, and we need a lot more information before we can draw conclusions."

"I believe I have plenty of information. Genealogically." Jillian leaned her head to one side. Her father knew what she did all day, every day. What she'd been doing for years. The kind of research companies—including his own law firm—paid her to do to establish family connections, or at least sufficient likelihood in the absence of available DNA. His caution came from nowhere, and it irritated her. Clients hired her because they didn't believe people just dropped off into nothingness. History was all about the trails people left.

Nolan drummed the table. "Last night, Luke said the same thing you've said. The records are incomplete and don't offer a particular interpretation of events. Doesn't that make it hard to say what's going on one way or another without more expertise? Or more information?"

"Pueblo?" Veronica said. "You found something in the property records since we talked last night."

Jillian nodded. "It started a few days ago when I began with a credible variant of Lynnelle's name and got a hit on a marriage record."

"It could still be someone else," Nolan said.

Her father's doubts were getting on Jillian's nerves.

"It's suspicious that the husband's name has only initials," Jillian said, "not even a full first name. Somebody is hiding something."

"People in that time often used initials," Veronica said.

"Legal documents require names," Jillian insisted. "He's listed the same way in the property records."

"So he's being legally consistent," Nolan said.

"Or deceitfully consistent. He bought a lot of land shortly after his marriage to someone who could very well have gotten her hands on Lynnelle's considerable assets."

Three sets of eyes stared at Jillian.

She glared back. "I know what I'm doing. I follow my nose all the time, and then I find the facts I need to confirm."

"Then that's what you'll do this time," Nolan said. "The situation is hardly dangerous. Eventually your research will tell you if you're on the right track."

"What about the people living in Pueblo?" Jillian said.

Nolan shrugged. "Even if there is an actionable inheritance issue—and I'm not saying there would be after all these years—a bit more time won't change anything."

Veronica's phone chimed with a text message. "That's the store. I can't stay much longer."

"I can go," Luke said.

"We should both get back to work." Veronica pulled a manila envelope out of her bag. "But if I forget this again, I'll kick myself. This was the whole point of this meetup."

"Let's see what it is," Nolan said.

Jillian nodded. Her father discouraging her path of questions was disheartening, but for now, a change of topic might be best. She opened the envelope and slid out a packet of about a hundred single-spaced typed pages.

In partial fulfillment of the requirements of the degree of PhD, it said. The year given was 1957. The school was one of Colorado's well-known universities. She flipped through pages.

Italian immigration.

Mafia families.

Transference of dominance.

New Orleans and beyond.

Influence on Denver culture.

The phrases jumped out.

"Wow," she said. "This is something."

"It seemed like something you ought to at least have a chance to look at."

"Thank you. I'll get into it the first chance I get."

Nolan pinched the last of his doughnut into his mouth. "Now that I have stuffed myself, I must return to the question of how to stuff two hundred people."

Jillian waited until they were inside their home before she spoke again.

"I'm telling you, Dad, my feeling about this is very strong. There's a ranch in the foothills to the San Isabel National Forest southwest of Pueblo that may not rightfully belong to the people living on it."

He nodded. "I understand your concerns. But even if you dig deeper and can put together a compelling case on the identity question, the legalities are what they are. Property law likes things to be tidy and settled. Nothing would be actionable."

"That's not right."

"I'm telling you the legal limits, Jilly." Nolan donned his apron. "We can gather some more information for the sake of the Owens House Museum—and our own curiosity—but we don't actually have an offended party that either of us is directly representing. No one could possibly still be alive who could be criminally charged for the financial misman-agement. We probably can't even uncover who failed to properly dispose of abandoned baggage from Union Station. I really don't think there's anything here, Jillian."

"You're going all lawyer on me."

"I am a lawyer." Nolan removed the London broil from the refrigera-tor. "Go sit with Lynnelle's trunk, if you like. Remember her. She deserves that. But you could probably fill your whiteboard with theories of why she left her trunk at Union Station, so let's not get ahead of ourselves."

"You don't understand."

Nolan met her eyes. "Actually, I think I do."

Jillian broke the locked gaze and shuffled to her office, where she kicked off one shoe and more carefully removed the other from her in-jured foot. Opening a folder on her desk, she studied the marriage record and property record she'd printed out.

The abandoned trunk.

A whole family disappearing from a census.

The missing financial records.

The name change, which she couldn't document. Yet.

The male initials hiding even a first name.

The ranch.

Legally actionable or not, no genealogist would like the way any of this smelled.

CHAPTER TWELVE

Denver, Colorado
April 13, 1909

Dear Miss Bendeure,

Per your instructions, we have conducted a number of illuminating discreet interviews, and within the scope of your retainer assigned an operative to the movements of the man your father engaged as his representative for his Colorado business investments. A number of irregularities have emerged, which I would consider to be worthy of legal action as soon as we have the required evidence. In the enclosed document, I have laid these out in chronology I believe to be accurate and the principal persons whom I hold in greatest suspicion. In the meantime, to mitigate further risk, I advise that your father conjure a passable reason to suspend all authorizations issued to this date for financial transactions and investments until such time as we have complete clarity in this matter. Alternatively, at any time, I would be happy to provide names of other representatives you and your father may wish to make inquiries about for future association. As always, I remain at your disposal and will issue further reports shortly.

Yours sincerely,
James McParland
Manager, Western Division
Pinkerton's National Detective Agency

The private compartment that seemed like the indulgence of her father's guilt for having gotten Bendeure & Company into the situation necessitating this journey now provided welcome respite. The train stalled for hours, while the maintenance crew, dispatched from Cedar Rapids, did their best to ensure the piston would hold during the painful, crippling limp to Luzerne, where it could be signaled off a main track and assessed. By the time they were underway to Luzerne, porters were on their rounds converting seats in the sleeping cars into berths for the night. No one would be making a midnight connection in Omaha. Lynnelle was not tall, and her build was "medium" rather than "slim," as indicated in the way her tickets were punched, but she considered herself reasonably fit and she suspected that in the right shoes she could have walked faster than the train was moving toward the nearest depot.

Strictly speaking, this was not true. As she sat up in bed and turned to gaze out the window, she knew the train was making progress. Compared to the usual speeds of a locomotive on a schedule with limited stops, however, advancement was laboriously diminished. And what would be the prognosis once they reached the depot? The silhouette of an unimpressive, isolated rectangular structure crept into view as the tracks took the slightest of curves, its contour uncertain and unpromising in the late evening shadows. Lynnelle was simultaneously relieved and discouraged. Once they reached the depot, the true repairs or the arrival of a replacement engine could begin. No doubt the porters would hand over stacks of telegrams for the telegraph operator to begin tapping, hers and Mrs. Sweeney's among them. But as near as she could discern under moon and starlight, the depot was nothing more than a platform and a small structure that could barely house a couple of desks to keep the small station functioning with occasional ticket sales and required signals as trains came through. Not all of the trains would even stop. This one wasn't scheduled to pause at this location if it hadn't become disabled. The prospects for swift resolution of an ejected piston, if that was truly the trouble, were not promising.

The train clattered to a halt. A dim light hung over the small platform, but Lynnelle could see little else.

And there was no point in trying.

She could not repair the train, nor hasten the process with her anxiety. Instead, she closed the shade and pulled up the bedding. An attempt at sleep seemed the best strategy. At least now they had reached a telephone and telegraph office, and by morning some arrangements could be made.

How Lynnelle wished her family Bible were with her in the compartment rather than packed away in the trunk in the baggage car. She would open it to seek words to soothe her anxiety at the delays the engine's incapacitation would cause and her inability to communicate with the people who needed to know. Instead, she beseeched the ones her mother had urged her to hide in her heart as a child. "'Thou wilt keep him in perfect peace, whose mind is stayed on thee: because he trusteth in thee.'" She settled into her berth, repeating the words to herself.

Eventually she slept, and woke when light broke through the shade and voices outside her window roused her. She peeked out and discovered workers passing by in a horse-drawn work wagon. The stallions that pulled it resembled her brother's horse, but older. Their speed would be no threat to anyone's safety. Why couldn't her brother have appreciated a fine service animal without insisting on championship speed as well?

Lynnelle's curiosity woke with her eyes. Yesterday they were rolling through freshly planted cornfields. Whatever today's scenery was, the passengers might very well stare at it all day. Had any information about the repair circulated during the night? She wasn't hungry enough for breakfast in the dining car yet—she might opt for one of the muffins in Cousin Marabel's basket—but a window with a more robust view would be welcome. She freshened up, allowed herself a clean blouse, and stood in front of the mirror to take a comb to her hair and arrange the pins to hold both her pompadour and hat before dipping one finger in a small pot of rouge and brushing it across her cheeks. Her satchel lay on the bench beside her wicker case. Lynnelle set her hand on it, hesitating. It was a nuisance to carry, and she wasn't planning to study the papers just now but rather simply to find the ladies' room and then see what the word was on the delay. They might yet be a full day from departing this tiny station. Between the Meades and the Hollises and Mrs. Sweeney, every excursion from the compartment turned into a social affair with the satchel slung awkwardly from her shoulder or strapped across her chest.

She reached under her waistband for the tiny keys and locked both the satchel and her case, pinned the keys back in place, and made sure she had the compartment key tucked deep in her skirt pocket. In a delay of any length, having her hands free would be a relief—and her mind would be free of the fear that she might accidentally leave the satchel somewhere about the train.

Finding the Meades' seats outside her compartment unoccupied surprised Lynnelle. She had expected people might still be in their sleeping berths—and most were—but some were stirring, no doubt for the same reason she was. At the moment, no porter was in the car. Unencumbered by her satchel and refreshed after a visit to the facilities, she strolled a bit farther forward to see what might be visible outside. From there at least she could see the side of the train where the breakdown had occurred. In the next car up, she found Mrs. Sweeney standing and looking out the windows on the open aisle. She stood next to her.

"What do you see, my friend?" Lynnelle said.

"Cows."

"Cows?"

Mrs. Sweeney pointed.

"I wouldn't think they would be allowed so close to the tracks," Lynnelle said.

"I doubt they asked permission. Must be a broken fence somewhere."

"We don't see too many cows in Cleveland. They're adorable. The open fields in the background. Their tails swishing. That one sitting like she's tired. It's all very pastoral."

"It gives us something to look at while we're stranded in the middle of nowhere."

"Mrs. Sweeney, we're not stranded. We're on a train with hundreds of people. We're at a depot now, which means the railroad will soon be involved in untangling this dilemma. I've given our telegrams to the porter, who will make sure the telegraph operator in the depot gets them, so your daughter won't be worried. We'll be in Denver soon enough."

Mrs. Sweeney leaned on her cane and tilted her head to look up at Lynnelle. "What about you? Aren't you going to be late for something?"

"I will revise arrangements, that's all. Let's not borrow trouble."

Mr. McParland did say in one of his letters that he might have travel to attend to, but he had not been specific about dates. Surely a day or two delay in her arrival would not thwart their meeting altogether. Though she did not know how long she would be at this particular depot, her telegram included her train information. He could send a reply anywhere along the route and it would reach her. At least this is what she understood from the porter.

Mrs. Sweeney nodded her head down the aisle. "There's your Mr. Meade now."

My Mr. Meade?

Lynnelle turned to see Carey. He had freshened his shirt and tie since the day before, and he looked quite smart.

"Hello, ladies." The dimple in his right cheek doubled the brightness of his countenance.

"Good morning," Lynnelle said. "Where's Willie?"

"We've been up for a while, and she was ready to sit already."

"I didn't see her in your seats."

He tugged at his necktie. "The library car, perhaps. She talked about finding someplace quiet before we investigate the breakfast situation."

"She should come here," Mrs. Sweeney said wryly. "The cows are the least disturbing thing to happen today."

Lynnelle laughed. "What about you, Carey? Haven't had enough of the excitement brewing outside?"

"Thought I might see about some coffee. Care to join me?"

"Don't you want to wait for Willie? Have coffee with your breakfast?"

He waved off the idea. "I don't think I can wait that long. She'll understand. Join me."

"You two carry on," Mrs. Sweeney said. "My berth should be a seat again by now." With her cane rhythmically one step ahead, she made her way up the aisle.

"You know, I'm not entirely sure she needs that thing," Lynnelle said.

"You're kind to look after her."

"Maybe she doesn't need as much looking after as we all assumed."

"She did survive a robbery," Carey said.

"And I'll bet she had some jewelry sewn into the lining of her coat that the thieves didn't get."

"I wouldn't doubt it. Let's have that coffee."

Lynnelle hesitated. His hopeful eyes entreated so persuasively. "Maybe Willie has changed her mind by now."

"She sent me on my way quite firmly. But I would love to have your company." He offered a hand.

Lynnelle tucked her fingers into her skirt pockets. *A married man.* "I really only came out to see if there was news circulating about the delay situation."

"Oh, that. Yes." Carey pointed outside. "I did hear that most likely they will decide to try to decouple the engine and bring in a replacement. But they have to locate one that can carry the load of this train and get it here. A small place like this is not going to have a locomotive hiding out back."

"So we don't know how long that will take?"

"I'm afraid not. Obviously we've all missed connecting to the Colorado Special once. Perhaps not again tonight, but one never knows. It's hard to say."

"If you had to guess?" She smoothed a stray hair back under her hat, conscious that it would already need repinning.

Carey scrunched his forehead. "We should wait for more complete information."

Lynnelle's booking at the Windsor Hotel in downtown Denver would be lost if she did not alert them as well as Mr. McParland.

"I should send a second telegram about my arrangements. If you'll excuse me, I'll go draft something for the porter."

He put a gentle hand on her wrist. "I'm sure there's plenty of time for that. We've only been at the depot for a few minutes, and whatever solution they work out will take a long time. The telegraph office will be mobbed. Another telegram will just go to the bottom of the stack. You may as well relax for a few minutes. Come have coffee with me. Maybe they have some apple cake in the dining car."

Her hand tingled under his touch.

A married man.

"I'm sure Willie must be wondering what became of you."

"Willie likes some time on her own. She's been known to tell me to get out of her hair." Carey's eyes drifted outside. "Is it my imagination or are there more cows now?"

Lynnelle looked. The bovines numbered at least a dozen now, and they were closer to the depot. "Where are they coming from? Mrs. Sweeney said there must be a broken fence."

"She's probably right. Exactly how big is a herd of cows?"

Lynnelle grimaced. "I don't believe it's a fixed number, but it can be quite large, can't it?"

"I might want to research that question, in case Willie and I should rule out farming or ranching as we look for a place to settle."

That dimple again, cleaving through his cheek in a most adorable way.

Lynnelle smiled. "It would seem advisable."

One of the depot employees had crossed the tracks and was trying to shoo the cows away, but the cows' response was to stare at him, unimpressed with the effort, and swish their tails.

"Enjoy your coffee and cake," Lynnelle said. "Perhaps I'll see you and Willie later."

"I hope so." Carey glanced at his watch. "I'll count the minutes. We both enjoy your company."

"And I yours." She palmed the key in her skirt pocket and made her way back through the cars and unlocked her compartment.

Willie was inside.

The wicker case was open.

The satchel was open.

Willie sat on one of the benches with half the papers in her lap and the other half beside her on the bench, facedown. Her eyelids flitted up, her hands flying into motion to order the papers.

Willie would have had to break into the compartment, the case, and the satchel to accomplish this chaos.

None of this was accidental.

And neither was Carey's charming attempt at distraction. They must have been watching to see when she'd leave. Watching to see if she'd ever leave the satchel behind. If she'd ever set it down. And she had.

They'd split up. Carey had been buying Willie time—but not quite enough.

Lynnelle lurched forward and scooped up the papers. "Get out."

"Let me explain." Willie jumped up.

"Get out."

CHAPTER THIRTEEN

Nolan scratched the side of his nose.

No coffee in the kitchen. Usually Jillian filled the canister with fresh water and hit the POWER button on the single serving brewer, and when he came downstairs on a Saturday morning, he could have his morning dose of caffeine in under a minute. Today the pot was idle, cold, and empty.

So was Jillian's office. Her favorite mug, still in the cupboard, showed no evidence of use.

Nolan had focused most of his brain power during the last two days on planning recipes, executing recipes, evaluating results, revising recipes, and cleaning up the mess he made. She'd probably said something about where she was going on Saturday morning, and he hadn't properly filed away the information for retrieval in this moment. Of course, he was capable of filling the canister and pushing a couple of buttons on his own, but there was also the question of breakfast. And he was tired of cooking. He would spend most of the day preparing food as it was.

He snatched his keys out of the copper bowl, picked up his stack of menu notes, and headed out the back door to stroll into town. Clark Addison could serve him a breakfast burrito and keep the coffee coming. When Jillian turned up, her first question would be whether Nolan had come to his senses and simplified his dinner menu yet.

Two hundred meals.

She was not wrong.

If he underwrote the food as his contribution to the evening, nearly all the ticket sales would go straight to the Heritage Society. Marilyn would clear more than five thousand dollars with just the dinner alone. The weekend was sure to yield the new windows the building needed.

Elegant. Worthy of a Victorian inn. But simplify. It must be possible.

Today Clark's gold wire-rimmed reading glasses sat halfway down his nose. Even the eyes of people who had trouble letting go of the hippie era aged eventually. Clark, at a small table with a stack of papers and a pen in one hand, looked over the lenses at two baristas working the counter. Nolan sidled over to Clark, glad as always to see brisk weekend business at the Cage.

"Did my daughter visit you for her morning libations?" Nolan asked.

"No sir. Haven't seen her."

"You've been here all morning?"

"Where else would I be?"

Nolan set his papers down. "Mind if I join you?"

Clark gestured acquiescence.

"I'll get in line," Nolan said, "and be back."

Saturday was always busy at the Cage. Nolan didn't mind the line. It gave him time to think. Jillian was right about one thing. The London broil would bankrupt him. He could do the beef Wellington or throw out everything he'd tried so far and go with a braised sweet ham. A ham would feed a lot of people. At the counter, a new barista, a young woman, seemed relieved with his simple order of a black coffee and a breakfast burrito, which she would only have to heat up. Nolan carried everything with him back to the table.

"A new barista," he said to Clark. "She seems nervous."

"My niece, Joanna Maddon. From Chicago. I promised her a job if she ever came to Colorado."

"Now she has."

Clark nodded. "Called my bluff. First time I'm hovering from afar rather than looking over her shoulder all day."

"You won't let her get into too much trouble."

"Nope." Clark pointed his pen at Nolan's papers. "What's all this?"

"Perhaps you've heard the rumor that I'm preparing a fancy feast for the Legacy Jubilee." Nolan unwrapped his breakfast burrito and inspected it.

"Same burritos we always serve," Clark said. "Made it myself this morning."

"Unquestionably delicious." Nolan slid it off the wrapper and onto the plate. "I'm trying to settle on a plan for what I'm going to serve."

"It looks like you've been scratching a lot of things off the list."

"The powers that be have vetoed some remarkable ideas." Nolan bit into his food.

"What hasn't been vetoed? Let's see." Clark picked up several half sheets of paper. "You've got some fancy stuff here, Nolan."

"It's at the Inn at Hidden Run. On china. With tablecloths and candles. I'm leaning toward the beef Wellington."

"I see your dilemma, but I still think you've overlooked an obvious choice."

Nolan sipped coffee and raised his eyebrows.

"Do your Irish spiced brisket," Clark said. "It's spectacular. Most people who've had your cooking like the Irish dishes best. The spiced brisket would be easy to make, it presents well, and you could slice it to serve a crowd rather than the individual meats some of these ideas involve."

"Are you sure you haven't been talking to Jillian?"

Clark held up three fingers, close together. "Scout's honor. I haven't seen her. I take it she would approve."

"It would meet a number of the specifications she has hammered on about." And the name would look nice printed on a menu at the place settings, which would please Marilyn.

"Do what you want with the side dishes. But I think that's your meat."

Nolan chewed and thought. "Have you got your ticket?"

"Me? At a fancy dinner? Should I wear the jeans with no knees or the ones with appliquéd flowers?"

"You could always help me cook. Eat in the kitchen for free."

Clark laughed. "I have no doubt you're going to need help, but I'm hoping to be very busy myself that weekend around here."

"I suppose so." Nolan swallowed the last bite of his breakfast and washed it down with coffee. "I haven't made one of those briskets in a while. I'll have to do one and figure out how many it takes for two hundred mouths."

"Two hundred! What have you gotten yourself into?"

"I'll have to go home for my truck so I can go to the butcher and buy a brisket." Nolan gathered his papers. "It takes five days to spice one of those properly, you know."

"I know now."

Outside the Cage, Nolan nearly collided with Marilyn.

"Oh good, I caught you," she said. "Someone told me they spotted you."

"Morning, Marilyn," Nolan said. "What can I help you with?"

"Menus, Nolan."

He waved the papers in his hands. "I just about have it narrowed down."

"Soon?"

"Soon."

"Friday at the absolute latest."

"I promise."

"Good. I'm so looking forward to your culinary creation." She looked around. "Isn't Jillian with you?"

"I'm afraid not. Do you need something from her?"

"Yes. Please ask her to call me today. I'd like to discuss the final title of her talk. We'll want to include that after the menu, don't you think? Make a small program card of the entire evening?"

Nolan nodded. "That does sound like a nice idea. I'll let her know."

At the corner of Main Street and Double Jack Street on the way home, Nolan paused for a vehicle turning toward the Inn at Hidden Run. Nia tapped the horn in the minivan she favored because she could easily remove seats to haul small furniture for restoration and use in the Inn. She slowed to a stop, and Nolan leaned in at the window she lowered.

"Where's Jillian?" Nia said.

"I thought she might be with you," Nolan said.

"I just came from the library, the grocery store, and Kris's ice cream shop. She wasn't in any of those places."

"You didn't spot her car?" Nolan asked. "Maybe you drove past it."

Nia shook her head and chuckled. "She dares to have a life neither of us knows about? When you see her, ask her to call me. I'm still trying to figure out how to have her seen and heard through several rooms—and whether she needs some sort of podium."

"Will do." Nolan stepped back, and Nia proceeded toward the Inn.

When Nolan left the house, he'd assumed Jillian had simply gotten a head start on him. She wouldn't be running—not on her injured foot—but she could still be doing errands around town. But if her small SUV was parked anywhere along the path Nia had taken, which covered a good portion of the Canyon Mines shopping loop, Nia would have spotted it. Nia was one of Jillian's best friends, and she didn't know where she was.

Marilyn had been in the shops and on the lookout.

Even when he sits at a table doing paperwork, Clark has a good idea of who passes by outside the shop.

Nolan let himself in the house, checked her office, and went upstairs. Her bedroom door was open. Jillian wasn't in the room. He opened the door to the attic, but the light was off.

The house was empty.

Nolan scrolled the contacts in his cell phone and found Luke's number.

"Hey, what's up?" Luke sounded cheerful.

"I seem to have misplaced my daughter," Nolan said. "Thought maybe she was there with Veronica talking about old trunks or something."

"Can't help you there. Veronica went to a huge estate sale. You know how she is. Looking for the right stuff to sell to our more discerning collectors."

"Okay. She'll turn up."

Nolan ended the call and retraced his steps to Jillian's office. He had all day to try cooking some more dishes, but before he forgot, a note was in order. On a bright pink self-stick note, he wrote *Call Marilyn. Call Nia* and stuck it to the bottom of Jillian's computer monitor. Turning, he saw the address scrawled at the base of the whiteboard, near the name she had circled several times.

Southwest of Pueblo. Near the San Isabel Mountains.

Nolan hustled outside and checked the garage. The slot beside his truck was occupied. Wherever she'd gone, she'd gone on foot.

Or in someone else's vehicle.

Nolan punched Luke's number again.

"Where is this estate sale Veronica went to?"

"Near Pueblo. She'll be gone all day."

"Find somebody to mind the store, Luke. I'll be right there."

"Nolan, I can't—"

But Nolan ended the call. Jillian's absence and Veronica's excursion to Pueblo were no coincidence.

Nolan burst into the Emporium, crowded on a fair-weather spring

Saturday as all the Main Street shops would be, and threaded his way toward Luke.

"Did you find somebody who can be here all day?"

"You called exactly six minutes ago," Luke parried. "And you gave me no explanation. I'm a little busy."

While Luke waited on a customer, Nolan tried Jillian's number for the third time. The call went to voice mail for the third time. He sent a text but received no response.

Luke finished his sale and turned to Nolan with an impatient huff.

"Your wife has a good reason to go to Pueblo," Nolan said, "but my daughter has attached a wild-goose chase to the trip."

"What are you talking about?"

"Jillian isn't answering her phone," Nolan said. "Try Veronica. If we get a good explanation, I'll call off the chase."

Glancing between Nolan and his phone, Luke made the call.

Behind the counter, Veronica's cell phone rang. Luke swung around to grab it and then looked up at Nolan.

"It could all be innocent," he said.

"Veronica forgetting her phone is innocent. Jillian finding a way to get to Pueblo when her foot is too sore to drive that far? Not so innocent."

"Maybe she's just keeping Veronica company."

"Does Veronica like company when she goes to estate sales?"

Luke pinched his eyes closed. "No. She likes to put in an audiobook while she drives and focus on the negotiating while she buys."

"It's a three-hour drive," Nolan said, "and they have a big head start."

"Why do we have to go chasing after them?" Luke raked a couple of fingers through his hair. "Veronica must have agreed to the plan. At least you know Jillian's not on her own. She's all right."

"She's not all right, Luke." Nolan craned his neck forward to capture Luke's attention. "Veronica might have agreed, but Jillian's not all right."

Luke blew out his breath. "It's Saturday. It's busy enough with Veronica gone. I don't think I can get away—and I don't think you should go either."

Halfway up an aisle, a box tipped off a low shelf, clattering replica Victorian ladies' fans to the floor. The responsible party, an unattended child, scampered away. Luke paced up the aisle to inspect the damage and clear the mess. Nolan followed to help.

"This isn't like Jillian," Nolan said.

"She must be persuaded she's onto something." Luke straightened the box and began arranging the fans in it again.

Nolan shook his head. "It's deeper than that."

Jillian had never been a temper-tantrum child, but she could be persistent. As a preschooler, she'd decide she *must* clean her toy box, and only in the process of helping her would Bella discover that something upsetting had happened during her half day at preschool, and the little girl needed someone to guide her through her own emotions. As an older child, the projects got more complex, but the pattern was the same. Jillian would choose to stay home and work on something nonurgent rather than go to the movies with her friends, or she'd make a detailed list of supplies she needed for reorganizing her closet. Nolan and Bella would look at each other, knowing one of them was going to have to come alongside their daughter and gently uncover what was going on inside her. When Bella was gone, and Nolan was left with a fourteen-year-old grieving puzzle, he realized how often he had left the task to Bella.

Jillian was twice as old now. She wasn't a child. She was a successful adult who made Nolan's chest crack open every day with a glistening surge of pride. But she was still his daughter, and he knew when the project that consumed her was not the whole story. He was starting to be sorry he'd ever gotten involved with that steamer trunk. If he'd gone somewhere else for his coffee one morning months ago, or popped into that same shop twenty minutes earlier or later, then he might never have met Rich, and this drive—this chase—wouldn't be happening.

"She'll come home," Luke said, "and she'll tell you what she found. She always does."

Nolan nodded. Luke's point was valid, though the same compulsion that sent Jillian jaunting to Pueblo had made her so exhausted she picked up a baking casserole dish without sufficient hot pads and stepped in the broken glass that resulted.

"I suppose she has to get this out of her system," Nolan said, "even if nothing any of us finds will change anything."

"It's true we don't have records from the bank itself," Luke said. "But if this Lynnelle Bendeure was carrying a document authorizing her to act as an agent of her father's company, the bank would have had to be satisfied they were acting on a signature the officers deemed lawful at the time.

Otherwise they would not have allowed a transfer of assets."

"That makes a lot of sense to me," Nolan said. "But Jillian is a geneal-ogist. Signatures and assets are not where she starts."

"People."

"Right."

"Family lines."

"Correct again."

"You never know," Luke said. "Something may turn up in the compa-ny records. I haven't heard from my forensics people."

"But under any circumstances, who would contest the outcome of whatever happened? None of us has any standing with the court to undo the foul play."

"Come on, Nolan. You're an attorney." Luke straightened several box-es along the shelf before standing up.

"Your point is?"

"I don't blame you for thinking like a parent at the moment, even if your kid is all grown up," Luke said as he walked back toward the cash register, "but give her some credit. She wants to know the truth. The true story. And make it right if she can. Most of the time, I'd say that sounds a lot like you."

Nolan looked at Luke out of the side of his eyes. "She's using your wife, you know."

"Nobody uses Veronica. She makes up her own mind."

Nolan couldn't argue that point. Veronica O'Reilly. Nia Dunston. Kris Bryant. Jillian was the fourth in a quartet of strong women with businesses in Canyon Mines and intertwining friendships.

"Look, I've got a line forming, so I can't play detective today," Luke said. "But why didn't somebody claim that trunk? That's the persisting question Jillian can't let go of. What if Jillian's right and somebody stole Lynnelle's identity to get the assets, and everything after that was illegal, including a substantial property purchase?"

Nolan didn't answer. Everything Luke said was reasonable. Explain-ing that he knew his own child—even if she no longer was a child—was difficult, much less that she hitched a ride down I-25 with Veronica as much because of what she didn't understand about the trunk she owned as the one she had on loan. Nolan didn't want to regret bringing Lyn-nelle's trunk into his home if its presence was going to undo his daughter.

CHAPTER FOURTEEN

T his should be the last major turn." Jillian pointed to the right. "The photos from Google Earth show a black iron gate. Not too far. A couple of miles. But first we have to find the private road."

"Google Earth." Veronica glanced at her. "Only a little stalky."

"Had to be sure we wouldn't get lost." At home, she'd been elevating her sore foot more than she realized. Even though she'd slipped it out of her shoe, it ached. She could never have driven down here comfortably on her own.

"Wow, it's flat out here," Veronica said. "Have we even seen a hill since we left Colorado Springs?"

"This here is ranch land!" Acres of grazing land sprawled on either side of the arrow-straight two-lane road that shot off the highway out of Pueblo, pockmarked by vegetative tufts foreign to the landscape around Canyon Mines. The same boundless sky, blue and bright and definitively Colorado, beckoned their eyes toward the horizon.

"I think my ears finally popped," Veronica said.

"We're down close to five thousand feet from home."

"I haven't been to Pueblo in years, much less south of there."

"Me neither. It's a whole different view of Colorado."

Veronica gestured forward through the windshield. "They do have mountains. Over there. We're just used to living *in* the mountains. We made good time though."

"Because you have a lead foot."

"Better than your sliced foot."

"I won't argue with you." Jillian leaned forward slightly. "Slow down. I think we might be getting close."

Veronica let her foot off the gas, and the vehicle's speed diminished enough for them to discern a series of small signs fifty yards apart leading to the one they sought. They made one final right turn. The fencing did indeed suggest they had entered private acreage.

"This is a gorgeous piece of God's earth," Veronica said. "You've made me very curious to see it. You're sure it's the same ranch as a hundred years ago?"

"I've checked and double-checked the property records," Jillian said. Pieces of it had been sold off—perhaps as much as half—but not the heart of it. It was family land, still more than five hundred acres. But if she was right, an undeserving family had been living on it all these decades and had profited from selling off the other five hundred acres.

Veronica braked.

"Why are you stopping?" Jillian said.

"Are you sure about this?"

"The gate is right there, and it's wide open."

"It's still private property." Veronica pointed at a sign. "And you didn't make any advance arrangements."

"How will we find anyone to talk to if we don't go through the gate?" Jillian grimaced as she tied her shoe back on her foot.

"That's all you want to do, right?" Veronica said. "Talk. Not interrogate."

"I'm not the CIA. Yes. Talk. I might ask some friendly questions. I'm a curious person."

Veronica accelerated cautiously, keeping her speed under ten miles an hour on the dirt road.

"Look!" Jillian pointed out her side of the car. "Mule deer."

A buck and two doe foraged, raising their heads slightly at the sound of the vehicle and turning to run.

"More up ahead," Veronica said. "We must be on a migration path. They go up to higher elevations for the summer, right?"

"I think so." Canyon Mines already was at a higher elevation. Jillian wasn't sure how much higher the muleys climbed. "Until the snow forces them back down for food. Something like that."

"The creek bed has some running water. Spring snow melt must have started already."

Jillian raised her eyes toward the western mountains, still solidly white. They could look that way for several more weeks while water flowed to the plains below.

"I don't see any cattle," Veronica said.

Jillian shook her head. "More of a legacy ranch now than a working ranch."

"How do you know that?"

"Way too small to be profitable in today's beef market."

"And how do you know that?"

"I read. I learn things."

"Well, even I know you saw that on a T-shirt," Veronica said. "There are some buildings up ahead."

"Stop here for a few minutes."

Veronica eased the car alongside a fence, and they both got out. "How's your foot?"

"I can tolerate a little exploring." Jillian hadn't come this far to be foiled by pain in her foot.

Veronica hit the Lock button on her key fob, and they sauntered forward at a pace that allowed Jillian to be cautious about how she stepped.

"A Quonset hut barn," Jillian said.

"It looks original," Veronica said. "Not Victorian, obviously, so not my specialty, but World War II surplus Quonset huts were used for a lot of things."

"I'm sure you're right."

"You probably looked at Google Earth images of the whole property," Veronica said.

Jillian turned up one corner of her mouth. Acreage. Number of outbuildings. Property taxes. County assessment. In a job like hers, she'd learned to dig for information of all sorts, but once she'd found that first suspicious name from 1909 on a marriage record, the rest had been easy. Most of it would be accessible to just about anyone. What she needed was some clue about the origin of the name.

The fault line that would trace back and prove the family story was all fabrication and the money ill-gotten.

Getting people to chat was more her dad's easy way, but he would never have agreed to come on this outing. She was on her own.

Not entirely on her own. She had Veronica, whose inquisitiveness could be charming.

Behind the Quonset hut barn stood a cluster of much smaller structures, likely storage sheds and perhaps a long-idle chicken coop. Jillian wasn't enough of a farmer or rancher to speculate, and probably their original purposes had been adapted through the decades to a chain of more convenient uses.

The path was uneven, making it hard for Jillian to put her injured foot down with steady compression and disguise the urge to limp. Yet the panoramic invitation to ramble on a spring day evoked the sensation of being in a state park or historic preserve featuring a living history museum. If the walls in her office at home weren't covered with correspondence and financial records from an abandoned steamer trunk, she'd be tempted to let go of the mission that had brought her down here—and the private property sign she'd urged Veronica past. They could soak up the sensations of a bygone era for a few minutes and be on their way to Veronica's estate sale.

"Uh-oh," Veronica said. "I think we're busted."

Astride a white horse, a man cantered toward them, pulling on the reins when he got close. Jillian blinked at the image. Against the scenic backdrop, with ranch land and mountains behind him, he was like an illustration torn out of a book.

Or the cover. The handsome hero. Dark hair, with tangled curls clinging at the base of his neck, scruffy cheeks that suggested he hadn't bothered to shave that morning, and a bemused dimpled smile taking form.

"Can I help you?"

A horse. An actual man on a horse. Well, it was a ranch. People still rode horses on ranches, apparently, even if there wasn't a cow in sight. Among all the questions swirling in Jillian's mind, though, she hadn't thought how she might answer this simple question, one someone who lived—or perhaps simply worked—on the land had a right to ask.

"The gate was open." Veronica's words came to the rescue as they looked up at him. "I drove through it. It's so beautiful down here. I suppose we wanted to see more."

His smile flashed. "My eyes never get their fill. That's why I prefer a horse rather than my truck. I get the whole experience."

Jillian recovered herself. "This is your land?"

"Not mine personally," he said. "But it's family land, and right now I'm living in one of the houses."

"One of the houses?" Veronica said.

Jillian knew the answer but held her tongue. Listening, her father always said, was the best way of learning. What would this man tell her that she might not already know? He was young, not much older than she was, if at all. Living on family land—had he grown up here?—he must know family stories.

"There are two," he said, "the main house and the little red house, as we call them. I live in the little house."

"We've been admiring the history in the buildings we've seen so far." Jillian shielded her eyes to get a better look at him. It was silly, but with brilliant Colorado sunlight filling the day, he seemed to glow on that white horse.

"We do try to keep them from falling down around us," he said.

"We're both sort of history buffs," Veronica said. "Two houses? There must be a story to that."

Bless you, Veronica. Bless your curiosity.

"One is original," he said. "It predates 1910, though it's been added onto and fortified a few times, so the original footprint is hard to see from the outside. The other was built a few years later and has never been much more than a nice cozy cabin. That's why I get to live there. I'd sleep in a covered wagon if that's what it took to be out here."

Veronica and Jillian laughed.

"We live in Canyon Mines," Veronica said. "Do you know it?"

"Only by name. Haven't been there. It's a bit off the beaten path, even when I get to Denver."

"Part of why we love it," Jillian said.

"What brings you all the way down here?" the man asked.

Veronica ran a hand through her sophisticated hair layered in a cut just to the shoulders. "We didn't come strictly for trespassing purposes, I assure you. I buy small antiques for my shop. There's an estate sale not far from here."

"So you're just taking a drive first?"

"Something like that," Jillian said. "It's such different landscape than where we live. We couldn't resist."

"I'm Drew Lawson."

"Jillian Parisi-Duffy."

"Veronica O'Reilly."

"Come on, then," he said. "I see no reason you can't have a look around, as long as you're on good behavior."

"That's very gracious." Drew Lawson. Jillian stored the name in her mind. Later it would become a leaf on a genealogy tree, a starting point to work backward toward the name she'd found. He was walking and talking DNA. Maybe there was hair in the hatbox in the trunk, fibers trapped in a hairpin or under a feather.

She was getting ahead of herself. She could hardly ask a stranger to let her swab his cheek.

"I'll tell you what," Drew said. "I have to put the horse away, but if you want to see my place, I don't mind. For the cause of history. It's the little red house next to the curve in the creek bed."

Jillian and Veronica looked at each other.

"We'll go back for the car," Veronica said. "We'll find it."

"Just don't poke around too much."

"Right," Jillian said. "Private property."

"Not everybody is as friendly as I am." Drew clicked his tongue, and the horse went into motion.

"What do you suppose he meant by that?" Jillian asked.

"I don't know," Veronica said, "but I think we should respect the boundary. Let's just get the car and find the little red house."

At the car, Jillian sank with gratitude into the passenger seat, glad to have the weight off her aching foot. She reached into her day bag for two items, her water bottle and over-the-counter pain relievers. Her knuckles brushed her phone, dropped into the depth of the bag hours ago with the ringer off. She'd heard it vibrating a couple of hours ago and ignored it—she knew who it would be.

Nolan would have discovered her gone.

She looked at the phone now.

Five missed calls. Six text messages. All from Nolan.

"Everything all right?" Veronica started the car.

"Yep. Just need to send a text."

Don't worry. Everything is fine. She hit Send. Then she powered off her phone.

CHAPTER FIFTEEN

Denver, Colorado
April 21, 1909

Dear Miss Bendeure,

While I don't purport to be a financial or business
adviser, because of the nature of our discussions, I'm
pleased on your behalf that your father has taken the decision to communicate to his representative his instructions
that for the time being he is suspending business in Colorado. As you have observed, it is not necessary to withdraw
his registration and licensing with the state. I do have
a short list of recommendations for representation if you
should decide to take up activities after our business together is concluded and you are confident that it is fully
safe to continue. Of course, it is my intention to make
sure you feel such confidence without the least hesitation.
To that end, I will conduct further inquiries regarding
the names on my list to reassure you that the person you
select, should you select one, has not crossed paths with
the representative you have discontinued. In the interests
of both justice and business, I am sure we share the goal
of expeditious resolution of these matters. In the meantime, I suggest your father contact, personally or through
an authorized bank executive in Ohio, the bank holding his
funds in Denver and freeze all transactions immediately
pending further instruction. As I indicated in the telegram
I sent, because I believed the matter to be urgent, if you
have not already done so, impress upon the Denver bank that
Bendeure & Company has no authorized representative in Colorado until further notice.

Yours sincerely,
James McParland
Manager, Western Division
Pinkerton's National Detective Agency

Saturday, May 22, 1909
Traveling across Iowa

Cousin Marabel's picnic basket, which Lynnelle had tried so politely to refuse in Chesterton, now allowed her to remain in her sleeping compartment nearly all the time.

Two days ago. It *had* been Willie ducking into that shop in Chesterton.

But why?

Lynnelle wasn't sure she wanted to know—at least not while she was on the train. Mrs. Sweeney might be right. They were trapped in the middle of nowhere—in the middle of hundreds of people. Lynnelle needed Mr. McParland's help. He would know what Willie—and Carey with his shiny dimple—had to do with all this.

They weren't on an adventure to find a place to settle down.

They probably weren't even Willie and Carey Meade.

Somehow, they knew she would get on the train in Cleveland.

Somehow, they made sure they had the seats outside her compartment on the train that left Chicago.

How was this even possible?

Bribes, she supposed. Bribes could get a person the seats he wanted no matter who else was inconvenienced.

She'd tried to change to another compartment where she didn't have to think of the Meades—or whoever they were—sitting on the other side of a shared wall, but the accommodations were all booked, and she didn't dare expose herself by moving to another car to sit up and not be able to lock herself away at all.

The knock on her door made her jump. "Who is it?" Perhaps the porter had a telegram for her.

"It's Clarice. We're worried about you."

Lynnelle checked her reflection in the mirror before opening the door.

"You're not unwell, are you?" Clarice's blue eyes clouded.

"A smidgen overtired."

"You need something to eat."

"I've been eating from Marabel's basket."

"Biscuits and green olives are hardly enough. Come out with Henry and me. The railroad brought in food from the countryside somewhere. The dining car has a whole new impromptu menu. Hearty fare. It's all the talk."

Lynnelle glanced at her basket, still half-full. "I haven't had much appetite."

"Soup, then. Something hot will do you good."

Lynnelle looked in the mirror again, considering. "Have you seen Willie and Carey Meade lately?"

"Only in passing."

"They weren't outside?"

"Not when I went past their seats."

"Give me a moment to pull myself together." Lynnelle tidied her appearance and picked up the satchel. She didn't know what Willie had seen or how many of the pages she had digested before Lynnelle returned to the compartment, but she wouldn't take another chance. The Moroccan red satchel would go where she went, hanging across her body by its long strap so she could not forget it even while she ate a bowl of soup and was distracted by conversation.

"Ready?" Clarice opened the door.

Henry was waiting outside. Moving single file up the aisle, Lynnelle fell in behind Clarice and ahead of Henry, welcoming the safety of the Hollises and the relief of not spotting the Meades as they moved through several carriages.

"The cows!" Lynnelle said when she took her eyes off the aisle and looked out a window.

Dozens. A hundred. Probably more.

Clarice laughed. "This will make a great story to tell the aunts. We've been outside to see for ourselves."

Lynnelle's nose wrinkled. "How did I not smell that before?"

"You probably haven't had your window open," Henry said. "The wind shifted a few minutes ago. They say that the replacement engine is almost here, but now there are cows all over the tracks."

"Mrs. Sweeney was right about a broken fence, I guess."

"It would seem so. Now they have to be sure the cows are off the tracks, and no one seems to be able to find the farmer who owns them."

"He must not be a dairy farmer or he would have noticed by now that they'd wandered off," Clarice said. "Trying his hand at raising beef, I suppose."

"So now we have to wait for the cows, of all things," Lynnelle said.

The Hollises both nodded.

"This is slightly less endearing than it was earlier." Surely the men who worked at the depot knew the farmers in the area. How difficult could it be to track one of them down and hold him responsible for his herd?

"On the other hand, supposedly the chickens in the chicken noodle soup were clucking only yesterday," Clarice said. "I'm almost tempted to come back later in the summer and see what the fresh sweet corn tastes like."

"Country living at its best." Lynnelle did her best to keep up with the light tone.

They found a table in the dining car. The elegantly printed menus were partially obsolete because an entire passenger train was parked miles away from the usual places where food stores were replenished. Instead, waiters were verbally listing the substitutions available. Based on the options, Lynnelle concluded someone had negotiated an impressive supply of eggs from area farms. Deviled. Poached. Scrambled. Omelets. Benedict. Egg salad. But the knot in Lynnelle's stomach prevented her from dabbling in anything but soup and the quota of coffee she'd missed when she skipped breakfast.

"I don't know what ails you," Clarice said, "but the aunts would say you must keep up your strength."

"I'm probably just afflicted with a bit of impatience," Lynnelle said. "You said you got off the train. Perhaps I need some air as well."

"A constitutional. We'll all go. As long as the new engine is not here, there's no fear of missing the train! But we may have to pinch our noses against the bovine invasion."

Lynnelle made herself smile. Apparently, nothing squelched Clarice's cheery disposition, though every hour lost took her perilously closer to missing her cousin's wedding the next evening, if it wasn't already too late. This was already Saturday, and the Hollises already planned to begin the journey home on Monday morning. They might just as well reclaim their luggage and get on the next train going east right now.

Lynnelle didn't have that option. Getting to Denver was imperative.

"Let's have some dessert first," Henry said. "Lynnelle can forget the soup and skip right to the cherry pie."

"Yes, let's," Clarice said. "Oh look, here are the Meades. We can make room, can't we?"

Lynnelle moved both hands to the satchel as Clarice waved hers toward Willie and Carey.

Henry shifted his chair to make space. Willie and Carey approached, smiling.

"Here we all are," Carey said, seeking Lynnelle's gaze, "together again."

That dimple. That hair. Those eyes.

No.

Lynnelle pushed her chair back. "Here, take my seat. I was just about to leave."

"What about our constitutional?" Clarice said.

"Perhaps there will be time later if the new engine has not arrived." Lynnelle stood. "At the moment, I think I'll rest."

"Shall I check on you later?"

Lynnelle nodded. Agreeing seemed the quickest route to an exit.

One advantage to the stalled train was the ease of walking through the carriages, and stepping between the porches, without constantly rebalancing to the sway of the train. Lynnelle went directly to her compartment and heaved out her breath. Going out again would require a very good reason. An open window could provide all the fresh air she needed. She raised the satchel strap over her head, unlatched it, and pulled out the dog-eared sheets yet again.

It was all there.

Every suspicion her father feared.

Every conjecture Mr. McParland intimated. More than intimated.

The more Lynnelle reviewed the financial lines and the hidden agenda in the dismissed agent's correspondence, the more the narrative took firm shape. She was right to make this trip. To go in person. To take the evidence. To carry the files in the steamer, but most of all to keep these pages on her person.

The steamer.

Surely not.

It was one thing for Willie to know which compartment was Lynnelle's, and even to somehow arrange berths near it, but the steamer trunk had been in the custody of the railroads since Lynnelle boarded the first train in Cleveland.

Surely not.

How complicated would it be to intercept its transfer from one railway to another in Omaha, to see for herself that it had not been tampered with? The normal transfer schedule between the Chicago and North Western and the Union Pacific was only twenty minutes in the middle of the night, but with a large enough tip to a porter, what might be possible? And now, of course, the baggage car had been just as idle as every other car for all these hours, and why would there be any reason for anyone to pay particular attention to it in the face of the larger calamity of rescuing the entire train?

Right now, the thing to do was to get off the train, march to the minuscule depot office, and demand to use the phone and call Pinkerton's in Denver. The rear door of the carriage was just outside her compartment. Lynnelle stuffed the papers back in the satchel. This time, with no eyes on her, she reached under her waistband for the key and locked it before hanging it over her head again.

She slipped off the train and traipsed forward on the uneven shallow embankment toward the platform. Dozens of passengers milled around, especially families with children eager to burn off some energy in advance of the coming confinement. Handwritten signs on every train car reminded passengers not to stray beyond the sound of the whistle that would announce departure.

Lynnelle wasn't the only one asking questions at the office. The line inched forward, one beleaguered question at a time.

First she asked about a return telegram from Mr. McParland.

"No, miss."

Had her message been sent?

"Yes, miss."

Could she place a phone call?

"No, miss. Railroad business or medical emergencies only."

It was urgent.

"Everybody's business is urgent."

This truly was.

The man shrugged.

She would end the call if the operator asked for the line.

He shook his head and gestured to the queue behind her. The telephone line would be tied up constantly if they let everyone on the train make calls.

"I must insist," Lynnelle said.

He chuckled out of one side of his mouth.

She settled for sending a second cryptic message to Pinkerton's and the message she had drafted asking the hotel to hold her booking for a later arrival than reserved and surrendered her place in line to the next person. She would have to try her own hand at enticing a porter to help her gain admittance to the baggage car to see for herself whether her trunk had been compromised. How did one determine a suitable amount of enticement? She refused to call it a bribe. It was her own trunk, after all.

When Lynnelle turned the corner of the building to return to the train, the engine whistle nearly made her jump out of her Oxford shoes. She pivoted toward the sound. The new locomotive was approaching. The disabled engine had already been decoupled and moved to the side in its own strength, leaving the train like a decapitated serpent awaiting the growth of a new mighty head.

Good. Find the farmer. Wrangle the cows so the engineers could accomplish their mission and a cheer could rise up from the entire passenger list.

She rotated again in the direction of her compartment—and nearly ran into Willie.

Lynnelle backed up three steps and two to one side. "Excuse me."

"I just want to explain. Sixty seconds. If you don't like what I say in sixty seconds, you don't have to listen to anything more."

"I don't have to listen to anything at all. You broke into my compartment and got into my personal belongings. You're lucky I didn't have you thrown off the train."

"And I appreciate your mercy. Please. It's in your best interest."

"I can decide what is in my best interest for myself." Lynnelle pushed past Willie. Mercy had nothing to do with it. If the Meades stayed on the train, and they were involved in the matter Mr. McParland was assisting with, they would be one step closer to arrest when they arrived in Denver, but she did not have to speak to them further.

With her window cracked, Lynnelle heard periodic shouts and whistles from outside suggesting progress toward clearing the tracks and coupling the locomotive to the train. It was not at all an expeditious process. A couple of horse-drawn wagons arrived to deliver food supplies to the kitchen and dining cars. Was that to equip them for the journey or to supply them for further delay? Two hours after the first whistle signaling the engine's arrival, there was no sign of imminent departure. Yet she had been peremptorily denied the opportunity to investigate the state of her steamer. All passengers were required to remain in passenger carriages, ready for departure as soon as the train was declared fit. She lacked the courage to offer enticement to circumvent the order and was left with berating herself for not attempting the strategy sooner.

Lynnelle went to her little sink to splash water on her face. When the knock came, she turned off the pitiful stream.

"Yes?"

"Please open the door."

Mr. Meade.

"No thank you."

"We must speak. Please."

She unlocked the door and yanked it open. "Mr. Meade, I would ask you to leave me in peace."

"I thought we were on a first-name basis."

"No longer."

"I know you're upset."

She glared.

"You must listen."

"Must I?"

"We're your friends—at least we want to be." He smiled, flaunting his secret weapons. The widest dimple she had known anyone to have, eyes that were persuasively, profoundly sincere. If there was anyone on the train she *wanted* to trust, to listen to, to accept friendship from, it was Carey Meade.

Lynnelle closed her eyes for a few seconds and pictured Willie sitting on the bench three feet away with the case and satchel open. That was all the image she needed to steel her nerves. Carey had known Willie was there, all the while trying to woo her to the dining car in the other direction to buy her a piece of apple cake. Under the circumstances, she couldn't trust anyone that charming.

"They found the farmer," Carey said. "He brought some men to help him with the cows. It shouldn't be much longer."

"Thank you for that important information. I hope you enjoy San Francisco." *I hope you are arrested in Denver.*

Another knock. They both turned toward the sound on the open compartment door. Mrs. Sweeney was there, with her cane in one hand and a covered plate in the other.

"I heard you were unwell," she said. "I thought you could use some proper food from the dining car."

"Thank you, Mrs. Sweeney." Lynnelle took the plate. "Mr. Meade was just leaving."

"I heard back from my daughter."

"I'm glad. I'm sure she appreciated knowing you are all right." Lynnelle couldn't help disappointment that her own telegrams had brought no replies.

At least Carey Meade was gone.

CHAPTER SIXTEEN

$\mathbf{H}$e seems really nice." Veronica's voice was half whisper. "When he said we could see his house, I thought he just meant the outside."

Jillian nodded. She'd never expected to be inside the house either. When Drew said he lived in a cabin, she'd imagined something campier, that "little red house" was merely a sentimental moniker. This home had never been a ranch hand's cabin or bunkhouse and showed no sign of neglect or disuse. It was cozy, but it had always been a home. While she and Veronica waited for Drew to return from wherever he stabled his horse—she hadn't figured that out—they'd taken the liberty to walk around the outside of the trim simple frame structure painted the popular color of barns in bygone decades. A gravel path designated a spot to park a couple of vehicles, and someone had cleaned the winter off two large green planters outside the front door, though it was still early to expect anything to be growing in them. The windows had been modernized with double panes. The little house might be a cabin compared to the main house, but clearly it was valued.

Now, unexpectedly, they were inside. Drew had disappeared around a corner into the kitchen with the promise that he could scrounge up some cold bottled tea, leaving the two of them to soak in as much of the main room as they could. There could only be one bedroom, and it couldn't be large. The whole house was barely eight hundred square feet. Kitchen, bath, bedroom, main room with space for a table, a fireplace, a wall of bookshelves, and eclectic furniture likely left from previous occupants.

Veronica was right. Drew was nice. Jillian hadn't expected that. She hadn't *not* expected it. In her focus on information and the truth of what happened to Lynnelle, she hadn't thought about how she would feel about who she might meet in the present day. Getting inside the house was all Veronica's doing. She started talking about the sort of small antiques she collected when she visited estate sales of homes that had been in the same family for a long time, and the next thing they knew Drew insisted they come in to see some of the old belongings he'd inherited along with the house.

Drew came out of the kitchen with three bottles of iced tea between the knuckles of one hand and a bag of pita chips in the other, bachelor-style hospitality.

"This is a nice piece." Veronica lifted a jewelry box from one of the shelves. "It's quite old—in remarkable condition for its age."

"A wedding present to some great-great-great somebody." Drew extended a bottle of tea.

Veronica returned the box to the shelf and took the tea. "I hope somebody knows the story."

"I'm sure somebody does. You have to excuse my ignorance. The rule for anyone staying here has been not to move things around too much. Old family stuff."

Staying here, he'd said. Not *living here*. Perhaps his residency in the little red house was transitory.

Jillian took the tea Drew offered and wandered to the other side of the room, drawn to the photos, while Veronica's and Drew's voices murmured about various items that obviously had lived on the shelves for longer than Drew's lifetime. The designs on the shoeboxes Jillian saw suggested they were from decades earlier, though structurally they'd held up well. The mantel drew her attention. There was no telling what they held now. A few knickknacks plainly were Drew's personal additions, but on one end were three silver frames from long before his birth. Out of one of these a face she'd seen before stared at Jillian.

The photos in the trunk. The assorted family photos. The younger woman she decided must have been Lynnelle. Not the one with the children, but the other one, clearly unattached in a three-generation family photograph.

This woman was decades older than the woman in those photos.

But the face.

If Jillian was right about the face, then she could be wrong about nearly everything else.

Veronica and Drew were still gabbing. Jillian dug in her bag for her iPhone and powered it on. Ignoring the new messages from her father, she opened the camera app and snapped a picture of the vintage image.

The click made both Veronica and Drew turn their heads.

"See something interesting?" he said.

"I do have a question." Jillian jammed her phone in a pocket. "About this photo."

"Which one?" Drew asked.

"Here." Jillian pointed. "This woman. When was this taken?"

The door opened again. An older woman, gray-haired with a scowl etched in her squarish features, stood in the doorframe, her hands plunged into the big pockets of a tan barn jacket above her dungarees. She had to be pushing eighty, Jillian thought, but looked like she pulled her own weight with whatever work the ranch still required.

"Aunt Min." Drew lost his casual stance.

"I saw the car. When I spoke to you this morning," she said, "you didn't mention having friends in."

"I didn't know," Drew said. "We have some visitors from Canyon Mines. This is my Aunt Min. Great-aunt, actually."

In Jillian's mind a new leaf sprang out on the family tree.

"I buy antiques," Veronica said. "We were in the area and found ourselves admiring your beautiful land."

"Trespassing, you mean," Min said.

As likable as Drew had been a couple of hours ago, his great-aunt was the polar opposite.

"I assure you, in the most respectful way," Jillian said.

Aunt Min drew in a long breath and exhaled through her nose, unimpressed.

"Your family has some lovely pieces," Veronica said.

"They aren't for sale," Min said.

"I didn't mean to suggest they were. Just admiring."

"I'm a genealogist," Jillian said. Given Min's disposition, she had nothing to lose. "I was noticing the photos. They seem to go back quite a ways as well."

"Family is important to us." Min turned her head to one side and eyed Jillian.

"In my line of work, that's music to my ears." Jillian gestured toward the fireplace. "Who are these people on the mantel?"

Drew had withdrawn from the gathering and now stood with his back against the farthest wall. If he took another step out of the close space, he'd leave the room. Jillian tried to meet his eyes, but his gaze was angled toward the kitchen window. Away from whatever he thought was going to happen next. Or was afraid might happen.

"These questions." Min waved them away. "I'm not sure what brought you people onto private land, much less into a private home, but I'm sure you have things to do, and I know we do."

Jillian's eyes fixed on that photo. If she went home now, she could at least compare the snapshot she took with the photograph in the steamer trunk and make sure the resemblance was not her imagination. But she'd come all this way. So many genealogy hunts began with educated hunches and ended with the facts that strung the pearls together. Leaving now, going home without the answers that might be standing right here in front of her—she just wasn't going to do it.

"May I please ask the name of the woman in that photo?" Jillian said.

Min glowered.

"Something about her piques my curiosity," Jillian said.

"Did your parents teach you no manners?" Min said. "You've overstayed your welcome."

"Jillian, we should go now," Veronica said.

"No," Jillian said. "I think there was foul play in 1909, and somehow this ranch being in this family has something to do with it."

"I beg your pardon," Min said.

Drew was out of sight. A back door clicked closed.

"Jillian," Veronica said softly.

"You weren't born in 1909." Jillian squared off toward Min. "You didn't have anything to do with what happened. But if something affected your family—which you said is important to you—wouldn't you like to know the truth? I can help you."

"You need to go. Now." Min opened the door and stood with her hand on the knob.

"Fine." Jillian knew she was beaten—for now—but she took a couple of cards from her wallet and dropped them on the coffee table. "But I would love to be in touch, in case more information emerges and you change your mind about whether you want it. And there is a steamer trunk that should come to the rightful family once we can sort everything out. You have so many lovely things. Wouldn't you want that as well—just in case it should be yours?"

"I believe I've made it quite clear that I want you to take your nose out of my house." Min glared. "Keep it in your own business and out of mine."

Veronica touched Jillian's elbow, and they walked through the door Min held open. It thudded closed behind them.

"That was something," Veronica said, hustling Jillian toward the car as quickly as her injured foot would bear.

Jillian pressed a hand against her forehead. "Did you see the way Drew just checked out? Where did he even go?" She leaned in one direction to look around one side of the cabin, even though she knew Drew could be well out of sight by now.

"I think it inadvisable to stand here and dissect the experience." Veronica unlocked the car doors, holding one open for Jillian.

Min stared out the front room window.

"This slays me," Jillian said. "We're driving away from something. I just know it. The key to the trunk is in that cabin. Or on this ranch somewhere."

"We don't have a choice." Veronica backed up the car. "Let's just go find the estate sale and then try to find a normal note in this day while your little gray cells work out the problem."

The drive back toward Pueblo.

The estate sale, where Jillian spent most of her time looking for someplace to sit down but didn't dare turn on her phone unless she wanted to actively ignore her dad's calls.

A late lunch after Veronica made a few purchases for the Emporium.

Loaning her phone to Veronica to call Luke, when she realized she'd been driving around all day without hers.

The drive back to Canyon Mines, knowing Nolan would be waiting for her.

Jillian went in the front door. Nolan was in the cozy end of the long front room that they used as a TV area, near the piano he tinkered with occasionally. He turned off the television and closed the file he had in his lap.

"I know what you think, Dad."

"I imagine you have a good idea."

"If I'd told you where I was going, you would have told me not to go."

"Probably. But you did go, and you're probably worn out, and you're too old for a lecture. So maybe you should just put your feet up and tell me what happened while you were incommunicado for twelve hours, and we'll go from there."

Jillian winced. She'd hurt him.

She ran her tongue over her lips, swallowed hard, and dug in. The ranch. Drew. The photo. Min. The flip side of Drew. Finally she powered on her phone.

"Ah, the phone works."

"Dad, please."

"I'm sorry."

"I want to show you the picture I took of the photo on the mantel." She pulled it up and handed him the phone. Then she went to the trunk and found the family photograph. "Do you see the resemblance?"

Nolan tilted his head. "It's hard to say. The old photo is grainy, and there's quite an age difference. No particular distinguishing marks."

"But it *could* be her."

"Yes, I suppose it could be."

"Don't you see?" Jillian took back her phone. "I said I was going to find Lynnelle, and I did. Now I just have to figure out why she's on that mantel. And we wouldn't know that we're close if I hadn't gone to Pueblo."

"Jilly, I have every confidence that you would have found another way to substantiate your theory, if that's what this was about."

"What else would it be about?"

"It's unlike you to gallivant off in person without very strong evidence."

She sank slightly in her seat. "Something happened to Lynnelle. She deserves justice."

"But when you took off without telling me you'd be gone all day, you weren't expecting to see a photo you think might be her. You had a quite opposite theory in mind. And you didn't want anyone's advice about it."

"No one with her name is legally associated with the history of that property," Jillian insisted. "If anything, I'm even more curious why her photo would turn up in that little red house."

"Maybe we'll figure it out and maybe we won't," Nolan said, "but I care a lot more about whether we figure *you* out."

"What are you talking about?"

"The trunk in the attic, Jilly. Please be careful that you understand what opening the trunk in the living room stirred up in you, and use careful judgment. In the meantime, please don't tangle with Min, whoever you think she might be."

CHAPTER SEVENTEEN

Denver, Colorado
April 29, 1909

Dear Miss Bendeure,

I am certain that with not much more investigation, and
the assistance of some of my best operatives, I will come
to timely conclusions and prevent the damage to Bendeure &
Company from taking root. It is unfortunate that it seems
clear that there has been some loss, but relative to the
overall strength of the organization and your father's
business acumen and early intuition, wise preventive steps
have been taken. In my experience, it would be highly unusual for only one company to be targeted, and my inves-
tigations have borne out the improbability of this in the
current circumstances as well. In fact, for the sake of
their own reputation and potential liability, the banks
have cooperated by supplying the names of other companies
whom the same agent claimed to represent, and I am in the
process of verifying the legitimacy of these organizations
and the transactions made on their behalf, many of which
predate your father's discomfitures with the nature of the
agent's correspondence. Many may prove to be aboveboard.
We need only find the one loose thread which may unravel
the enterprise and lead us to the key figure who will be
far more significant to apprehend. If that happens, or if
I might say, when that happens, we will have your father
to thank.

Yours sincerely,
James McParland
Manager, Western Division
Pinkerton's National Detective Agency

Lynnelle pressed her hand to her forehead. The late afternoon departure from Luzerne meant they could make Omaha only twenty-four hours late, and the Union Pacific would attach extra cars to accommodate the overflow passengers the train's late arrival caused to its schedule. She only wanted to be left alone for these remaining torturous hours.

For heaven's sake, why was there yet another knock on her door?

"Hear me when I call, O God of my righteousness: thou hast enlarged me when I was in distress; have mercy upon me, and hear my prayer." The psalmist's cry vaulted through her spirit. If she had any righteousness, it surely was not her own. Nor mercy. If Willie or Carey Meade was knocking at her door again, she would march straight up the aisle until she found a porter or a conductor or a guard or a waiter. Anyone. She would bang on the door to the locomotive and demand to speak to the engineer if necessary, but she would not tolerate harassment all the way to Omaha and certainly not to Denver. Someone in authority could make clear that they *must* leave her alone.

"Yes?"

"Miss Bendeure?"

"Yes?"

"I have a telegram for you."

She leaped off the bench and opened the door to the porter.

"When did you receive this?" They were nearly two hours out of Luzerne.

"I'm sorry, miss. The depot master gave us quite a stack of replies just before we pulled out. It has taken some time to sort them out and match them up to everyone."

"Thank you." She scrambled for a coin to press into his palm. "Thank you very much."

"You're very welcome, miss. I hope it's the news you've been hoping for."

"Thank you again." Lynnelle closed the door behind the porter and sat on the forward-facing bench to tear open the telegram. Almost immediately another knock sounded. Perhaps the hotel had also responded to her message—hopefully with reassurance that her delay did not imperil her accommodations arrangement. Lynnelle popped up to open the door for the porter again.

Clarice Hollis stepped across the threshold with her incessant smile. "I haven't seen you in hours and hours. Did you ever get that bit of fresh air before we *finally* got underway again?"

"Yes. I felt better after a short rest and ventured out. I'm sorry I didn't come looking for you. I wasn't sure how much time there would be at that point."

"No trouble at all." Clarice sank into one of the benches. "Just wanted to be sure you're all right."

"My case of impatience should be cured now that we're moving again." Lynnelle casually stepped over to the small cushioned bench opposite the sink, where her wicker case was opened, and let the telegram drop in next to her folded nightdress and dragged the hem of a pale pink blouse across it. She joined Clarice on the benches, though she would have preferred Clarice to make a polite inquiry and leave, not settle in.

"I think everyone is quite relieved!" Clarice slapped one knee. "My aunt Ida—or was it Iola—tells a story of being stuck on a train during a blizzard. I think that's probably worse. At least we could get off and go outside. Every time she tells the story, the snow gets deeper. For all I know it was a passing rain shower, but I tend to believe there was at least some snow. There must have been. Something stopped the train. Rain wouldn't stop a train, but deep snow would."

Lynnelle managed a polite smile. "I've never known rain to stop a train."

"Ivy says the whole thing never happened." Clarice got up and wandered three steps to the mirror and leaned toward it, examining her reflection. "At least not to any of them. It was in Wyoming, according to her, and Ida—or Iola—read about it in the newspaper decades ago and transported the whole thing to New Jersey where they grew up."

"I suppose anything is possible," Lynnelle said. "Does it really matter?"

"No. The aunts are ancient. And they bicker about memories all the time. Who knows what's true?" Clarice pivoted and leaned her wrists behind her back against the sink as she surveyed the compartment. "I've never actually traveled in a compartment. I'm lucky if I get a sleeping berth instead of sitting up all night."

Lynnelle waved a hand. "As you can see, you can practically trip over yourself."

"At least you've got space for a small case out of the way from where they make the bed." Clarice took two steps toward the wall beside Lynnelle's wicker case. "What's this? A cabinet?"

"Yes. If you really wanted to, you could hang a couple of blouses in there."

Clarice opened the cupboard door. "But you haven't."

"Not on this trip. I brought so few things into the compartment."

"Just the one hat?"

Lynnelle's eye followed the end of Clarice's finger to where Lynnelle's gray hat hung from a hook. "It seemed bothersome to bring more than one on the train."

"I agree. Of course the aunts would never travel with fewer than four."

"Another era."

Clarice returned to the benches and patted Lynnelle's satchel. "I've been meaning to tell you how much I admire this piece. Elegant but practical for travel. A rich color. The aunts would approve."

"Thank you."

"Henry won't let me carry anything important. He insists on having everything in his pockets."

Lynnelle smiled. "Enjoy the advantages of traveling with a man."

"True enough. I've also been admiring your brooch. It's absolutely divine."

"Thank you." Lynnelle's hand went to the piece. "It was my mother's. I'm very fond of wearing it as often as I can."

"I can see why." Clarice stood. "With your case of impatience cured, will we see you out and about again?"

"We'll see. I have some reading to catch up on." The miles to Omaha were shrinking rapidly now.

"Henry and I would be happy to see you anytime."

"You've been lovely companions."

Finally Clarice left. Lynnelle latched the door behind her and stepped to the wicker case to retrieve the telegram from between her spare blouse and nightdress.

It wasn't there.

She dug through her clothes.

She emptied the case.

She picked up the case to be sure she hadn't misjudged where she'd slid it, and perhaps it was underneath or had fallen to the floor. She even opened the cupboard, which she had never opened before Clarice entered the room.

She checked the benches, and the satchel, and the back of the sink.

The telegram was gone.

Clarice. It was the only explanation. Was there no one on this ghastly trek worthy of her trust?

Lynnelle had to find the porter, the one who delivered the telegram. Unpinning her keys from her waistband, she locked her wicker case, though it held only clothes for which she cared nothing at all at this point, snatched up her satchel, and left the compartment.

Willie jumped out of her seat as soon as Lynnelle stepped into the aisle. "What's wrong?"

Lynnelle stiffened. "Why should anything be wrong?"

Carey stood now as well, withholding his dimple. "You do look upset."

"I'm sure I don't."

"If there's something we can help you with—"

Help from the two of them was the last thing she required. "Thank you, but I'll manage."

She ignored the way they glanced at each other and proceeded in search of the porter. Not just any porter. The right porter.

Finally, she found him. "I wonder if by chance you read the telegram you delivered to me."

"No, miss! That would be wrong."

She was quick to reassure him. "I'm not accusing you. I seem to have misplaced it before I had a chance to read it, and I very much need to know what it said."

He shook his head. "I just put it in my pocket until I found you. Only the telegraph operator in Luzerne might remember what it said. But he was taking so many messages, I would be surprised if he did."

"It's my own silly carelessness," Lynnelle said.

"If you'd like to send another message, just write it out and pass it to me. The next time we slow to pass a depot, I'll make sure to pass it along to someone in the mail car who will pass it to an operator."

Pass. Pass. Pass. That was quite a bit of passing along. A lot of chances for a message to get lost.

Or intercepted.

Lynnelle walked slowly back toward her compartment, positive she didn't lose the message. Even telegrams were too risky. She'd just have to contact Mr. McParland when she reached Denver and checked into the Windsor.

"Lynnelle, dear, were you hungry again?" Mrs. Sweeney was in her seat. Lynnelle must have walked right past her while seeking the porter.

"I'm glad to find you," Lynnelle said. Mrs. Sweeney was the clearest, most unassuming soul on this entire journey. "Maybe you'd like to come and enjoy the peace and quiet of my compartment."

"Indeed I would." Mrs. Sweeney pulled herself upright. "Perhaps you can explain to me why your mood has changed so much since we met."

CHAPTER EIGHTEEN

I'm okay, Dad." On Sunday after church, Jillian flipped a page in her genealogy magazine and bit into a grilled cheese sandwich. "You don't have to hover."

Veronica sure wouldn't aid and abet her again.

Nia had her hands full on Sunday afternoons recovering from weekends with every room at the Inn full.

Kris opened her shop between one and five for the weekend tourist traffic, especially at this time of year when spring weather brought more families out on mountain excursions.

Jillian was in no danger of another breakout.

"Did I tell you Clark thinks I should make an Irish spiced brisket?"

"Mmm. It's a good idea." She flipped another page.

"Jilly."

"I'm okay, Dad." At least she would be. Tomorrow, or maybe tonight, she'd go back to work on a long to-do list for the week. She wasn't giving up on Lynnelle—not after meeting Min—but she did have obligations. Her dad was right. She'd nearly lost herself. After church, he busied himself rubbing the brisket he'd bought from the butcher with brown sugar, covered it, and put it in the refrigerator—day one of the spicing process.

While he puttered in the kitchen with his lists and recipes, he hummed snippets of arias, but he restrained himself from bursting out in song. Jillian felt responsibility for his subdued mood but not remorse. Not yet anyway. She said good night early and went upstairs to bed. Maybe a good sleep would reset her own mood.

On Monday morning, he popped his head in her office.

"I'm *okay*, Dad," she said again.

This time she looked up and met his gaze, and when he left for work in Denver it was with a nod and a smile. She had three video calls on her calendar and an article due by the end of the day. Probation and an ankle bracelet would have given her more flexibility to get out of the house. She even cleared her whiteboard of the distracting list of name variants and colored arrows. Only one mattered, and it had already led where she'd hoped it would go. As a peace offering, for supper she warmed some of the many leftovers Nolan's cooking experiments had produced and had a meal ready by the time he was home.

On Tuesday morning, Nolan worked in his office upstairs, and Jillian plodded along in hers downstairs, as they did most Tuesdays. Occasionally one printer or the other would spit something out, or a phone would ring. At ten thirty an alert on her computer's calendar reminded Jillian they both had promised Nia they'd take a break and visit the Inn to discuss their needs for the weekend of the dinner. Jillian closed the file she was working on, stepped to the bottom of the stairs—her foot was feeling much better—and called up.

"Dad?"

"Coming." His footsteps, answering in tandem with his voice, were right on time. "I'll get my truck out."

"I feel up to walking."

"Are you sure?"

"I'm okay, Dad." Her foot was okay. Her mind was okay. Her mood was creeping toward normal. He could stop worrying.

They grabbed light jackets and set off down the street.

In the Inn's large kitchen, Nia set the agenda. The last time they were there, they'd never gotten around to having Nolan inspect her assorted pots and pans, small appliances, and variety of utensils.

"Nobody wants any last-minute surprises," Nia said. "I promised Marilyn this will be a precision operation."

Nolan opened an oven door. "I must confess I have coveted your double ovens since the day you had them installed."

"I wouldn't be without them," she said, "but are they going to do the job for you?"

Nolan raised his hands as if he were framing photos and squinted.

Nia looked at Jillian. "What is he doing?"

"Measuring."

"Should I get a measuring tape?"

"If you want the measurements to be correct."

"You mock me," Nolan said. "I have to know how many baking pans I can get in each oven."

"Doesn't that depend on the size of the baking pans?" Nia said.

Jillian twisted her mouth in an effort not to laugh for the first time in four days.

Nia opened a small drawer and extracted a measuring tape, a pen, and a notepad. "Here. The ovens are extra wide, but measure so you know."

"Refrigerator space?" Nolan asked. "Once I start shopping, well, it's a lot of food to store."

"We may need to beg, borrow, and steal some large coolers," Jillian said.

Nolan pointed at her, pleased with the idea. "We can always cook in both kitchens and shuttle food back and forth. I'll need my good electric knife."

"Who's 'we'?" Nia asked. "Did you find someone to help?"

"I'm working on it."

From there they moved on to opening cupboards and listing available pots, saucepans, skillets, and baking dishes. Jillian silently excused herself from the commotion, until Nia was ready for the questions she wanted to direct at her, and walked through the Inn to sit in the library. She'd always liked this room, cozy and apart from the larger main rooms, designed for quiet with a view of the front porch through its lace curtains. She sat in one of the matching champagne-colored Victorian spoon-back tufted armchairs, where the hum of spirited conversation in the kitchen was barely audible, and gazed out. If the Inn had any guests in the middle of the week, they were either upstairs or out for the day.

At the sound of car doors slamming, Jillian's eyes focused on the view beyond the porch.

She popped out of her chair.

Two figures came up the sidewalk, one straggling behind the other, and up the broad steps to the porch. Jillian's heart raced, and she went to the front door to open it before they even rang the bell.

Min stared at her. "Good. You're here."

At least Min hadn't torn up her business card and tossed the pieces in the fireplace the moment Jillian left the little red house.

"It's good to see you," Jillian said. "Please, come in."

Min strode into the main hallway. Drew shrugged a little as he followed, his neck buried in the collar of his jacket.

"We can find a place to talk," Jillian said. "How did you know where to find me?"

"You're not the only one who dropped a card," Min said. "It turns out your friend Veronica left a card with Drew. When you weren't home, we went there, and she suggested you might be here."

"I'm glad you found me," Jillian said. "Did you decide you wanted to hear about the trunk after all?"

"Don't flatter yourself," Min said.

Nolan and Nia entered the hall from the dining room.

"May I help you?" Nia said.

"This is Min and Drew," Jillian said.

Nolan stepped forward to offer a handshake. Drew took his hand. Min did not.

"Are you interested in staying at the Inn?" Nia asked.

"No." Min turned back to Jillian. "My only business is to ask Jillian to mind her own business."

Jillian's stomach clenched. "You've come all the way to Canyon Mines to say that?" Min had made her feelings quite clear on Saturday.

"Don't take me for a fool," Min said. "Drew is driving me to Casper for a visit with Michelle."

"Michelle?" Jillian would grasp at every name she heard.

"My daughter. Not that this is any of your business either, but I don't do distance driving on my own. People seem to think I'm too old for that. It didn't seem that far out of the way to stop here and make sure you understand my position."

"I do. Very well." Jillian searched for Drew's eyes, but he refused to offer them. The friendly, dimpled man on the horse was still lost in whoever his great-aunt caused him to become. Compassion climbed through the core of her, but no words that would diffuse the clinched mood came to her. She glanced at Nolan, the one who usually knew what to say, wishing he could have met the Drew she first met.

"We promise to respect your home and property," Nolan said.

Thank you, Dad. He hadn't said they wouldn't get at the truth. His answer allowed ample latitude to do it from a distance.

"You'd better," Min said. "And tell your friend at the Victorian shop that I made note of her license plate the other day. If I see her vehicle on my property again, I promise I will call the police."

Jillian glanced at Nolan, whose eyes implored her to remain calm. Drew blanched in silent embarrassment. Jillian hid her fists behind her back.

"The trunk is in my living room," Jillian said. "You could still see it, since you're here." It was a risky offer. Min might get it in her head to abscond with it—and all the evidence it contained. But if she'd been home when Min and Drew marched up her porch steps rather than Nia's, the trunk would have been standing right there. Maybe seeing it would soften Min. Make her curious. At the very least, a few minutes of less hostile conversation could rule out that the photo on the mantel had anything to do with Lynnelle Bendeure. And if Min saw a connection—well, the path of conversation would change.

Min scoffed. "It's as if you're not listening to a word I'm saying. Just mind your own business, please. Come on, Drew." She pivoted and went out the door, dragging Drew in her undertow.

"What just happened?" Nia asked once Drew's truck pulled away.

"What just happened," Jillian said, "is that we found out where another branch of the family lives!"

"Also what just happened," Nolan said, "is that I've decided Jillian is right."

"Dad?"

"It's just plain odd for people not to be a *little* curious about their family from a hundred years ago," Nolan said, "and it's close to incriminating for them to go this far out of their way to tell you for a second time to back off."

Jillian smacked a big sloppy kiss on her father's cheek.

"Despite his demeanor, my gut tells me Drew is plenty curious," Nolan said.

"What is the power she has over him?" Jillian asked. "I wish you could have met him before she showed up the other day. His personality changed completely when she came in. Now today he didn't say a single word. I don't think he even wanted to come inside."

"Your methods were rather like a search without a warrant," Nolan said, "and I still want you to be careful, but I agree it's a little hard to walk away from what she just stirred up."

"I've got a family tree to work on."

"You still don't know that it's Lynnelle." Nolan's tone carried caution.

"No, but I sure plan to find out."

"What are you people talking about?" Nia asked. "Who is Lynnelle? Where did you meet those people? And what did you do to make that woman so angry?"

Jillian and Nolan laughed.

"It's a long story," Jillian said.

"Well, hold that thought then," Nia said. "Right now I need to know if it's really going to work to have you standing here in the hall for your talk."

They returned to the preparations for the Legacy Jubilee meal. Between her guests and the dinner, Nia would be swamped. She couldn't get caught up in last-minute problems that could just as well be worked out now.

Back in their own home, Nolan mixed salt, chopped onion, bay leaves, pepper, dried crushed rosemary, thyme, and cloves to rub into the brisket before returning it to the refrigerator—day two. He would turn and rub the salt mixture into the beef once a day for the next two days before roasting the meat with vegetables. Then they both went back to work.

In the evening Jillian turned her attention to the family tree she was trying to build. Now that she had Drew Lawson's name, she could work backward as well as forward from the names of the couple who bought the ranch so long ago.

In theory.

Even using *Andrew* in place of *Drew* didn't get her what she wanted. It must not be his given first name. She didn't know Michelle's last name—or Min's. And Min was no doubt short for something. Minnie? Minerva? It could be short for a given name, or it could be a family nickname. Jillian needed a day clear of other commitments to devote to sleuthing through this conundrum. She couldn't stay up all night again.

Nolan had checked the locks and gone up to bed an hour ago. Now Jillian shut down her computer, turned off the lights in her office, and went up the back stairs. On the landing, though, she hesitated. Instead of going toward her bedroom, she opened the door to the attic and flipped the light switch.

The trunk. She blew out her breath and put a palm to her forehead.

Her father was not entirely wrong. He rarely was. The arrival of Lynnelle's trunk cranked up and triggered every emotion she felt about her own.

Jillian climbed the stairs. The trunk's shape beckoned from under the blankets. She wanted to turn around. Retreat down the stairs. Go to bed at a sensible time, just as she'd planned.

She swallowed and moved toward it. Dragged it out from under the eaves. Uncovered it. Raised the lid. Removed the tray.

She had to be missing something. A small thing that could make all the difference, something she hadn't seen all these years.

Jillian lifted the box of odds and ends and stared at them. What happened between those two letters addressed to her great-great-great-grandfather Sal? She'd always surmised, without proof, that Lou was another brother. And Geppetto? Growing up with the story of Pinocchio, it hadn't occurred to her that real people had that name. Because of its fragility, she still hesitated to unfold the streetcar map, but with great care she spread it under the brightest light in the attic. It was unremarkable in every respect but one. *Hotel.* The black ink word was scrawled in tiny letters next to a lopsided star at an intersection that would have been a good distance from downtown Denver at the time. Not until she was in college and had access to the university library, with its historical images, did Jillian find an early twentieth-century five-story building on that corner and references to a brief period of time in its history when it had been a hotel.

But if there'd ever been a family story for why it should be marked on a streetcar map, she'd waited too long to be curious.

Jillian's hands shook as she folded the map and replaced it in the box. Could she never forgive herself? She packed the trunk, closed it, and covered it. She should have just gone to bed rather than torturing herself.

In her room, changed and ready for bed with teeth brushed, she climbed under the quilt. Veronica's oddball dissertation on the history of Italian immigration sat on the nightstand. Jillian thought she'd read everything under the sun on that topic years ago, but she'd never seen this. She picked it up and turned to the index at the back, a research habit that she found gave her an idea of what to expect in a large document before she dove in. Many entries were what she expected, including the long section on the Mafia.

Then there it was.

Parisi.

CHAPTER NINETEEN

Just watching Marilyn made Jillian antsy. The Legacy Jubilee was still two weeks away, and the museum director was getting more tightly wound by the day.

"She's got her clipboard," Jillian whispered to Kris Bryant in the community room at the Heritage Society during the assembly of business owners involved in the weekend's events.

"I'm ready." Kris slapped a fist into an open palm. "Supplies ordered. Extra temporary staff recruited. Machines in optimal working condition."

"Are you here to put the rest of us to shame?" Jillian leaned into her father's shoulder on the other side.

"Ahem," Nolan said. "I have. . .lists."

"Why aren't you in Denver today?" Kris asked.

"And miss all this?" Nolan said.

"What he means," Jillian said, "is that he has to go to Denver on Friday anyway, so he swapped work-from-home days from Friday to Thursday."

He checked his watch. "I do actually have to work at some point."

Jillian yawned and tried to push her eyes open wider. In the end, she'd stayed up later Tuesday night than she'd meant to. In fact, the dissertation had absorbed the last two evenings. The list of pages on which *Parisi* appeared numbered more than a few, and she would never have gone to sleep without at least scanning for some context. The first night, she'd gone downstairs, flipped on the lights, and made a photocopy of the entire document so she could mark it up when she had time for a more thorough reading. The second night, she'd dug in to begin a careful read.

Marilyn worked her way down her clipboard checklist. Silently, Jillian admitted the details were worth reviewing. Everyone would know what to expect during the Legacy Jubilee, and today's process likely would save the chaos and incessant questions on four very busy days two weeks from now. With all the participants in one place, before they opened their own businesses for the day, Marilyn could also ask her individual questions and save time chasing down people who weren't returning calls. As the meeting proceeded, Jillian's appreciation for Marilyn's organized analytical approach increased. If she ever ran for mayor, she'd have Jillian's vote.

Nolan's turn came. Marilyn pointed the end of her pen at him. "Menu, Nolan. By tomorrow."

"You'll have it."

"Can you give me some idea?"

"Choice of soup, salads, breads, one or two meats, side dishes, three or four vegetables, Irish specialty dishes for particular interest, vegetarian options, of course, and an array of desserts."

Marilyn's lips pursed. "That doesn't seem very specific. You do understand it is a sit-down meal and not a buffet."

"I'm still narrowing things down." He wagged one eyebrow.

Unimpressed, Marilyn nevertheless moved on, and Nolan exhaled. Jillian didn't blame him. While Marilyn's method was expedient, it was a bit like being called to the board at the front of the room to show your work in algebra class.

"Jillian has given us a lovely topic," Marilyn said. "She will speak on 'Your Family's Then and Your Now: Knotting the Threads Together.'"

"No fair," Nolan muttered. "You used that theme at a conference last year."

Jillian shrugged.

Marilyn finished her rounds and dismissed the group with a final admonition to read emails to remain informed of any changing details and gratitude for everyone's support for the museum.

"Gotta scoot," Kris said. "Carolyn and I are cooking up some Legacy Jubilee special combos with her Digger's Delight chocolates and my ice cream. We're still experimenting."

"You don't have to turn in a menu on Friday?" Nolan said.

Kris laughed and left.

Nia beelined toward them. "Nolan! Too many options! No wonder you're talking about cooking in two kitchens. Can't you simplify?"

"Simplify, schimplify," Nolan said. "It's supposed to be elegant. Do you think the Victorians ate simplified menus?"

"Jillian," Nia said, "somebody has to tame him, and I think it's going to be you."

"Me!" Jillian put her hands up, stop signs. "I don't control him."

Nia shook her finger at Nolan. "For the sake of Marilyn's sanity and the good of my kitchen, narrow down the options to something reasonable—and specific. And not too messy. Things you can prep ahead."

"What happened to everyone's imagination?" Nolan chuckled. "But all right. Message received. Final menu due tomorrow. Specific. Fewer options. Not messy."

Nia turned on her heel and went to consult Marilyn.

Veronica sauntered over. "Did Min and Drew find you? What a shock to see them!"

"They did find us," Jillian said. "Was Min as courteous to you as she was to us?"

"She's a piece of work."

"She slipped up a little," Jillian said. "She has a daughter in Casper. That's where they were heading."

"Ooh. Name?"

"She didn't slip up that much," Nolan said. "Just a first name."

"I have a leaf for the family tree in the generation between Min and Drew," Jillian said, "and I know that at least part of the family migrated to Casper. Maybe somebody with the family name did as well. I need a chunk of time to do some digging."

"You just made me promise to focus on the heritage event," Nolan said. "Don't you need to update your talk so it doesn't sound tired and recycled?"

"You wish. I could give that talk in my sleep." Jillian grinned. "But I do have some actual paying work that needs attention today."

"I'm supposed to tell you Luke has been emailing more people about the papers," Veronica said. "He's hoping to have something for you soon."

"Ah." Nolan inclined his head toward Jillian. "Another reason to be inquisitive but not headlong."

"Message received." Jillian saluted as she echoed her father's earlier words. "No more going off the grid." Some mental machinations would leave no outward evidence while she waited for Luke's results, and the dissertation now posed considerable distraction for the hours after she dispatched her professional obligations.

After four days of turning and rubbing the seasonings and turning again, the spiced brisket was ready to bake. Nolan filled the roasting pan with generous portions of onions, carrots, celery, and beef broth and roasted the meat all afternoon, filling the house with an aroma tantalizing Jillian's taste buds incessantly. Nolan's requirement for serving it, however, was her honest opinion.

She rolled a bite around on her tongue in three directions before finally swallowing it.

"Fewer cloves, more rosemary?" Jillian squinted her eyes at Nolan.

"Is that a question or advice?"

"My best guess." She stabbed her fork into the meat for another bite. "But it's good."

"It has to be excellent," Nolan said. "I have just enough days for another practice run before starting the real thing. But I'd better get my order in with the butcher."

"Two hundred meals," Jillian said.

"Where exactly is that butcher shop?"

Jillian rolled her eyes. He'd found the butcher on Saturday to buy the brisket they were eating now. He was just playing helpless. But she could do a little penance. "I'll go tomorrow. How many pounds do you want altogether?"

She cleared out of the kitchen after supper. Nolan donned his white apron and chef's hat and started singing Puccini. The Italian text was fitting to Jillian's reading material as she settled into her favorite chair and ottoman in the living room with the photocopied dissertation on Italian immigration, a yellow highlighter, and bright-colored self-stick notes in her hands to review again the details that had emerged over the last two evenings.

Three Parisi brothers arrived together from Sicily in the late 1800s. Jillian already knew this was an era of large waves of Italian immigration. The dissertation did not give birth dates or specific ages. This was not its purpose. The Parisi story was only significant for its intersection with the narrative of the Mastranga crime family in New Orleans, which used a saloon and a brothel as the base for its operations. Italian laborers of all sorts, but especially dockworkers, handed over a cut of their earnings or faced the prospect of having their livelihoods terminated. South African fruit. Produce. Grocery stores. Shipping. Wagons. It was one big network, a minefield of business monopoly. What good was it to have imported perishable produce, even the best quality, without a way to get it off the docks? And what good were agreements to sell it in stores without local transportation to get it there?

Mastranga.

Provenzano.

Warring crime families.

Plenty of commerce to go around, but the Mastrangas wanted it all and would do whatever it took.

Parisis and a string of others scrambling to make a living, to find a new dream in a new country, made choices they would never be able to take back.

Luciano was the oldest brother, arriving in the new country taking seriously the pledge he made to his mother to look after his younger brothers, still teenagers.

Luciano Parisi. *Lou.*

Jillian's mind's eye could see the swirly handwriting of the lengthy letter prevailing on Sal—Salvatore—to ease a transition to Denver. Her instinct that Lou was Sal's brother was correct. The author of the dissertation listed the brothers. Luciano. Salvatore. Giuseppe. Like many young immigrants of their generation, they'd simplified their names and were known in their trades by their more American sounding nicknames.

Lou. Sal. Joe. *Think of Joe.*

The Parisi brothers, like others, hedged their bets with their allegiances. All their livelihoods depended on their decisions—Luciano in transporting produce, Salvatore on the docks, Giuseppe climbing the ranks in a grocery store with aspiration of opening one of his own. Luciano paid for the protection the Mastrangas offered. He was the head of the American family and the first to marry and have his own children. But Salvatore resisted the violence with which the Mastrangas strangled entire industries.

As Nolan burst out with an Italian chorus Jillian didn't recognize, she flipped pages, scanning and homing in on relevant explanations. Conflict between the Mastranga and Provenzano families caught the attention of

David Hennessy, the police chief, who paid for his alertness with his life. In a chain of backlash violence and vigilante lynchings, the Mastrangas forced out the Provenzanos.

But not before felling a swath of opposition—including young Giuseppe Parisi, who had just opened his own small grocery store—who were caught up in the violence and lost their lives.

At least take Geppetto. Save him. Think of Joe.

Listening to her father's strains of Italian lyrics, Jillian took the front stairs as quickly as she could manage on her nearly healed foot. After not looking in her mother's trunk for six years, now she would open it for the third time in nine days.

What was she missing?

Jillian hadn't dragged the trunk back under the eaves after the last time she opened it, and the blankets were only roughly positioned atop it. She pushed them aside now and soon had the box out again. It must be in the photos.

She always focused on the little girls with the distinctly Parisi hair and secondarily the canopy with the Parisi name. The children remained nameless—Lou's children?—but above the letters of her family name was another. Smaller letters, perhaps, but at the time the bigger name.

Provenzano.

Whoever Geppetto was, Luciano had wanted to send him to Salvatore in Denver for a reason. Giuseppe had bet on the wrong side.

CHAPTER TWENTY

Denver, Colorado
May 3, 1909

Dear Miss Bendeure,

I am not persuaded that your physical presence in Denver is required, but I am not unsympathetic to the sense of urgency your father and you must surely be feeling for complete resolution of the matter. I assure you I have operatives on this case even when I need to leave the city or state. If you wish to make the journey, I suggest we arrange a date in the third week in May or the beginning of the fourth. This will allow me to dispense with another matter and meet with you personally. If you wish to arrive earlier, I can arrange for you to speak with a senior associate who is fully versed in the details of the investigation. Please make your wishes known, and we will make sure all is ready, not only with our own presence but also with the availability of others whom it will be important for you to meet, including the individual your father may wish to engage as the western agent for Bendeure & Company, rather than withdrawing completely, as you have indicated is his preference if it is possible to accomplish with confidence. It is my understanding that you will arrive duly authorized with appropriate documents to act on his behalf on all matters to which we will attend.

As far as accommodations, my recommendation is the Windsor. You will find them quite comfortable with every amenity you may wish during a pleasant stay.

Yours sincerely,
James McParland
Manager, Western Division
Pinkerton's National Detective Agency

"In case you haven't figured it out, I'm a stubborn old bird." Mrs. Sweeney's beady eyes were narrower every time she turned up at Lynnelle's compartment. "Something happened on that train in Iowa. You don't want to talk about it."

"It was lovely of you to bring me another sandwich, Mrs. Sweeney." Lynnelle picked up a quarter of the offering between thumb and forefinger. "Roast beef is my favorite."

"That's all you have to say for yourself?"

Lynnelle bit into the sandwich and chewed.

"You've barely left your compartment for more than twelve hours," Mrs. Sweeney said.

"I don't mind." Lynnelle dabbed her lips with the napkin that arrived with the food. At least on this leg of the trip the Meades weren't sitting right outside her door. That didn't mean they—or the Hollises—weren't watching her. She'd seen both couples the first time she ventured out after the train left Omaha, an experience that cemented her resolve not to leave her compartment unless absolutely necessary. "After all, I have you inquiring after my welfare at regular intervals and making sure I don't starve."

"When we got stuck in Iowa, I rather thought it was going to be the other way around."

"One must never assume, because one never knows what surprises a day may bring."

"Now you sound like Clarice and her infernal stories about the aunts. But of course you've spared yourself by hibernating in here."

Lynnelle swallowed. "Is she pestering you?"

"She does have a way of turning up."

"Yes, she does." *And telegrams have a way of disappearing in her wake.* "You've been a wonderful traveling companion, Mrs. Sweeney."

"My dear, why won't you tell me what distresses you? Perhaps I can help."

"It's a delicate matter."

"I'm an old woman. I've seen everything."

I hope you haven't seen this. "I have some cookies left in my cousin's basket. Oatmeal raisin. Would you like one?"

"I'm not so easily distracted, Lynnelle."

"Well, I'm going to have a cookie." Lynnelle opened the basket and took her time fishing around.

"It's only another three hours until we arrive in Denver," Mrs. Sweeney said. "Will you come to see me at my daughter's home while you're in town?"

Lynnelle nodded. "That would be lovely. Let's meet up when we get off the train and make some arrangement."

"I'll hold you to that."

"You won't have to hold very hard. I would love to meet your family." Not knowing how long her business with Mr. McParland might take, Lynnelle had not yet booked her passage home. Another day in Denver wouldn't matter. Once the matters were concluded, she could tell Mrs. Sweeney the whole story.

Mrs. Sweeney stood. "Then I have brought you your final sustenance for the journey, and I shall wait for you when we disembark. I'll find a bench after I have my trunks and make my daughter wait until we have spoken."

"You have my assurance." Lynnelle stood to see Mrs. Sweeney out and latched the door behind her. She turned again to Marabel's basket. The jar of olives was down to its last four. As Lynnelle scooped them out, she spoke aloud the verse her mother's cousin would have recited on such an occasion and tried hard to embrace it, whatever awaited in Denver. " 'But I am like a green olive tree in the house of God: I trust in the mercy of God for ever and ever.' "

The last few hours were the longest. The train would get into Denver midafternoon, and once she settled in at the hotel—assuming they could accommodate her altered reservation—a proper bath and a fine meal would help her resist the urge to try to reach Mr. McParland on a Sunday evening. First thing Monday morning she would telephone Pinkerton's.

When the final hour had arrived, and the conductor was coming through the cars announcing the imminent arrival in Denver, Lynnelle straightened up the contents of her wicker case, combed and pinned her hair, applied rouge to her cheeks, fixed her hat at a fetching angle, straightened the jacket of her navy plaid traveling suit, and made sure she had coins handy for tipping the porters, cabbies, and bellhops who would help her with her luggage along the way.

Lynnelle touched her mother's brooch at her neck. The reunion with her steamer would be sweet, with its photographs and the family Bible. If her father knew she had packed these mementos, he would have scowled over the top of his spectacles. He had never even been able to bring himself to enter the dates her mother and brother had died. Entries had always been her mother's task. But more than a thousand miles from Ohio she wanted to feel close to something familiar. The faces and names of her family would greet her every morning in the hotel and strengthen her in the unknown. At first she'd regretted not somehow fitting them into her crowded wicker case to keep with her on the trains. Now she was glad her most precious personal items hadn't been available for Willie Meade or Clarice Hollis to rifle through.

Who *were* they?

The massive lumbering train tempered and lurched into its berth at Union Station. With one last look in the mirror, Lynnelle blew out a breath, opened the compartment's door, and stepped into the throng gathering belongings and disembarking. Strapped over her shoulder, the Moroccan satchel was braced under one elbow. One hand held her case, and the other Marabel's empty picnic basket, which she couldn't bring herself to abandon after it had served her so well after all. Like most crowds that arrive in an unfamiliar station, people stalled at the bottom of the steps as they left the train to look around and get their bearings. Signs. Porters. Carts. Lynnelle chose to keep walking in the direction of where the baggage would be unloaded and find a porter there to assist with her trunk. After she spoke to Mrs. Sweeney, the hotel would be only a few blocks away by cab.

Closer to the baggage car, a porter with free hands looked at her hopefully. She nodded, and he stepped forward to take the claim check to her trunk.

Instead, another hand reached from the side. "I'll take that," Carey Meade said.

He grinned at her. That dimple.

"Mr. Meade!" Lynnelle reached for the claim check, ignoring the dimple. "I beg your pardon."

Carey tipped the porter twice what Lynnelle would have given him. "Thank you anyway, but I'm happy to help my friend."

The porter pocketed the coins. Someone else was already signaling for his assistance.

"What in the world?" Lynnelle braced herself. Carey was on one side and Willie on the other. "I will thank you not to interfere in my efforts to find another porter. You've done quite enough on this journey."

"Look." Willie lifted her chin, and Carey followed its direction.

Henry and Clarice Hollis were headed their way.

If the Meades had left her alone, Lynnelle would be within sight of her steamer by now and within a few minutes in the comforts of a cab. Tomorrow she would speak to Mr. McParland.

She took two deep steps backward.

"Oh no you don't." Carey caught her elbow.

The weight and warmth of his hand pressed through the fabric of her traveling suit, and whether she liked it or not, Lynnelle responded to his touch.

But he was a betrayer. And married. She tried to step out of his grasp, but his grip tightened.

"I beg your pardon," she said.

Willie looped arms with her on the other side and leaned in conspiratorially. "Trust us. It's for your own good."

Carey steered her away from the train, out of the main path of passengers, out of sight of the Hollises.

Away.

Lynnelle pulled against him to no avail. The temptation to release both her wicker case and the picnic basket in order to flee unencumbered was earnest and severe. She would telephone Mr. McParland from the nearest telephone.

"I demand you both unhand me!"

"Perhaps this would persuade you we're on your side." Carey reached into a suit pocket and pulled out a small folded paper.

"My telegram! Where did you get that? Why would you take it?" The fleeting urge to succumb to his charms of a few minutes ago had dissipated, supplanted with rage rising like water rushing over a broken levee.

"Have we been anywhere near you since it went missing?" Willie said.

"You know Clarice took it. The Hollises are the ones you have to worry about."

They were in a secluded corner now, and Carey released her elbow. Lynnelle snatched the telegram from his hand.

Lynnelle had to concede that neither of the Meades could have taken the telegram from her compartment directly. Yet they had it. Who was to say they weren't in cahoots with the Hollises? She scowled and fumbled with the crumpled message.

"Did you read it?"

"No. But I'm sure Clarice Hollis did." Carey's dimple had not appeared once during this exchange. Lynnelle met his unclouded gaze. This is what he looked like when he was all business.

"Of course, that's not her name," Willie said, "and she doesn't have three great-aunts from New Jersey or anywhere else."

"We've been watching out for you."

"Why would you need to?"

"We have our orders."

"From whom?"

Carey pointed at the telegram. "The same man who sent you that."

"Mr. McParland?"

"We're from Pinkerton's."

"Operatives?"

They nodded.

"On my investigation?"

"And related activities," Willie said.

"We have to go." Carey relieved Lynnelle of her case, and she did not resist. "Now."

She glanced back toward the tunnel of trains in Denver's Union Station. "What about my trunk?"

CHAPTER TWENTY-ONE

Swinging her arm away from her torso to prevent toast crumbs from dropping into her father's laptop, Jillian leaned over his shoulder to read the email he'd composed.

To: Marilyn.

From: Nolan.

Re: Final Menu.

She scanned the contents. "It's still too much, Dad."

"I've trimmed it down as far as I can."

"What happened to a salad *or* soup?"

"That was your suggestion. It was never my vision."

"Okay. But they're both vegetables. So do we really need *both* additional vegetables with the main course?"

"It's all about a colorful presentation."

"This is not the cooking channel. There's no prize."

"I have a plan."

"I have no doubt. I also have reason to believe Nia's plan is to serve the entire main course on one standard dinner plate."

Cucumber Soup
Watercress and Orange Salad
Irish Brown Bread
Individual Bacon and Cabbage Pies
Irish Spiced Beef
Glazed Carrots
Garlic Roasted Brussels Sprouts
Baked Barley and Wild Rice
Vegetarian Stuffed Portobello Mushrooms (upon prior arrangement)
Fruited and Cream Dessert Tray

"Nice touch with the cabbage pies." Jillian bit her toast and picked up her coffee from the breakfast bar.

"Thank you."

"You snuck in another meat *and* another vegetable," Jillian said, "*and* a second Irish dish to complement the brisket."

Nolan tapped one temple. "I've given this a lot of thought."

"I can see that. I still think it might be a bit much, Dad. It's a lot to make."

"I have a plan for that too."

At least there were no last-minute fancy sauces. The desserts and bread could be made ahead. The barley and rice casseroles could be prepped ahead, ready for the ovens on the day of the dinner. After four or five days of sitting in the seasonings, the briskets would only need roasting and slicing. Most of the meal could be prepared in stages during the days ahead of the meal. Jillian saw the logic of Nolan's selections. Compared to some of the dishes he'd contemplated, he'd made reasonable choices. There were just so many.

"Perhaps fresh green beans," he said. "Some people might appreciate something fundamentally familiar. Traditionally American. And the basic color will tie the palette together."

"Dad."

"It wouldn't be too much more trouble. Just wash them, snip the ends, and a quick blanching."

Jillian reached around him and hit SEND. The unaltered message whisked into cyberspace.

"Jillian Siobhan Parisi-Duffy!"

"Marilyn wanted the menu first thing," Jillian said, "and you have to go to work. I'm going with you today—to Denver, not to work—and I'm ready. I just need to get my pad and pencils."

"There's something you're not telling me," Nolan said.

"I'll explain on the way."

During the thirty-minute drive to Nolan's office, Jillian gave him the condensed version. She'd waited far too long to get to the bottom of the mystery of her own trunk, and she still had a long way to go. But she always knew the trunk would be there in the attic. Lynnelle's trunk was different. She didn't have time to dillydally. There had to be more to the story than just what was in the Pinkerton's letters. Maybe the Pinkerton's archives at the Denver Public Library would hold some answers.

"This has something to do with that name you circled in seven colors," Nolan said, "and you think is connected to the ranch."

"It was one color, and I *know* the name is connected to the ranch," Jillian said. "That's a matter of public record. I just have to connect it to Lynnelle's trunk." Nolan couldn't object. He had agreed Min's reaction suggested Jillian was on the right trail—as long as she didn't upset the family until she had something solid.

They parted at Nolan's downtown office. Jillian had plenty of time to walk to the library, even stopping for a second morning cup of coffee on the way, before the doors opened. Jillian carried a light bag. No laptop. No pens. Not even an iPad or a purse. Just a narrow-ruled yellow pad and pencils that were safe in the vicinity of volumes and documents that could not be easily replaced. She'd been around enough valuable documents to know she didn't want to be responsible for accidental defilements. If she found something of value, she could request a photocopy or snap an image on her phone.

Even dawdling over coffee, Jillian arrived at the library before it opened and was the first person through the door when a staff member unlocked it, and made her way to the Western History and Genealogy section on the fifth floor. Like most archival listings Jillian had come across in her years researching genealogy and historical events, the printout of the Pinkerton's archives of the historic Denver office that had once been housed in the same block as the famous Tabor Opera House wasn't exhaustive. Instead, it gave numbers and labels on boxes and the general nature of the contents of each box. Before requesting a box, however, Jillian asked a more general question of the archivist librarian on duty.

"How would I locate copies of correspondence from the Pinkerton's Agency to a client in 1909?"

The librarian looked over the top of her stylish blue-rimmed glasses. "You wouldn't."

"You don't have any in the collection from that year?"

"We don't have any at all," the librarian said. "Such documents would be rare. Pinkerton's was scrupulous about confidentiality with private clients. They made their reports to clients when the investigation was complete, but keeping files of any details was out of the question—certainly not any correspondence that could fall into the wrong hands and compromise their reputation."

She spoke with the clinical detachment of someone who disbursed information all day. What she said made sense but was of no help to Jillian.

"Some fragments of correspondence survived," the librarian said. "They don't tend to have identifying information, and they're not organized chronologically, but if you look through the right boxes, you never know what you might find."

Jillian glanced at the index she'd printed out. "What about this one about train robberies?" It was the best guess she had at the moment. Lynnelle's train journey to meet with James McParland was the only clue she had.

"Give me a few minutes. I'll bring it to you."

Jillian chose a table and spread out her legal pad and pencils. Ten minutes later, she had the train robberies box in front of her. She unpacked the contents, stacking them carefully on the table and looking for some pattern that would have made someone group the items in this box together. A couple of small bound books about train robberies bore faded stamps indicating they had belonged to the Western Regional Office of Pinkerton's National Detective Agency at some point, but as far as Jillian could tell they had not originated with it. Someone had compiled an annotated list of train robberies and the gangs alleged to have perpetrated them, organized by spurs of the major railroad companies of the late nineteenth and early twentieth centuries. Remarks included the ones Pinkerton's claimed credit for solving, though it seemed that most went unsolved or unprosecuted. Apparently, finding witnesses who were both reliable and willing was problematic, though when Pinkerton's agents were aboard a train at the time of the crime, they claimed a higher success rate. Whether that was true or meant to be advertising material, Jillian couldn't tell. She jotted names on her legal pad, though nothing stuck out as persuasive. The only correspondence in the box was addressed to bank executives, and none of it was dated in 1909. It couldn't have anything to do with Lynnelle Bendeure, but references to annual reports Pinkerton's made to the American Bankers Association caused Jillian to ask for a second box.

The librarian brought it to her with the caveat that it also would likely only contain fragments. Full reports to the American Bankers Association were prepared at the national level, most likely out of New York or Chicago. As far as she knew, they weren't a primary function of the Western Regional Office, though of course there were cases of bank fraud in the western part of the nation that would have been included if the Denver office succeeded in cracking them.

Jillian found pieces of reports—as if someone who learned how to write research papers in the days of index cards had made notes about what might or might not go into a first draft, never mind make the cut for a final draft. Some of the documents were typed on machines with ink-clogged letters and faded ribbons on pages yellowed and fragile with age. Others were handwritten notes with the swirls and elongated elegant lettering of the turn of the century. Nowadays so many people didn't do more than offer an opening letter and an illegible squiggle for a legal signature. When she read historical documents, Jillian admired the disciplined gentility that went into written records. Immediately, however, she knew she'd need to take notes to sift any organization that might emerge from the fragments.

Names mattered, and then dates. And bank names.

Some of the names included first and last names. Some were one name only—she presumed last names, but she couldn't always be certain—and some were merely initials. The person making notes, who presumably might also have written a fuller version that did not survive, at least not in this box, would have known what the abbreviations stood for. Some notes were so sparing that Jillian couldn't be certain they were meant to refer to a Pinkerton's operative or a con man. She could do little more than make a list and hope for a pattern. Beside names or initials, she included brief notes identifying the activities of the individuals.

Mr. Wills seemed to have been quite active in averting several disastrous fraud operations on the New York Central and Union Pacific.

Later Mr. Willis appeared. Then Miss Willis.

Lazy typing?

Jillian underlined the similarity of names in her notes and the frequency with which the same railroads were mentioned, even the same routes.

Cara Wills.

Carey Willis.

She circled both these names the third time they appeared. More careless draft recording? Surely Pinkerton's knew the names and genders of their own operatives. Carey could be a female name, or a misspelling of Carrie. The ink was faded enough that it was difficult to say whether there was an *i* in the last name. But none of what she'd come across so far occurred during 1909 anyway. It was all earlier. She would have a hard time arguing it was relevant to Lynnelle's disappearance.

The list of banks included fourteen institutions in the Western Region, but as far as she could remember none of them matched anything in the business listings in Lynnelle's trunk. None of them was even in Denver. What could this have to do with anything?

By now the librarian had been relieved for a lunch break and returned. Jillian ignored the grumbling of her own stomach. She'd promised Nolan she'd be back at the law firm in plenty of time to get a jump on the afternoon rush hour traffic, and so far she hadn't turned up anything she could use. As random as it seemed, she kept adding to her list of recurring or similar names as her primary focus for her remaining time.

Mr. Meade.
L. Carey.
K. Willis.
William.
Careys.
C.K.
K.C.
H.H.
Willis.
Hollis.
C.W.
C.M.
Hank Hills.
Helen H.
Krispin.
Kiplan.
Caroline.
Clara Hollis.
Clarissa Hill.

Liam Meade.

Carey K.

Kipling.

Jillian flipped back to the page of names from the first box about train robberies. Wills, Willis, and Kiplan were on that list as well. Whoever Meade was, it was hard to discern which side of the law he was on from the descriptions of his activities.

And still not a single reference to 1909. When she got back to her computer at home, she would dig a little harder into finding full copies of the reports from Pinkerton's to the American Bankers Association for 1909 and 1910.

Jillian made a clean listing of the documents she wanted photocopies of, which she had sorted into neat piles, and took them to the archivist.

"Does the library have copies of the Pinkerton's reports to the American Bankers Association for 1909 and 1910?" Jillian asked. As long as she was here, she might as well inquire whether she could save herself some research time.

"I've never seen them," the librarian said. "There wouldn't be one at all for 1910, because Pinkerton's lost their contract in September 1909, and the Bankers Association had stopped including the Pinkerton's reports in their proceedings book before then anyway. A bank officer who wanted the full report had to ask for it. I wouldn't say that it's impossible you'd find it in an average collection, but it would be difficult."

"Thank you for the information." Jillian slid her list across the counter and set down her stacks. "Perhaps I could just have these photocopies then."

"Of course." The librarian scanned the list of document titles. "Pinkerton's in 1909? That's what you're interested in?"

Jillian nodded.

"You probably want the trial transcript then."

"Trial transcript? I didn't see anything about a trial in the archives index."

"I keep telling the powers that be that we need to get the records updated. We have some other boxes stored off-site."

"What kind of a trial?"

"A big banking fraud trial in mid-1910. But the case happened in 1909. Is that what you're trying to find?"

"It might be." Jillian's heart pounded. "How do I see the transcript?"

The librarian opened a drawer and removed a form. "Fill this out while I make your photocopies. It will take a few days to get the boxes."

Boxes. Plural.

"Here," the librarian said, handing Jillian a pen. "Use ink for this."

Jillian raced back to Nolan's truck just in time to see him unlocking the doors.

"How was it?" he asked as he backed the vehicle out of the spot in the parking garage.

"Fruitful. I think. Confusing." It was hard for Jillian to know how to begin an explanation. "There's a trial transcript, Dad! When I get it, can you help me sort out what it all means?"

Halfway home, they agreed that in a house full of food, they had nothing to eat for dinner. Every available ingredient and space were waiting for Nolan to organize himself to begin assembling two hundred meals. They stopped and grabbed spicy Asian noodle bowls for an easy meal to take home.

Later, Jillian picked up a dry-erase marker and started another list of names on her whiteboard. This time, instead of listing names in the order in which she had come across them in her note taking, she reorganized.

Which initials might refer to the same people as full names?

Which single names might refer to the same people?

Which names were similar enough that they might be variants for the same person—code names, perhaps—used on different operations, whether referring to Pinkerton's operatives or to suspects perpetrating bank fraud?

Which descriptions of activities might tie unnamed participants to names on her list described elsewhere?

Several variations, or combinations that could lead to variations, could lead to the name of the man on the 1909 property records of the ranch. Jillian hadn't found him in a census either. It all smelled fishy. Two people married to each other who both potentially had wide name variants, one of whom turned up in Pinkerton's reports, and neither of whom was in the census under the names they used to marry?

They were hiding something.

CHAPTER TWENTY-TWO

Four to seven business days. That's what the archivist told Jillian. There was no way to know how many other requests to fulfill were ahead of hers, and sometimes a priority triage system was applied to determine urgency. Factor in a weekend—or two—and the wait for the mysterious trial transcript could try her patience. In the meantime, she had her photocopied pages, her lists of name variants, Lynnelle Bendeure of Ohio, the couple who bought the ranch in Colorado, and suspicions she couldn't prove for how everything connected.

Jillian wasn't sure which trunk was more distracting, the one in the attic or the one in the living room, but sitting in the rocker on the front porch with a photocopy of the midcentury dissertation and the odds-and-ends box of her Parisi family history, she buttoned the fleece-lined flannel jacket against the chill the spring morning still held in the shade and raised her eyes to the mountain view that daily reminded her why she was in no hurry to relocate to a loft condo in Denver or Chicago or Seattle the way many of her college friends had in the last few years. It was only the first Saturday in May. Snowcaps could greet her mornings well into the summer weeks. She flipped to a clean page in the yellow legal pad assigned to her personal genealogy project and clicked down the blue fine point on her favorite brand of rolling gel pen. In her work, she spent plenty of time staring at screens and crawling around the internet, but the best breakthroughs came when she wrote notes in her own hand. Raising her coffee mug, she fortified herself with a steaming gulp and began making her own manual index of the Parisi references in the dissertation with a record of the nuances of information surrounding them.

She didn't look up when the motor cut out on the vehicle that stopped on the street. Only when footfalls found rhythm on the porch steps did she glance up.

"Drew!" Jillian placed an orange self-stick note on the page she'd been reading to mark her place. She couldn't help her gaze passing over his shoulder toward his truck. "What brings you here?"

"Don't worry," Drew said. "Aunt Min is still in Wyoming."

Jillian's half smile was sheepish. "Pardon me."

"Who would blame you, after the way she spoke to you? Twice."

She met his eyes now, finding there the warmth and charm of a week ago when she had charged onto his ranch, past the notices of private property, and he nevertheless welcomed her with Veronica.

"Excuse my manners." She gestured to the cushioned double-wide wicker chair beside her rocker. "Please sit down. It's not quite the open land you're used to, but we enjoy the view when we can."

"As you should." Drew sat down. His dimple was back, unhindered. "It's a fine view. The mountains are very in-your-face around here."

Jillian laughed. "We like them that way."

"I can see why."

"Can I get you something cold to drink? Or something hot?"

He held up a hand. "I didn't come to trouble you."

Jillian waited, counting her breaths, as they stared at the mountains. She wouldn't have minded staring at Drew, but it would have seemed rude in the silence. She counted his breaths now.

"You sure I can't get you something?" Jillian said. "I make incredible coffee. Ask anyone in town."

Drew shook his head. "I'm just trying to gather my words."

"Oh." She looked at him now.

He ran his tongue over his lips. "Aunt Min. I wish there was a way to apologize for her, but I can't honestly say I understand her all the time myself. Mostly I want to apologize for allowing her rudeness when you'd done nothing to deserve it."

"I did trespass," Jillian said.

"But I invited you into my cabin. And I let her throw you out. And I was behind the wheel, so I could have driven straight to Casper instead of detouring here to let her yell at you again for no reason. Not my proudest moment."

A hundred questions tangled together in Jillian's mind, but she left them unasked.

"I accept your apology," she said. "I certainly didn't expect you'd be passing through again," Jillian said.

He chuckled. "No, I don't imagine you did. I left Aunt Min with my father's cousin, Michelle."

"Min's daughter?"

"Right."

"I assumed you were staying up there."

The dimple reappeared. "I only have so much tolerance. Michelle's son lives practically next door, and I like him. We spent a lot of time together as kids, so it's always good to see him. I even like his two little children, but they are of the especially noisy variety, and I find I reach my limit."

"Four generations!"

"It's great to see them, but I'm used to my peace and quiet. I never promised to stay the whole two weeks. This way Aunt Min can visit as long as she likes, and Michelle can drive her home when she's ready. Michelle always enjoys a couple of days at the ranch where she grew up."

With his apology off his mind, Drew relaxed back in the chair, setting one booted ankle on the opposite knee. The dark curls at the back of his neck and brushing his ears had lengthened since Jillian first encountered him on the horse. It was a good look for him. Jeans. Boots. The plaid shirt. The kind of hair that would let him go a long time between haircuts without looking shaggy. Jillian wondered if he'd ever had a beard.

She roused herself to return to reality.

"Somebody has to look after the ranch while Min is gone, I suppose," Jillian said.

Drew shrugged. "There's not too much to look after anymore. It's not the working ranch it was when Aunt Min and my grandma Gretchen and their brother were little."

Jillian's fingers twitched with the urge to pick up a pen and start recording the genealogical information Drew dripped into the conversation. Surnames would be helpful.

"Still," she said, "I saw animals. They need caring for."

"My sister," Drew said. "Josie. She and her husband live in Pueblo, close enough to run out and check on things, and we have a guy we hire from time to time. I'm entitled to some time on my own. My sister agrees."

Jillian twiddled her pen. "So you're not going home?"

He scratched the side of his neck. "Not directly, no."

They drank in the view together, his breath matching hers in companionable silence. Jillian often was alone on the porch in the morning with a coffee mug, or a legal pad, or a book, or all three. Those elements were familiar. The unaccustomed aspect was a man whose presence made her at once comfortable and curious.

And never had she sat on the porch with a man whose dimple and gray eyes made her stomach quiver in this odd way. Her pen slipped from her distracted grip.

"Oops." She bent to pick it up, but Drew had it already and handed it to her with a slight upturn in his lips.

He'd come for a reason beyond apologizing for Min. If her dad were home, he'd already have Drew talking about why he was really there. It couldn't be to sit on the porch and look at the mountains with Jillian. Could it?

"Am I interrupting your work?" He gestured at the yellow pad and photocopied sheets in her lap.

"Investigating some of my own genealogy." She nudged open the box of family mementos on the small side table between them. "Looking at the things in your home last week got me thinking about items I've never quite made sense of in my own family's history."

He nodded. "Glad I could be of assistance."

She smiled. "If only you could explain why my Italian ancestors seemed to be tangled up with the Mafia."

His eyes widened. "For real?"

"I think so. I haven't figured it out yet." She did her best to measure his expression. He was here—without Min—and the trunk was still in the living room. "Would you like to see the trunk that sent me trespassing on your land? It's just inside."

He glanced behind them through the front windows. "I don't see how that would hurt anything."

"Then let's have a look." Jillian led him inside the house, where she set her personal items down on the coffee table and gestured across the living room to where the steamer trunk stood open beside the piano.

"This really is old," Drew said. "If it had legs, it could walk onto the ranch and fit right in up at the main house."

"You really like the ranch, don't you?"

"It's a sweet spot for my soul."

"I didn't see the whole place, but from what I saw, I can understand why."

"Maybe someday I can give you the whole tour."

His eyes arrested hers, and she didn't want to look away.

"What about Min?" She stumbled over her own words. "I mean...I'm sorry. I would love to see more of the ranch—if that was ever appropriate."

Jillian let out a slow, controlled breath. She couldn't help but like Drew Lawson—when his great-aunt wasn't around. If the family had come to hold the property through nefarious means, it certainly wasn't his fault. But Min wasn't a puzzle she could ignore.

"Have you always lived on the ranch?" she asked.

Drew shook his head. "Hardly ever, actually. But Aunt Min has never lived anywhere else. Her mother married a rancher and took over running the property from her parents, and then Min did the same thing. Everyone else moved off the land at some point, but most of us love the place."

"So Min owns it now?"

"Technically a family foundation does. But Uncle Ron sold his interest to his sisters as soon as their mother died, so it's really just been Min and my grandmother from that generation. Various other descendants might be entitled to something if it were sold. Now my grandmother passed last year. But no one can do anything as long as Min chooses to live there. That's one of the terms of the foundation."

"Would anyone want to sell the land?" Jillian asked.

Drew shrugged. "Not if we can afford the upkeep. Parts of it have been sold off over the years to keep it afloat, but now that it's more recreational than commercial, it's not as expensive. Others come back for an occasional vacation, and it's *the* place to be at Thanksgiving. Someone might like to live in the main house someday, but it would take some serious renovating."

Jillian turned back to the trunk before them. "You can look at things if you like."

"It belongs in a museum," Drew said. "A lady's clothes, and all that."

"There are a few personal items." Jillian pulled on the white gloves and opened a drawer. She didn't want to rush or overwhelm Drew, but he was in a chatty mood, and she might not get another chance to gauge his reaction to the pictures. "The owner traveled with several photos."

Drew took the multigenerational family photo Jillian handed him, holding it lightly around the edges, and studied it. She resisted prompting him with any commentary or speculation. He studied it for a full minute before speaking.

"This is why you were so curious about the old photo on my mantel." Jillian nodded.

"I can see the resemblance in the shape of her face, and something about her eyes, but this is a much younger person, so it's hard to say it's the same woman, isn't it?"

"It would help to have someone who knew the person in your photograph look at this one."

"Like Aunt Min." Drew handed the photo back to Jillian. "What do you know about the person who owned this trunk?"

As much as Jillian wanted to deluge Drew with information while she had him to herself, away from his imposing aunt, she curbed the inclination. "Her name was Lynnelle Bendeure," she said, "and she was from Cleveland, Ohio. She traveled to Denver in 1909 for business purposes. That's about it. Then the trail goes cold."

"Ohio?" Drew's face lengthened in sobriety.

"Yes. Does that mean something to you?"

"I'm not sure." Drew pushed his palms down the front of his jeans. "I suppose in your line of work, people spit in tubes all the time."

"It's been known to happen, yes."

"A friend gave me one of those DNA kits for Christmas, so I spit in the tube. Aunt Min saw it before I got it mailed off and blew a gasket. You've met her. You know she can be harsh. But despite what you might think, most of the time she keeps her nose out of my personal business as long as I do what I'm supposed to do around the ranch to satisfy her that I'm earning my keep. But when she saw that box ready to mail, we had a huge argument."

"Why?"

"I have no clue what set her off. But she actually took the kit out of the stack of stuff I was taking to the post office for her, opened it, and threw out the sample."

"Whoa."

"That's what I thought. She's two generations closer to the beginnings of our family history—*my* family history—but if I ask about it, she brushes me off. She remembers her grandparents. I know she does. My grandmother—Min's sister—is gone, but she used to talk about the old days of being a child on the ranch once in a while, and Min is older than Grandma Gretchen was."

"What did you do after she destroyed your tube?"

Drew set his jaw. "I bought another kit. I spit in the tube, and I sent it off. The results say I'm related to a bunch of people in Ohio. Fourth or fifth cousins or something like that."

"So now you wonder about this trunk that came from Ohio and led me to your land."

"It's a lot of coincidences. When I saw on your card that you're a genealogist, I thought you might be able to help me."

"Help you how?" Jillian returned the white gloves to the top of the trunk. This was a twist she hadn't expected.

"If I give you my log-in, will you look at the DNA results, poke around a little, and tell me if you think I'm really related to those people?"

"Those DNA companies are very good at what they do," Jillian said. "I've had a lot of clients use them. They give you solid statistics about the likelihood of the relationship."

"I know. But before I upset Aunt Min by asking her what she knows about the results, I'd like a professional opinion I personally trust."

"I would be glad to help," Jillian said. She was tempted to try out some of the names she suspected. Would he recognize the names of his great-great-grandparents enough to tie them to any family stories about them?

No. She'd promised Nolan. The trial transcript could answer questions irrefutably. Patience. No more rankling the family—not even the family member who showed up on the doorstep with questions and offering his DNA.

Drew reached into a shirt pocket and pulled out a slip of paper. "This should get you into the account. I already started building my family tree with information I know, so you don't have to worry about that."

Jillian hoped her face didn't show the thrill she felt. Direct access to

Drew's family tree. Min's name. Cousins. Last names. A trove of information that would save her hours—days—of digging with dubious purpose.

"Hello!" Nolan's voice rang from the back door. "Do we have company?"

"Hi, Dad," Jillian called down the hallway. "Drew stopped by."

"Welcome to our abode." Nolan came in from the kitchen, bewilderment plastered on his face. "It's nice to see you."

"Likewise," Drew said. "I was just about to scoot though. I'll leave you both to your Saturday."

"I'll check this out," Jillian said. "How will I reach you?"

"I'll find you." Drew was out the front door before she could propose a more specific plan.

"What was that all about?" Nolan asked. "Did I scare him off?"

"Keep in mind," Jillian said, "that I was minding my own business and *he* stopped by here." Then she gave her father the gist of what had transpired.

Nolan pulled out his phone.

"Who are you calling?" Jillian asked.

"Luke. Something tells me he needs to lean on his forensic accountant friend to speed things up."

CHAPTER TWENTY-THREE

Denver, Colorado
May 7, 1909

Dear Miss Bendeure,

I hope you will find your journey by rail comfortable
and reliable. I have traveled by train many times between
various major cities both before and after assuming my
responsibilities in Pinkerton's Denver office. I find it
can be useful time to mentally take stock of the task before me and confirm my strategy. Because of the nature of
my work, I take certain precautions in the conversations
in which I engage with strangers. Due to the nature of your
excursion, I advise you to do the same. Enjoy the comforts
of the train and the companionship of fellow travelers—
there are always those eager to converse—but remain focused
on your purpose. When I meet you, we can talk at length
about the agenda I have in mind, since this may fluctuate
according to events that are yet unfolding. I expect we
can conclude our business in a matter of a few days. You
may want to arrange your return travel at a time that
allows you to enjoy some of the culture Denver has to offer
or even an excursion into the Rockies. They are quite
impressive.

Yours sincerely,
James McParland
Manager, Western Division
Pinkerton's National Detective Agency

"You have to leave your trunk." Carey's tone left no room for argument.

Lynnelle protested nevertheless. "My things! I have business documents related to the reason for this trip, along with irreplaceable personal items. I have a claim check in my possession, and I intend to claim my steamer."

Her mother's steamer. Her family's Bible, handed down from her mother. Her mother's handheld mirror and brush. The only copy Lynnelle had of the photograph of her brother's family taken before his death, before his widow cut off contact between his children and the Bendeure family.

Willie put her hand on Lynnelle's forearm. "It must be unbearable to think of leaving your things behind, but we believe it is not safe for you to retrieve your trunk. Or anyone. Undoubtedly it's being watched."

Heat oozed up Lynnelle's neck. "What are you saying?"

"We can't go back to the baggage car," Carey said. In a face devoid of smile or pleasantries, no dimple afforded allure, but the deep gray of his eyes drew her in.

"Later, then," Lynnelle said. "Surely the Union Pacific has a procedure for baggage that is not claimed immediately. A locked room somewhere until I can return."

"That might not be possible," Carey said. "For now, you can't go any-where near it."

"But they won't just pitch it or give it to just anyone. I have the only claim check. Eventually they'll try to reach me, won't they? Perhaps a letter sent to my home in Cleveland?"

"Possibly," Willie said. "We can't worry about that right now. Time is of the essence, Lynnelle. We must leave."

Lynnelle reached for the case Carey had taken from her earlier. "How do I even know you are who you say you are?" She would not be caught up by a man's eyes. Her mother had not raised her to be that dim-witted.

"We'll take you to see Mr. McParland," Willie said, "just as soon as we take care of those papers you've done such a fine job protecting."

Lynnelle drew back and glared at Willie. "You only know about that because you went through my things."

"I'm sorry about that. We had to know. I had my orders."

"That's proof of nothing."

Carey pointed at the telegram still crumpled in Lynnelle's fist. "Read it."

Willie stepped back, glanced around, and then shook her head at Carey.

Lynnelle untwisted the paper. "If you haven't read this, how do you know what it says?"

"McParland knows what he's doing."

Lynnelle focused on the words. ALL IS WELL WITH DELAY *Stop* SPECIAL ARRANGEMENTS REGARDLESS OF ARRIVAL *Stop* IN GOOD HANDS *Stop* WHEN I MEET YOU, WILL DISCUSS WHAT HAPPENED *Stop* McPARLAND.

"I don't understand." Could Mr. McParland not have spent a bit more money for a few more words? *Will discuss what happened.* The phrase was in the past tense. What happened in Denver while Lynnelle was riding a train across the country? What happened on the train? What was happening now?

"They're coming." Willie's voice was low and even.

"Then we're going now." Carey's hand went to Lynnelle's back, pushing her forward. "We can't afford any more time discussing."

"Where are we?" Lynnelle said. "Are we even supposed to be in this part of the building?"

"That's not an important question at the moment." Carey grasped Lynnelle's hand and towed her. Willie was right behind. She could not escape.

"I don't even know what I'm running from."

"But we do," Willie said.

"Keep your head down," Carey said. "We have to cut through a corner of the main hall, but it's a good place to get lost in the crowd. Give Willie the picnic basket."

Lynnelle followed the instruction on instinct rather than will. Carey looped her hand through his elbow and covered it with his other hand, leaving Willie to look like the unattached woman carrying a case and a basket as they ducked through the flowing crisscrossing paths of passengers of Union Station.

And then they were outside, blinking in the afternoon sunlight.

"We need a cab." Willie shifted the basket in her arms.

Lynnelle turned her head in both directions at her first view of Denver's downtown brick structures. The Welcome Arch, which she expected to bring relief upon arrival, was not meant for her after all.

"Lynnelle!"

She flinched at the sound of her name. Mrs. Sweeney clomped toward them from the corner with her cane, leaving a younger woman behind with several trunks.

"I waited for you inside as long as I could," Mrs. Sweeney said.

Lynnelle glanced at Carey and removed her hand from his arm. "I'm sorry I was delayed."

"Lynnelle isn't feeling well," Willie explained. "We're going to make sure she gets some rest."

"We were going to arrange for her to visit my family," Mrs. Sweeney said. "My daughter is just over there. It will only take a minute."

"That would be lovely, I'm sure," Willie said, "but I'm afraid Lynnelle isn't up to it at the moment."

Mrs. Sweeney looked at Lynnelle, confused.

"What's your daughter's name?" Carey asked. "We'll make sure to help Lynnelle find her when she's recovered."

"Elizabeth Owens. Mrs. Herbert Owens on Logan Street."

"Very good. We'll find it, then."

"When?"

"A few days at most."

Lynnelle nodded. "That's right. When I feel less stricken."

Mrs. Sweeney glanced over her shoulder twice as she shuffled away.

"I hated that," Lynnelle said as they moved toward a cab. "Lying to her."

"Don't you feel stricken by all of this?" Willie asked.

"Of course."

"There you go."

"Will I really see her later?"

Silence.

"The Windsor is close by, as I understand."

More silence.

"You're not taking me there, are you?"

"We have other accommodations in mind." Carey opened the door to a hansom cab and assisted her with a display of politeness she did not welcome.

She was in a strange city, with people who might or might not be who they claimed to be, going who knew where. Certainly she wouldn't know the route back to Union Station without further inquiry of more strangers. Inside the carriage, Lynnelle hinged forward at the hips slightly and dipped her head to look out the window. Every landmark she saw would be important.

Willie smiled. And drew the curtains closed. Lynnelle's stomach constricted.

When they stepped into the hotel lobby at least thirty minutes later, it was discordant from the accommodations she had in mind. Two settees, three chairs, and two side tables crammed the small space across from the registration desk. Everything looked like ragged castoffs from another establishment that had long ago been renovated with better taste.

"We seem to be quite a distance from downtown," Lynnelle said.

"It's better that way," Willie said.

"How so?"

"Safer for you, to begin with." Carey stopped at the desk only long enough to sign the registry—Lynnelle could not see what he wrote—and receive a key. He pointed to the stairs in a manner suggesting great familiarity with the establishment.

They climbed to the fourth floor. Surely there was an elevator, but seething over that question was the least problematic matter Lynnelle faced.

Carey unlocked a door, and they entered a room every bit as shabby as Lynnelle suspected it would be. A dingy green rug covered half the floor but failed to disguise the deepest gouge in the wood. A bedspread might have once been yellow, but its color lacked reasonable description now. Floral wallpaper peeled at the seams. A spider-thin crack wove through the frameless mirror above the chipped bureau. Two hideous pink upholstered side chairs were the least offensive pieces in the room.

Lynnelle put up both hands. "Surely you don't think—"

Willie cut her off. "It's not the Windsor, but it's secure. We have eyes we trust here."

The phrase made Lynnelle's stomach tighten, still uncertain whether to trust the two pairs of gray eyes, in two different shades, that she looked into.

"We'll talk through the plan," Carey said, "and then Willie and I will implement it."

"What about me?" Lynnelle slanted one eye toward him.

"You'll wait here."

"No."

"Yes."

"No!"

"I'm certain not to like it if this is the way it starts out. I want to speak to Mr. McParland first thing in the morning before anything happens."

Willie turned to Carey. "You'll have to show her."

He sighed and nodded, reaching into his inner suit pocket. "You'll want to sit down."

Lynnelle glanced at the bed and instead opted for the edge of one of the pink chairs. She took the pages—written over the same signature she had come to recognize in her own correspondence—to read and then examined Willie in a way she hadn't up to this point.

Their height and build were similar.

Their hair coloring was nearly identical.

Their faces were even the same shape.

Lynnelle's eyes were pale blue and Willie's light gray—close enough.

Of course, the people meeting her—Willie pretending to be her—had never met Lynnelle and wouldn't know the difference anyway, but the impersonation would be credible.

"But my signature," she finally said. "It's on the authorizing documents."

"Willie is a quick learner," Carey said, "and we have the whole night."

I take certain precautions in the conversations in which I engage with strangers. Due to the nature of your excursion, I advise you to do the same, Mr. McParland had written.

"Then how do I know Willie didn't learn Mr. McParland's signature?" Lynnelle said. "You could have stolen this stationery. I need to speak to Mr. McParland. Even this questionable establishment must have a telephone downstairs."

"Actually," Carey said, "generally it's not in working order."

Lynnelle still clutched McParland's telegram. *In good hands.* Did he mean *these* hands?

"I have the proper authorization to act as my father's representative," she said. "Why shouldn't I go myself and affix my true signature?"

"The papers you've carried, along with what you provided Mr. McParland, have helped us set a trap," Willie said.

"A trap?"

"If you will. We cannot risk that it snaps closed without catching anything."

"So you—I—am bait."

"And a valuable witness," Carey said. "We will want you to speak to the authorities. Mr. McParland will explain everything."

When I meet you.

Lynnelle exhaled in uncertain surrender. "I like to use a good solid black ink."

"We'll need to change clothes also," Willie said.

"My *clothes?*"

"Your hat, the brooch."

Lynnelle's hand flew to her mother's jewelry. "I can't part with this."

"Someone on the train would have seen you with it," Willie said. "You never took it off. I promise, you'll get it back."

Carey turned toward the door. "Geppetto will have some paper. I'll be right back."

"Ask him for food as well," Willie said. "And lots of coffee."

The hours swept by. As pink crept across the eastern skyline above the city, Lynnelle examined her name on a clean sheet of paper and found the signature indistinguishable from her own swirls and strokes. Without the steamer, the only clothing to trade with Willie was the traveling suit she'd worn across the rail miles and her final fresh blouse. Carey left the room again and procured breakfast from somewhere. His departing advice was for Lynnelle to sleep while she could. Geppetto would inquire later whether she was ready for lunch. They would be back as soon as possible.

And she was alone.

In a stranger's clothes. Without most of the contents of her satchel.

Sitting on the edge of the bed, with the spread gingerly pulled back, unable to imagine sleep in these circumstances.

Geppetto came to the door to collect the breakfast dishes.

"I thought I would come down to use the telephone," Lynnelle told him. Call Mr. McParland. Call her father. Let someone know where she was.

"It is not working," Geppetto said.

The truth, or convenient fabrication? There would be other telephones in the neighborhood. She could pay someone for the use of one.

"That's all right. Perhaps I'll go out for some air," she said lightly. "I've been cooped up on a train for days. I could do with a walk."

"Mr. Meade—he would like you to stay here and rest after your trip." Behind Geppetto's bland smile was firm enforcement of Carey's definite instruction. "I'll bring you a hot lunch, Miss Bending. You like Italian food, yes?"

Geppetto left without awaiting an answer.

Miss Bending? In what manner had Carey butchered her first name in the register along with her last?

CHAPTER TWENTY-FOUR

N ow Nolan could get down to business. Working from home on Saturday afternoon and twelve hours in the Denver office on Monday had cleared the decks to stay in Canyon Mines the rest of the week organizing himself for next Saturday evening's meal, squeezing in essential legal memos and phone conferences when necessary. His assistant, paralegal, and junior associate all had instructions not to add anything to his schedule this week, however. Starting Tuesday morning, the Duffy kitchen would transform into Legacy Dinner Central.

Three. Two. One. Go.

He'd spent Sunday afternoon clearing the refrigerator of anything that didn't absolutely have to occupy space in it. Soups from leftovers now stocked the freezer in the garage. A shepherd's pie made from the last of the beef from his second practice brisket had been their supper last night. The shelves of the garage refrigerator were empty most of the time because Nolan had been expecting it to give out for years, and with just the two of them in the house, they rarely needed the overflow space. Now he was grateful for it and crossed his fingers that this would not be the week the old appliance gave up the ghost one night as he innocently slumbered while the cool shelves housed a city of vegetables. He was taking no chances with the briskets. Those would stay in the house. Right now they were lined up in eight aluminum roasting pans ready for spicing.

Jillian wandered into the kitchen to refill her coffee mug. Nolan rolled over one of the briskets to inspect it.

"Something wrong?" Jillian asked.

"I suppose not," Nolan muttered. "This might have been trimmed a little better."

"I still wish you had found somebody to help you." Jillian pushed a button, and one of the fancy machines Nolan never bothered with whizzed and hissed. "Maybe it's not too late."

"First I just have to rub the brown sugar in," Nolan said. "The rest is organizing. Washing all the fruit and vegetables. I can't actually start cooking this far in advance."

"Okay, but tomorrow or the next day, you're really going to wish you had some extra hands," Jillian said. "I'll see what I can do to lighten my work schedule."

"No need."

"Big need. Two hundred meals."

"Did we buy any brown sugar?"

"Dad, don't mess with my head."

"I'm serious. Where's the brown sugar?" He only needed three cups. It was a staple, and it hadn't occurred to him to put it on a shopping list.

Jillian pointed. "There should be plenty in the canister behind you."

"Right. I'll be fine. Go back to work."

Jillian's phone rang from her office, and she scooted off to answer it. Nolan reached for his white apron and chef's hat. Even just for rubbing sugar into eight briskets, he might as well get in the groove. As he rolled sugar between his fingers and laid his hands on the first brisket, a pensive melody began in his throat, and he hummed as he worked. Italian opera, of course. The best music to cook by. Puccini this time. The Nessun Dorma aria. Nolan would never sing it as wondrously as Luciano Pavarotti or Plácido Domingo, but he enjoyed trying from time to time. "None shall sleep." Nolan hoped the phrase was not a portent of what his week would be like. By the fifth brisket, he was singing, full voiced, of Calaf's determination to win Princess Turandot's hand. By the eighth, Nolan laughed at the thought that if anyone asked for his recipe for the spiced beef, he might respond by singing, "*Ma il mio mister è chiuso in me.*" But my secret is hidden within me.

"Dad!"

Nolan knew the tone in his daughter's voice. "I'll turn it down."

"Thank you!"

Despite his promise, her office door clicked closed against future disturbance while she took another call.

Nolan ran his hands under a warm stream from the faucet and dried them before beginning the task of covering the roasting pans with foil and transferring them back to the refrigerator, where he had calculated carefully how they would fit. He wiped the breakfast bar clean and lined up heaps of celery, carrots, brussels sprouts, cucumbers, strawberries, blueberries, raspberries, cabbage, spinach, mushrooms, onions, watercress, and oranges. Everything had to be cleaned, pared, sliced, diced, pureed, and crushed in the right quantities before being stored in containers or zip-top bags that would keep everything handy when the moment came to add ingredients to recipes efficiently.

He would require a steady stream of Italian arias over the next few days. "Work smart," he told himself, "and make sure you sleep."

Nolan opened the pantry door looking for ten pounds of onions. They weren't there. He checked the back porch, where they might have been left to save space in the kitchen. Not there either. This would not do. He needed at least ten pounds if the briskets were going to have the desired effect, and more for seasoning the soups. He yanked off his apron. The only solution was to dash out to the grocery store. Despite Jillian's assessment of the general inefficiency of his shopping patterns, he did know where the store was, and he was capable of selecting onions. He jumped in his truck, drove directly to the store, and marched down the produce aisle. The avocados looked good—not too green, not too ripe. He put four in the cart. And tangerines would always come in handy. Neither item had any relationship to the weekend's menu, but that was hardly relevant. Nolan preferred to be prepared for inspiration. Before the onions, he debated between sweet Vidalias and the more peppery red onions.

Someone slid next to him in front of the onion bushel baskets.

"Hello, Mr. Duffy," Drew said.

"Please call me Nolan."

"Onions." Drew planted his feet and crossed his arms. "Big decision."

"The nuance in flavor can completely transform the dish," Nolan said. "I've always favored the red, but I find myself wondering what Vidalia would do in this case."

"Nothing wrong with experimenting."

Nolan began filling a bag with red onions. For this occasion, the days of experimentation were over. "What brings you into the grocery store?"

"Hiking snacks. Apples. Granola bars. That sort of thing."

"I could do with a hike." Nolan dropped three extra onions in the bag for good measure.

"Then come along."

"You tempt me."

"I'm serious." Drew pointed at the onions. "Anybody who needs all of those is working too hard."

Nolan chortled. "Where are you planning to hike?"

"I hear interesting things about the glacier."

"Might still be a little muddy, or even snowy at this time of year. But it's not far, so if you don't mind the risk, it's worth the drive."

"Then come along."

Nolan considered the unexpected opportunity. "What would your aunt think?"

Drew gave an impish smirk. "She's not invited."

"I think I could manage a quick dash out to the glacier." This was only Tuesday. He still had the rest of the week to panic about pulling together two hundred meals in time for Saturday.

They both checked out, and Nolan left his truck in the lot so they could ride together in Drew's and he could serve as navigator.

"A personal tour guide is so much better than a brochure," Drew said as they parked.

"It's not a difficult hike." Nolan closed the passenger door. "And you couldn't ask for better views. Quite a bit different from ranch living, I imagine."

They sauntered up the trail as they talked.

"I do get off the ranch." Drew handed Nolan an apple. "But southern central Colorado is nothing like this."

"Do you work full-time on the ranch?" Nolan pointed to a turn on the trail.

"The work is erratic. I like taking care of the animals, and I'm there for whatever Min thinks needs doing, but I have opportunities for other work as well."

"And what line of work are you in?"

"This and that, here and there. But living on the ranch cuts expenses and allows me to give some other things a shot at least for a while. If they don't work out, then at least I'll know I tried."

"Well, then I hope they do work out," Nolan said, "and you find great satisfaction."

"I'm not unsatisfied now," Drew said. "All my life I've loved going to the ranch, and now I'm living there. And Aunt Min—she's the person who first put me on a horse. I was scared half to death, but by then, she had so much experience helping children learn to ride. She was incredibly patient, even when I wanted to get off almost immediately. Aunt Min is the reason I love horses, the reason astride a horse is my happy place. She *gave* me my own horse. Because of Aunt Min and the ranch, I have my own horse and can ride whenever I want. I know you find it hard to believe, but she's very generous."

"In my experience," Nolan said, "people do not have just one facet. Different people experience them in different ways for all sorts of reasons."

"She's smart as a whip. The way she ran the ranch before she retired and decided to sell off parcels of it—she learned the best from her own parents and grandparents."

"That's a wonderful legacy."

"It is. I'm in awe. But sometimes she has a way of making everyone have something else they'd rather do, someplace else they need to be. Even my own grandmother, her sister, never understood what could set off her sometimes, and Aunt Min's husband and daughter would just sort of work around it until she got out of whatever funk she was in. I know I sure just want to get out of the way until it's over."

"Sometimes pain is underneath moments like that."

"But about what? None of us can figure that out."

They walked awhile before pausing again to gaze at the always-wintry view of the glacier's height.

"The other thing I don't understand," Drew said, "is all the boxes."

"Boxes?" Nolan raised an eyebrow.

"Everywhere. Min holds on to everything. She's incredibly decisive about every other area of her life except which old documents to throw out."

"So she keeps it all?"

Drew nodded.

"Always?"

"As far as I know. Boxes it all up and stacks it in the outbuildings. She won't listen to anyone about it. As old as she is now, I think everyone is finished arguing with her. They'll just pitch it all when she passes without opening any of it."

"Some people are hoarders," Nolan said. "It can be a form of mental illness."

"She doesn't keep anything and everything. It's about documents. And she won't put them in files. It has to be boxes."

"Sounds like that can be frustrating for the family."

They were looping back down the trail now.

"Is Jillian home today?" Drew asked.

"She was when I left."

"I was hoping to see if she had a chance to look at my DNA results. Maybe she can tell me what she thinks—speaking of things Aunt Min is irrational about."

"Come back to the house with me and we'll find out."

CHAPTER TWENTY-FIVE

A narrow smile twisted at one corner of Drew's mouth as he followed Nolan into the kitchen and set the onions on the counter. "I don't think I ever heard what you do for a living."

"I'm an attorney."

"Do you represent a major bakery corporation? Or a small restaurant chain?"

"Family law, mostly. Some mediation work."

Drew's eyes, puzzled, flicked over to Nolan's limp chef's hat and apron on the back of a stool.

"Oh that," Nolan said. "When Jillian's mother died, I had to learn to cook so my child didn't starve to death. A little help getting in character is not a bad thing."

"No, sir."

"I have a few things going on at the moment."

"I see that." Drew's eyes pinched together. "It's just the two of you living here, right?"

"That's right."

Drew gestured to the heaping produce Nolan had assembled earlier.

"There's the small matter of a dinner party on Saturday night," Nolan explained.

"I've seen restaurant kitchens that look less frenetic than this."

Nolan wiggled an eyebrow. "Have you seen a lot of restaurant kitchens?"

"A fair number." Drew's gaze strayed to the counter where Nolan had laid out the final recipes, though he had not yet rewritten them for the quantities involved. "I'd say you're expecting some pretty brisk business."

"All prepaid." Nolan ducked into the cabinet under the breakfast bar for his two largest colanders. "I can't disappoint."

"There's enough food here for, what, a hundred and fifty?" Drew said.

Nolan panicked and popped his head up to stare at Drew. "You don't think it will feed two hundred? Maybe I need to go shopping again."

Drew laughed. "It's hard to tell with the way things are piled. And I'd have to see the whole menu without all the scribbles."

"How do you feel about peeling carrots?"

"I've peeled a few in my day."

"I'll clean. You peel." Nolan set a colander in the sink and laid a large group of fresh carrots in it. "Wait a minute. You said you wanted to talk to Jillian."

"Right."

"She's in her office. Let me check if she's free." Nolan stepped across the short chunk of hall that separated the kitchen and Jillian's office and quietly turned the doorknob. Immediately he saw she was on the phone with her back to the door, so he withdrew. "On the phone. I'll check again in a few minutes."

"Then let's have at those carrots. Glazing them?"

"Honey butter, I thought," Nolan said.

"Try some rosemary with that. Halve the carrots lengthwise, add the glaze and roast them. Much tastier than boiling."

"I might not have the oven space for that," Nolan said, "but I have another proposition."

"Let's hear it."

"I need help putting this dinner together. Can you stick around town between now and Saturday?"

"Depends. Do I get to wear the hat?"

Nolan snatched it off his stool and tossed it to Drew, and they started in on scrubbing and peeling what Nolan estimated to be six hundred full-size carrots. He started humming again, the same melody from earlier in the day. The words returned to his mind as well. *None shall sleep.*

Drew picked up the tune and started singing—with the sort of tenor mastery Nolan envied but had never achieved no matter how many compliments he received on his voice.

"*Nessun dorma. Nessun dorma. Tu pure, oh Principessa. Nella tue freddo stanza, guardi le stelle che tremano d'amore e di speranza.*"

Nolan couldn't help but join. "*Ma il mid mistero è chiuso in me il nome mid nessun saprà. No, no, sulla tua bocca lo dirò quando la luce splenderà ed il mio bacio scioglierà il silenzio che ti fa mia."*

They finished with their arms around one another's shoulders, heads tilted together. "Vanish, oh night. Set, stars! At dawn I will win!"

"Wow!"

Nolan turned to see Jillian standing at the kitchen entrance. "I'm sorry, Silly Jilly. I forgot about the noise."

She laughed. "There are two of you! He's wearing your cooking hat and singing opera!"

Nolan beamed. "It's beautiful, isn't it? You wanted me to find help, and I have."

"I think maybe help found you."

"Only because you were on the phone."

Beneath the chef's hat, Drew grinned. "Aunt Min needs more help than she likes to admit, so I moved to the ranch. It makes everybody feel better about her staying on there, since she refuses to leave. But I've had some pretty good stretches cooking in upscale places. Not everybody in Pueblo is a cowboy."

"You looked like a pretty convincing cowboy yourself," Jillian said, "that day we first met. Riding a horse. Living in the cabin and all."

Drew cocked his head to one side. "Most of my things are in storage. No one has lived permanently in the little red house in a long time."

"So it's temporary?" she said.

"To be determined. A lot of people have lived there over the years. Some staff, some family. But these days, it's a place to stay for the short term and not mess with the way Aunt Min leaves things. It's my turn right now."

"We bumped into each other at the grocery store," Nolan said, "and had a nice chat on the glacier. Now it's time to do something about all this." He gestured expansively.

"I don't know what to say," Jillian said, "except thank you, if you're really going to help my dad, who also is somebody who needs more help than he likes to admit on this particular occasion."

"I'd love to help."

Drew's eyes were fixed on Jillian now—and even Nolan could tell the interest was not strictly professional. He was curious. Friendly. Talented. Jillian had tried to tell Nolan that Drew's personality had morphed in the presence of his overbearing great-aunt, and Nolan could see for himself now what she was talking about. And he was not so doddering that he couldn't see how Jillian perked up when Drew was in the room.

Nolan said, "Actually, Drew was looking for you."

"Yes," Drew said quickly. "I wondered if you had a chance to look at my DNA results. Should I believe I have distant relatives in Ohio?"

"Absolutely," Jillian said. "You're related to those people. I see no reason not to think so."

"There are no Bendeures in the family tree," Drew said. "Isn't that the name you were trying to connect to my family?"

"Yes, but names change for all sorts of reasons. Lack of registration of a birth. Adoption after remarriage. A simple lack of a male offspring in a generation can change everything."

"Right!" Drew said. "I'm the only male cousin in my generation. Not that I have the same last name as the great-great-grandparents who settled the ranch in the first place anyway."

"I saw that your family tree only went back as far as your grandmother and Min," Jillian said.

"That's right. Farther back, things get sketchy. I do know my great-grandmother had a sister who died in childhood and a couple of brothers. We never hear from those branches of the family. It was so long ago. But I imagine some of the distant cousins that turned up in my results could be from those brothers. I don't even know if they had kids."

"Your family is a perfect example of how easily a surname can just drop away even when there are lots of descendants," Jillian said, "but give me a little more time. I might still find the connection."

Nolan transferred his weight at the sink, where he had quietly returned to cleaning carrots, and searched for Jillian's eyes. She did not yield them. She wasn't telling Drew everything she already knew, which might be for the best, but Nolan hoped she would respect the shifting balance for how hard to probe for what she did not yet know.

"I'm still not clear how you got from that trunk to our ranch," Drew said.

Jillian shrugged. "A hunch. Playing around with the way names change and checking marriage and property records."

"I've been thinking about that photo you showed me. I still can't be sure it's anyone in my family. Aunt Min would be the one to ask, if she was ever in the right mood. But I remember my grandmother used to say that *her* grandpa and his sister used to borrow each other's names like a game all their lives."

Now Nolan turned off the water running from the faucet. He wanted to hear this. "What do you think she meant?"

"I'm not sure. Just that her grandpa liked it a lot. That's how Aunt Willie got her name."

"Aunt Willie?" Jillian asked. "Your genealogy didn't include anything that far back."

"It was sort of a family name. For most of the world she used Helmi. Short for Wilhelmina."

"Willie?" Jillian said again. "Willie Kyp?"

"I guess. Kyp was her maiden name. But I don't think anyone ever called her Willie Kyp. Willie was just a family nickname because her brother called her that sometimes."

"Kip Carey? William Kip? Liam Meade?" Jillian threw out some of the names from her somewhat research.

Drew shook his head. "I've never heard those names, but I never really kept up with the family tree that much. Are they distant cousins?"

"Did your grandmother ever say *how* her grandfather and his sister traded names?"

"Maybe. I didn't pay the best attention. It was just a game."

"What was your grandmother's grandfather's first name?"

Drew shrugged. "I'm terrible, aren't I? I should know. The ranch has been in the Kyp family all this time."

"It's all right," Jillian said. "You're pretty typical, actually. Does C. M. Kyp sound familiar?"

Drew nodded. "I know that's right. My grandmother said that's how he got *his* nickname—'See 'em Kyp.' The joke was when he went hunting, he could see the deer before anyone else. So they called him See 'em Kyp, because of his initials and his talent. Pretty soon, no one used his name."

Nolan laughed. "I can see how something like that would stick, and people wouldn't care what your name was anymore."

"Right," Drew said. "Tiger Woods. Not his name."

"Bing Crosby," Nolan said. "Totally a nickname."

"Red Skelton," Drew bantered.

"Babe Ruth."

"Sundance Kid."

"Scarface Capone."

"Some dudes were way more famous for their nicknames than their real names," Drew said. "Why not See 'em Kyp? Especially back in those days."

"Exactly," Nolan said.

"Can I ask one more question?" Jillian said, her tone departing from the playfulness.

"Of course." Drew turned from Nolan to Jillian.

"Did you ever hear any family stories about your grandmother's grandparents being involved with Pinkerton's detectives?"

Drew scrunched up his face. "Involved how? Working for them? Hiring them?"

Jillian finally glanced at Nolan. He shook his head half an inch. The line was bold and wide, and she was about to step over it with insufficient information. She looked away. *Oh Jillian.*

"I'm not sure," she said. "Caught by Pinkerton's, perhaps. Or almost."

"No!" Drew said. "What are you getting at? Illegal activity in my family history?"

"Unquestionably there's foul play involved in the story of that trunk in the other room," Jillian said. "That's why it was separated from its rightful owner. I'm still working on how it all fits together."

"And you think my family is incriminated."

And bam.

"I'm just trying to find the truth," Jillian said.

"You're the one related to the Mafia."

Crimson rolled through Jillian's features before her face blanched.

"You said I was related to the people in Ohio. If anything, doesn't that mean that trunk might belong to my family? Why the accusations?"

"I'm not making accusations!" Jillian recovered her voice.

"Let's not get ahead of ourselves," Nolan said. "The curator of the museum where the trunk surfaced asked us to look into a few things, and that's all we're doing. When Jillian has solid answers, you'll be the first to know. Let's all take a breath. In the meantime, we have a lot of work to do with all this food and at least two dozen operas to sing."

"This isn't what I was expecting." Drew removed the chef's hat from his dark head and set it, listless, on the counter. "I'll have to think about this."

CHAPTER TWENTY-SIX

Denver, Colorado
May 13, 1909

Dear Miss Bendeure,

Our frequent courier correspondence allows us to be fully prepared for the greatest benefit from your presence in Denver. With the imminent date of your departure from Cleveland, it will not be possible to apprise you of every operation between now and then. At this stage, new information arises daily. I have put into motion several provisional scenarios in order to be confident that we not miss any key opportunity not only to bring this matter to a satisfactory result for Bendeure & Company but to uncover other related activities of which the authorities will be pleased to be fully informed.

Yours sincerely,
James McParland
Manager, Western Division
Pinkerton's National Detective Agency

Monday, May 24, 1909
Denver, Colorado

Lynnelle accepted Geppetto's Italian food, even expressing gratitude. Her excursion would require fortification, after all. She ate in her room, which clearly was Carey's plan, and surveyed the view from her fourth-floor window. With no familiarity of Denver other than photographs she'd seen in the newspapers over the years, Lynnelle had little to go on. She'd expected to be in a downtown hotel with a concierge, only blocks from Mr. McParland's office. Instead, she couldn't even see the landmark Welcome Arch of Union Station that the city prided itself on.

But she could see streetcars. And they seemed to go everywhere.

Geppetto couldn't remain at the front desk every single minute. The Meades had been gone hours now, and there was no telling when they would be back. *If* they would be back. Or what would be the state of her father's assets if they did return? Lynnelle freshened up and put on the shoes Willie had left behind. They were larger than her own—how did Willie pinch her feet into Lynnelle's Oxfords without complaint?—but she tied them snugly and slipped some folded bills from the pocket of the wicker case in alongside one heel. A hat or a handbag would look suspicious for just a walk to the lobby. Instead, she picked up the remains of her lunch, arranged them on the tray, and carried it down three flights of stairs to the lobby.

Geppetto hopped off his stool. "I would come for the things."

"It's no trouble." Lynnelle smiled. "I'm here now."

"Yes, yes. I'll take them." Geppetto came around the desk to relieve Lynnelle of the tray.

"Perhaps I could have a cup of coffee."

"Yes, yes. I'll bring it to your room."

"I don't mind waiting. I could do with a change of scenery." Lynnelle smiled again. "I could use something to read. Anything will do."

"Yes, yes. Magazine. I'll bring it. To your room." Geppetto's tone stiffened under his steely geniality.

Lynnelle chose the least offensive of the settees in the dilapidated lobby, sat down, and crossed her legs. "This seems quite comfortable." A spring jabbed into one hip.

"Mr. Meade said you should rest."

"Perhaps Mr. Meade is more tired than I am." Another vacuous smile.

Somewhere deep behind the desk, beyond a closed door, a telephone rang.

Lynnelle's politeness evaporated. "I see your telephone is working. You probably ought to answer that. It might be Mr. Meade with more instructions."

Only Geppetto's eyes scowled above his plastered upturned lips. The telephone stopped ringing, the door behind the desk opened, and a young boy, also Italian in Lynnelle's assessment, signaled to him.

Geppetto hesitated. "Please. Wait here. I will return with your coffee."

But Lynnelle did not wait. Geppetto was never going to let her use that telephone. She was out the front door before the young boy could come out from behind the desk to stop her. He would not have been able to—he couldn't have been more than ten or twelve years old. Glancing back over her shoulder, she noted the hotel's name and looked for a street number before hustling to a corner to discern the street name and repeating the address under her breath four times. When she saw a rack of streetcar maps inside a small shop window, she ducked inside. She bought a trinket with a bill from her shoe just to get some change for the streetcar and got on the next one that came past the corner.

Only then did she unfold a map to study where she was headed.

She needed a telephone. A larger hotel. A department store. A police station. A pharmacy. A newspaper office. In other words, she needed to be closer to downtown Denver than the miles away that Carey and Willie had dragged her in the seclusion of the carriage. The print on the map was small, but Lynnelle looked up at passing streets as the car stopped intermittently, and gradually got her bearings. If she transferred twice, she could even be back at Union Station. She groaned. She hadn't thought to bring the claim ticket for her trunk when she left the room. In fact, she was fairly certain Willie had surreptitiously retained possession of it.

The car stopped again. Four passengers got off and two got on. Friendly dark eyes caught Lynnelle's glance, and a couple who might have been approaching forty years of age sat in the seat in front of her.

The woman twisted around, her hat sliding loose. She caught it with one hand. "You are visiting Denver, yes?"

Lynnelle nodded. Did she stick out so badly?

The woman reached over the bench and tapped Lynnelle's map, open in her lap. "Streetcars very good, but still confusing. Where you stay?"

It was a reasonable question to ask a visitor, so Lynnelle answered with the name of the hotel.

The couple grinned at each other. "Our nephew Geppetto works there! You know him?"

Lynnelle nodded. "The front desk."

"Manager! And our son Aldo helps him. He will learn good profession this way," the woman said. "I am Annamarie Parisi. This is my husband, Salvatore."

"You no need map," Salvatore said, sliding it from Lynnelle's lap and folding it. "We take you."

"No, that's not necessary." Lynnelle's heart pounded. All she'd accomplished was to ride the streetcar out of the neighborhood to exit Geppetto's sight as quickly as she could. She'd wasted the time she could have been looking for a telephone.

"Oh, no trouble," Annamarie said. "We say hello to Geppetto and Aldo, yes, Sal? He's a good boy."

"You must have things to do," Lynnelle said, "somewhere you were going."

"Plenty of time," Salvatore said. "We transfer at next stop, take streetcar in other direction, and you be back at hotel in no time."

Annamarie grinned mischievously. "I think Geppetto will ask Caterina to marry him soon. His father say he is young, but he send him to us from New Orleans, so we say is okay."

"Annamarie." Sal's tone turned sharply somber.

"Is nothing, Sal," she said. "Many people come from New Orleans for many reasons."

The streetcar stopped.

"Here we are," Annamarie said.

"Please," Lynnelle said, "I don't want to trouble you."

"No trouble! We make sure Aldo do a good job."

At least in Cleveland Lynnelle had been allowed to come and go at will. Between the Meades and the Parisis, she had no control in Denver.

"I thought I would find a telephone while I was out and call my father," Lynnelle said.

"Geppetto will let you use his telephone," Salvatore said.

"I was told it was out of order."

"It comes and it goes. We ask. Come. We don't want to miss the transfer."

Lynnelle would have lost them in the crowd—if there had been one. They were the only passengers to get off, and the Parisis flanked her, extolling Geppetto's virtues steadily.

Sighing deeply, but politely hiding exasperation, she stepped back into the lobby of the hotel a few minutes later. Geppetto's features were both relieved and annoyed, but instantly he put on his mask of indulgent hotelier as he received his aunt's kiss.

"Would you still like a cup of coffee?" he said.

"Yes, that would be lovely," Lynnelle said evenly. "I met your aunt and uncle while I saw a bit of Denver, but I'll let you have a visit while I go upstairs and rest."

Geppetto snapped his fingers. "Aldo, walk with Miss Bending up to her room."

"I am quite capable," Lynnelle said.

"Aldo will tell me if you need something."

I'm sure he will. Miss Bending. Not very imaginative for a Pinkerton's operative. Unless that's not what Carey Meade was.

In her room, she dismissed the boy, kicked off her shoes, and sat in one of the pink side chairs to await the coffee. No doubt Carey and Willie would get a full report of her escape—unless Geppetto protected himself by withholding the information. Thanks to his aunt and uncle, the evidence remained that she did not escape on his watch.

Lynnelle answered the knock on the door without getting up. "Come in." Geppetto had a key. Why should she exert herself?

He set the coffee tray on the small table. "Mr. Meade will return soon."

"Oh? Is your telephone working now?"

Geppetto bowed slightly and backed out of the room, clicking the lock behind him.

Lynnelle drank two cups of coffee, splashed water on her face, and paced the small room, periodically standing at the window to peer down at the sidewalk and look for signs of the Meades. She ought to recognize her own hat and traveling suit progressing toward the hotel if they were coming from this side of the building.

Far from her own city.

Far from home.

Far from anyone she knew—or trusted.

To whom could she draw near? Lynnelle murmured the words where her mother kept the bookmark in the Bible she might never see again. *"But as for me, I will come into thy house in the multitude of thy mercy: and in thy fear will I worship toward thy holy temple. Lead me, O LORD, in thy righteousness because of mine enemies; make thy way straight before my face."* She'd never been very good at surrender, but if she must surrender, it would be to God's mercy and not merely to the scheme of Carey Meade.

The tall buildings around the hotel began to block the rays of the setting sun, and shadows fell.

CHAPTER TWENTY-SEVEN

I t was all her fault.

Her dad told her to tread carefully, and she'd blurted out all the wrong things at the wrong moments. Again.

Now Drew was gone. Jason Andrew Lawson, Jr. At least she knew his full name now, from looking at his DNA results and the family tree he'd started. For a man of his age, he left almost no social media footprint. She'd looked, under the guise of professional information gathering. Facebook. Instagram. Twitter. Snapchat. Of course she'd looked for any sign of a relationship status, but Drew Lawson was not very self-revelatory online.

It was crazy to think the way he looked at her meant anything.

Or that the way she *wanted* to look at him, to be in the room with him, meant anything.

After his visit to Canyon Mines with his Aunt Min, he was memorable enough that if he'd tried to book a room at the Inn at Hidden Run, Nia would have sent Jillian a text message immediately. So he wasn't staying there. Jillian had driven out to the chain motels at the far end of town, where Nia sometimes directed people looking for rooms if she couldn't accommodate them, to look for Drew's truck before circling around Canyon Mines a couple of times hoping to spot it. The downtown blocks buzzed with preparations for the Legacy Jubilee to begin the following day. Pop-up vendor booths and food trucks were showing up in the park and some of the sidewalks and parking lot spaces. A temporary outdoor stage and sound system for the nearly continuous schedule of regional bands Marilyn had booked was almost complete. Banners hung from the major shops, and most of the store display windows posted event schedules. Jillian returned the waves of workers and kept driving, looking for any sign of the truck that had turned up twice in front of her home. She even called Veronica, doing her best to sound casual, to ask if he'd dropped by the Victorium Emporium lately.

If Jillian found him, she'd grovel. She had three different scripts mentally prepared, all with the same theme. It was all her fault. Don't take it out on Nolan. Please help him. She would eat worms from the backyard if it would change things. Please forgive her. Please.

But nothing.

By Wednesday noon, she gave up and straggled home with a peace offering, Nolan's favorite bacon and avocado sandwich from the Canary Cage and the resolve to do whatever he needed in the kitchen. Hand him any utensil he required with surgical precision. Scrub every pot before he needed it again. Wipe down and disinfect every surface to health department standards. Sweep and mop every crumb and splotch he dropped. The *perfect* cooking companion had walked right into their house just when Nolan needed him most, and Jillian spooked him right out the door. The least she could do was rearrange her schedule, pull a couple of all-nighters if necessary—whatever it took to make sure her father succeeded.

She'd closed up the trunk in the living room on Tuesday as soon as Drew left. If it were possible, she would have moved it into a closet. Out of sight. In a dark place. Maybe they should call Rich and schedule a time to return it to the Owens House Museum—but not this week. Not when Nolan was up to his eyeballs in cooking. The impetus of her misjudgment taunting her every time she raised her eyes from her desk or padded through the house only strangled her stomach. Jillian wiped off the whiteboard and snapped down the easel pad sheets still hanging in her office.

The back porch was lined with the largest coolers they could beg and borrow, and Kristina Bryant's freezers at the Ore the Mountain ice cream parlor were stocked with bags of ice Nolan could access with a quick phone call no matter what time of day or night he needed to fill one of the coolers this week. Already three were loaded with the fruit and vegetables Nolan and Jillian morosely washed and packed side by side after Drew left. Nolan hadn't lectured Jillian. Her silent lecture to herself played on a constant loop.

Entering the house through the back door now, Jillian expected singing. There should be Italian opera with that Irish lilt only Nolan Duffy could deliver. She'd seen the day's scheduled activities. By the end of the afternoon, there would be gallons of creamy cucumber soup that could easily be warmed through on Saturday just before serving. The kitchen's aroma told Jillian the chickens that would provide the base for the broth—Nolan refused to take any shortcuts—were still simmering. He was at the nook table tucked into one corner of the large kitchen with his master recipes spread out in front of him.

"I brought lunch," Jillian said.

"Good." Nolan looked up. "I thought I might have to make a chicken salad or something, and we don't have any grapes."

"I know you like grapes in your chicken salad." Jillian removed the sandwich from the sack and set it down in front of Nolan.

"Nothing for you?"

She shook her head. "I don't feel like eating."

"Jilly."

"I'm going to help you, Dad. That's all there is to it."

"You don't have to do penance."

"You need help, and I need to help. I don't cut fancy julienne strips and stuff like that, and I can't suggest that you add rosemary to the carrot glaze, but I can fetch what you need and clean up as we go and throw a load of dish towels in the washer."

"You mean business."

"I do."

"Will you let me sing?"

"I demand it."

"Then we have a deal." Nolan offered a hand, and Jillian shook it. "You know, of course, Min is the linchpin."

"Well, duh."

"She's a puzzle even to her own family. Drew made that clear on our little hike. The reason he lives in that cabin in the middle of someone else's storage is because Min is afraid of doing the wrong thing with ranch documents."

"Min has been running the ranch for a long time. She must have mounds of records."

"I think we both know there's more to it than that." Nolan proffered part of the sandwich. "Here. Eat half."

"You eat it," Jillian said. "I'll go clean up a little bit and be right back down ready to work."

She climbed the back stairs and shuffled to her bedroom.

From the dresser, the box of family mementos, atop the photocopied dissertation, taunted with shouts of failures that had followed her for years.

Now that was something she could put out of sight in a dark closet. It should go back in the attic, back in the old trunk, back under the blankets in the unlit corner. For now, Jillian shoved the box onto an overhead shelf in her closet and closed the door. She had an orderly life. Good friends. Work she excelled at. Enough paying clients to keep her more than occupied. A town she loved. Views she never tired of. A decade out of high school, her years of track and cross-country training at high altitude meant she could still outrun anyone she knew. Until recently, she would have said she made good decisions. Slicing her foot open had been a dumb thing to do, but it was nearly ready to run on again, and she wouldn't allow either of the old trunks to shake her focus like that again.

And Drew. Well, he was gone. She'd seen to that. Now she wouldn't have to wonder why her stomach heated up when he was around or why something in her melted when he aimed his smile at her or why a silly dimple had the power to make her go irrationally soft at the center like a piece of chocolate from the Digger's Delight candy shop. What was important now was supporting her dad through the challenge of two hundred meals.

Jillian went into her bathroom to splash water on her face and fasten back the mass of dark curly hair. The Parisi hair. The same hair in that old photo in the box.

No. She wouldn't think about that. Keep a clear head. That was the goal for the rest of the week.

Music wafted up the stairwell, her father's voice. He was singing, which meant he was cooking and happy doing it. Jillian smiled. At the last minute, she decided to change into an older shirt she wouldn't think twice about if food splashed its fibers and it didn't quite come clean. The personal concert paused briefly, but by the time Jillian was ready to leave the room, the singing had resumed.

But it wasn't the usual Italian opera Nolan favored while he cooked. He did appreciate other music as well. This was Latin and a modern composer—Andrew Lloyd Webber's music.

In the hall on her way back downstairs, Jillian realized there were two tenor voices winding around each other in the spellbinding "*Pie Jesu.*" She crept quietly down the stairs, sitting on a step halfway down, flabbergasted at the sight.

Drew and Nolan, stopping time as they sang about Merciful Jesus who takes away the sin of the world and grants eternal rest.

Jillian held her breath. Whether hearing the piece in concert in person or in recording by the many artists who performed it, she'd never been able to breathe normally amid its ethereal loveliness. And now to have it coming from her kitchen, with one of the voices being one she had not expected to hear again. This memory, of how thick her throat was when she didn't dare breathe for fear of desecrating the moment, would never leave her.

With the final *sempiternal requiem*, everlasting rest, Jillian eased air out of her lungs and whispered, "Thank You, Jesus." Mercy wrapped her spirit, and she yielded to its solace.

Rest from her own bumbling, tangled pain.

Rest for her own sweet mother, who might have had answers to Jillian's questions and might not have, but who was in the arms of her Savior in her own eternal rest.

Rest for Lynnelle, whatever had happened to her.

Rest for Drew, who was alive and well—and standing in her kitchen—but seemed to die in himself at times and find himself again.

Jesus' mercy covered it all and gave rest for the heavy laden.

The oven timer went off, and the spell broke.

"Time to turn the briskets," Nolan said.

Jillian stood on the stairs, her movement rustling, and Drew turned toward her.

"That was beautiful," Jillian said, eyes misting. "Stunning, actually."

"Thank you. It's a pleasure to sing with someone like your dad."

"I'm sure he feels the same." Jillian pushed out more air, trying to find her normal voice.

Nolan plopped the first of the briskets on the breakfast bar. "You sing circles around me. I can tell you've got more experience than my old college ensemble or a church choir."

"Lamont School of Music," Drew said.

"At University of Denver?" Jillian and Drew were almost the same age. Their college years overlapped—and they'd both been in Denver, their schools not that far apart. What if she'd met him at a party or a concert?

"Voice. Performance major," Drew said.

Nolan lined up two more of the briskets.

"What are we doing with these things?" Drew asked.

"I sugared them two days ago," Nolan said. "Today we put on more of the good stuff."

We. They both said *we.*

"My expertise is more in the pastry department," Drew said. "Show me what to do."

With the three of them rubbing the mixture of salt, chopped onions, crushed bay leaves, pepper, rosemary, thyme, and cloves into the meat, the roasting pans were returned to the refrigerator quickly.

Drew picked up Nolan's master list. "Looks like you're planning to work on the make-ahead mixtures today to bake later."

"That's right," Nolan said. "I don't want the pastries to get too soggy. Besides, I forgot to buy those puff pastry sheet things, and now I'll have to drive all over creation looking for enough of them for the cabbage pies and the fruit tarts—or try to persuade Ben at the bakery to make them. And he'll complain that they take too long."

"Nonsense," Drew said. "That was my specialty in culinary school."

"Culinary school?" Jillian said.

"Johnson & Wales University. Also in Denver."

"Before or after the music degree?"

He toggled his hand. "Sort of a dual time line. My father was concerned singing great music was not actually a way to earn a living but baking great pastries might be. We negotiated a compromise."

They all laughed. Jillian scouted the best pastries in Denver during college. Had she passed Drew on the streets, like one of those cheesy scenes in a movie?

"So these restaurants you worked for?" Nolan asked.

Drew shrugged. "Started out as master baker and turned into head chef."

"And singing?"

"Let's just say my father has been pleasantly surprised. Not the fastest way to get rich in southern Colorado, but steady opportunities. Right now, living and working at the ranch lets me take advantage of some possibilities with more flexibility than when I'm tied to a restaurant job."

But then Aunt Min, Jillian wanted to say. She didn't dare. If she was ever to know what had brought him back to the house, it would be on his terms.

"Nolan, it would be my pleasure to help you cook," Drew said, "especially the pastries—though I am particular about my flour, and they do require a shocking amount of butter."

"Jillian," Nolan said, "it would seem your services will not be needed after all. You may return to Plan A for your afternoon. But I will hold you to your agreement to let me sing."

One side of her mouth quirked in amusement. That Drew had returned to help Nolan was a mercy. That they had sung a song reminding her that her own shortfalls would not hound her forever was another. Today they could sing whatever they wanted and at whatever volume.

"Thank you, Drew," Jillian said. "My office is right there. Knock if you need something."

"Will do." He smiled. With the dimple.

"We shall get the barley and wild rice going and fry up some bacon," Nolan said. "Once that is accomplished, we shall go in search of this young man's perfect flour and butter."

"Then I'll get out of the way." Jillian withdrew and closed her office door. In her chair, she expelled a long breath. The day had taken a decided turn. For an hour or so, noises from the kitchen—including the occasional tidbit of an aria—indicated a companionable culinary flurry. Against the backdrop, Jillian focused her efforts on polishing the family tree for the woman she'd met at the genealogy conference. She'd been so hungry to know everything and get the facts right before sharing them with her wider family. Attendees at genealogy conferences were, of course. Most people Jillian met were at least a little curious about her work and offered a story or two from their own families.

And then there was Min. If she knew something, she didn't want anyone else to know it.

Jillian shook away the thought, which had already gotten her in so much trouble, and abruptly realized the men must have left the house. All was quiet.

Her phone rang, jarring her thought. It was the special collections archivist from the Denver Public Library.

"I have the trial transcript boxes for you," she said when Jillian answered. "I can keep them for seven days unless you need to make other arrangements to visit on a date later than that."

"That's not necessary," Jillian said. "I'll come tomorrow."

"I'll warn you, there's quite a bit to read. It looks like both the prosecution and defense presented complex cases, and I see no evidence that it has been digitized, obviously, or I would have offered that to you sooner."

"Thanks for the heads-up," Jillian said. "I'll aim to get there early in the day."

It was one thing to close up Lynnelle's trunk in the living room, wipe clean her whiteboard, and pull down oversize sheets hanging in her office. It was something else altogether to turn away the chance to read the trial transcript.

If it was irrelevant and had nothing to do with Lynnelle Bendeure, she would let it all go.

If it was *not* nothing, it might unlock everything. Drew might still want to know, even if Min did not.

Before she went to bed, she gave Nolan a brief summary of what she might—or might not—find at the library. The next morning, by the time she gathered her things and was ready to leave for Denver, Nolan and Drew were in full bakery mode. Puff pastry dough took hours to make between mixing and kneading and relaxing the dough and chilling before anything could be rolled out. In between these cycles, the day's schedule called for Irish brown bread, which Nolan could make in his sleep, and the fillings for the pastries. Drew had revamped the dessert plan according to his specialties, and as long as it matched the menu listing of "fruited and cream dessert tray," whatever they made was sure to go over well. Between the two of them, their phones were loaded with operatic playlists they could blast through the kitchen speakers at full volume with Jillian out of the house.

Drew dusted flour off his hands. "Mind if I walk you out?"

The suggestion surprised her, but she welcomed it. Her stomach quivered as they went out the back door.

"I'm so sorry," she said, "about the other day. You trusted me, and I let my own stuff get in the way of helping you the way I should have."

Drew reached out and touched her elbow. "No. That's not why I wanted to walk you out."

Jillian paused her steps. Those eyes. Jillian looked down at her key fob and jiggled it.

"I'm the one who gave you the log-in information to my DNA results because I wanted to be sure what was true," Drew said, "and then when you asked questions to get to the whole truth, I got bent out of shape and said something snappy and mean. I sounded like my aunt Min, and I don't want to be like that. Ever."

Jillian raised her eyes. "You came back to help my dad. That's what's important."

"He's not the only reason I came back." The dimple was creeping across his cheek.

Jillian moistened her lips and swallowed. "He's not the only one who's glad you did."

Drew nodded. "Good. Glad we got that cleared up. I don't know what's eating Min, but I don't want it to eat me. It's a busy week. I promised to help your dad. But I want to understand your theory, whatever it is."

She nodded. "I promise to tell you. But my dad's right. I should wait until it's solid. I may know a lot more after today."

"Will you be gone all day?"

"I'm not sure. You never know with genealogy research. Libraries can be rabbit holes, so I might be." She wouldn't tell him what she was researching. Not in this moment of fresh mercy blossoming between them.

They resumed walking toward the detached garage, and she entered a code to raise the door.

"Maybe I'll still be here when you get home," Drew said.

"That would be nice."

He stood in the driveway and waved at her as she backed out. She wouldn't lie to him, but she wouldn't speculate again without facts. She'd never done that with a client before. Technically Drew wasn't a client, but that was no excuse for cutting corners.

Jillian reached the library just as it opened, and within fifteen minutes she was settled at a table with her boxes of trial transcripts. The trial lasted eight days, and most days court was in session at least six hours. There was no way she could read deeply and get through everything in one day, even if she remained in Denver until the library closed in the evening. But if she rushed, she might miss the details that mattered most. Even if she simply asked for copies of everything regardless of the cost, it would take hours of someone's time to handle the volume of old documents. Almost certainly she would be told she must return on another day or wait for the copies to arrive in the mail.

Jillian laid the individual documents out to glean some system. In a transcript, chronology was the primary organizer, but if she could discern which portions were routine court procedures, which were witness testimony, and which were summary arguments, perhaps she could prioritize her entry points into the wealth of data before her.

An hour ticked by. And another. And another. Jillian scanned some sections and read closely in others. She filled page after page of her narrow-ruled yellow legal pad with notes and questions for which to seek answers as she continued to read. Separately, she made a careful list of pages she would want copies of before she left that day. In the early afternoon, she took a short break to grab a fast sandwich but did not stay away a minute longer than necessary. The transcript entranced her, tedious as it was to wade through.

In the late afternoon, she took another short break to refresh herself and send Nolan a text to let him know not to expect her until later in the evening. She would be sorry to miss Drew, but when she saw him again, it would be worth it.

It was all there—information to support her theory.

Pinkerton's role.

Why Lynnelle Bendeure disappeared.

Who the Kyps were.

Who Ela was.

How Ela Kyp ended up on the ranch where Drew Lawson lived now.

Jillian laid her pencil on her pad and stretched her neck in both directions. She hadn't read every single word, but she had what she needed, and she could ask for copies of some portions she didn't get to. But she couldn't wait until the last minute if she wanted to take them with her that evening. She pushed her chair back and took her list to the librarian on duty for the evening. By the time she had what she needed, announcements came over the public-address system warning patrons the library was about to close.

She made the thirty-minute drive home and entered the familiar terrain of Canyon Mines, altered slightly with evidence of a successful first day of the Legacy Jubilee. A cleanup crew stabbed trash with their pointed tools and collected the remains of the day into large black trash bags. A foursome straightened chairs around the bandstand, and lights flicked off in shops and restaurants that had stayed open later than usual. Tomorrow the town would do it all again but probably for even larger Friday crowds as the weekend commenced.

Jillian pulled the car in the garage and went in the house through the back door. The kitchen was dark. In fact, the whole house was. It wasn't so late that Nolan would have gone to bed—especially without a text message or a note on the kitchen counter. And his truck was in the garage.

But no one was home.

CHAPTER TWENTY-EIGHT

Just to be sure, Jillian went upstairs to check Nolan's bedroom. The door was open, and the room was dark. Again.

She pulled out her phone and opened a text message. HOME NOW. WHERE ARE YOU?

The reply came quickly. OUT WITH DREW. NICE FELLOW! DON'T WAIT UP.

Out with Drew? Out where? It was nearly ten o'clock. Beyond a couple of bars, which were not Nolan's favorite form of recreation, Canyon Mines didn't offer much to do past ten o'clock on a weeknight. Even the Legacy Jubilee festivities she'd passed coming back into town appeared to be dissipating for the evening, though there might still be something going on indoors.

Jillian was too tired to rummage around for a schedule and speculate further. Instead, she crossed the hall to her own room and dumped her bag, with a full pad of notes and a thick stack of photocopies, in a chair in the corner. Her stomach growled. It would have been smart to stop for some real food before coming all the way home. There wouldn't be much in either refrigerator that wasn't dedicated to Saturday night's meal. A few minutes later, after placating her stomach juices with crackers and peanut butter, she brushed her teeth and went to bed.

When her alarm sounded in the morning, Jillian's first thought was that she'd never heard her father come in. But as soon as she opened her bedroom door, she smelled coffee. It would be unadulterated black, of course, the only way he ever drank it. She'd set him straight by filling her mug with a creamy vanilla-cinnamon blend and waving it under his nose. Raking fingers through unbrushed hair, Jillian headed downstairs in the flannel bottoms and T-shirt she slept in.

Nolan was dressed in jeans and a light pullover. Rather than on a stool with his breakfast, where Jillian had expected to find him, Nolan was lining up large empty food storage containers on the breakfast bar.

"Dad, it's barely six thirty."

He glanced at her. "Is it that late already?"

Jillian rubbed one eye. "How long have you been up?"

"I'm not sure. I woke up early, so I just got up and got started."

"But you were out late."

"I think I'm old enough that we can do away with my curfew."

Jillian stuck her tongue out at him and punched the POWER button on her preferred coffee machine. "Have you eaten?"

"I'll grab something later. Maybe from the Cage."

Jillian opened the fridge. If there was any half-and-half in there, it was well hidden behind—she wasn't sure what was in the assorted glass and aluminum baking dishes that seemed to have multiplied during the day she was gone yesterday. Coffee without cream. She could bear it when necessary, but she sure wouldn't grin.

"What is all this?" Jillian gestured to the containers on the counter.

"Nia and Veronica are expecting me at the Inn this morning. Nia only has a couple of guests. Joelle is looking after their breakfast so Nia can help me start moving food over there. She will have made room for the desserts by now." Nolan smacked his lips. "If Drew lived in town, Ben's Bakery would have stiff competition."

"Is Drew helping you take everything over?" Panic struck at the thought Drew might walk in the door while Jillian was a rumpled mass of bed head and flannel.

Nolan wagged that eyebrow that seemed to be its own creature. "You're safe. He had to take care of a family situation, so I'm on my own for now."

Jillian resisted taming her hair. "I wasn't worried."

"But he made enough pastry for the cabbage pies. I just have to roll it out."

"Sounds delish," Jillian said. That explained the big blob she didn't recognize in the refrigerator. "I think I might have some good news for him."

"And I'm sure he'll want to hear it. We just have to get through tomorrow night." Nolan pulled open a drawer and rattled the utensils. "If I take my good bread knife and my best whisk to the Inn today, am I going to miss them around here?"

"Probably not." Jillian put her mug under the dispenser and pushed a couple of buttons. The machine hissed. "I found some great stuff at the library yesterday."

"That's terrific." Nolan dropped several utensils into a rectangular bin and scanned the breakfast bar. "I guess I don't need all these containers. I want to put the mushrooms in some of them to make sure they don't get smashed before I even get a chance to stuff them."

"Sounds smart." Jillian sipped her coffee, giving up on the notion that Nolan would focus on details from the trial transcript right then. "Where did you and Drew go last night?"

"One of the bands Marilyn booked for the stage on Main Street announced they were doing an impromptu show at the high school later on. We thought it would be fun. The vocalists were terrific."

"Opera?"

"Don't be silly, Jilly. Smooth jazz."

"Drew will be back for tomorrow, right?"

"I have every reason to believe so. Maybe later today. In the meantime, do you have time to help get some coolers over to Nia?"

"Of course." If Jillian wanted a real breakfast, Nia's leftovers or the Canary Cage were better options than her own kitchen. "Let me get showered and dressed."

Publicly presentable twenty minutes later, Jillian grabbed the original dissertation on Italian immigration off the bookshelf in her office. If Veronica was supposed to be at Nia's, this would be a good chance to return it.

In the daylight, Jillian saw that the number of coolers on the back porch had increased along with the mounds of food in the refrigerator. No doubt the fridge in the garage was stuffed to capacity as well. If it weren't for the charm of the Inn at Hidden Run, a venue with a larger working kitchen would have made much more sense. Whether a church hall would have had the same draw as the historic Victorian home was doubtful, though, and both the third seating and squeezing in extra chairs at all three seatings had increased the mountains of food required.

And then, of course, there was Nolan's elaborate menu. There was no working around that.

Jillian flipped up the lids of the new coolers, larger by far than the others, and saw they held some of the scrumptious results of yesterday's labors. Her dad wasn't kidding about the threat Drew could pose to a local bakery. Éclairs. Chocolate mousse domes. Raspberry bread pudding. Key lime tarts. Cheesecakes. Lemon cakes.

"Don't get any ideas." Nolan reached around her and latched the coolers closed. "You can choose what you want for tomorrow."

"One of each, please."

"If you do a good job with your speech and make your father proud. Now let's get these things loaded in my truck."

Taking care to keep everything level, they placed the dessert coolers in the truck, and Nolan rounded up the other containers and bags he'd organized of pans and supplies. At the Inn, they pulled around to the small rear parking area and unloaded directly into the kitchen, trying not to disturb the guests lingering over breakfast. Nia steered Nolan to the empty spaces she'd cleared in her side-by-side oversize refrigerators, and they discussed the logistics of the rest of the food. Kris Bryant had offered to keep the barley and wild rice casseroles in the large refrigerator at her ice cream shop if Nolan could get them over there once the coolers were freed up for another load. Stuffing mushrooms. Making the cabbage pies. Counting up pans for roasting the vegetables that just kept coming.

Jillian left them to it and wandered through the dining room, smiling at the guests and envying their breakfast, and into the hall looking for Veronica. She'd seen her car parked in the back. Several trunks lined the hall as if awaiting orders. Transforming the decor for the dinner must be underway in one room or another.

She found Veronica in the library, which had already been rearranged to accommodate an intimate collection of ten diners on matching rented chairs. A crisp ivory cloth was neatly draped across the back of one of the champagne-colored chairs Jillian found so comfortable, awaiting the moment when it would be unfurled across the round table.

"Hey, you." Veronica straightened a stack of small cases well suited to the size of the room.

"That looks nice," Jillian said.

"It's a start. We have a long way to go."

"I would have been happy to help. You didn't ask for my mother's trunk."

Veronica lifted one shoulder and let it drop. "It seemed a little sensitive, with everything that's happened. Besides, I was able to round up quite a few things. Luke is bringing over more as soon as he's sure someone shows up to open the Emporium."

Jillian nodded. "Good. My dad had help, and then he didn't, and then he did, and now he doesn't for today, so I'm it. Otherwise I'd stay."

"But he has Drew tomorrow, right?"

"You heard."

"They were hanging out pretty late last night."

"You were there?" Jillian asked.

"Lots of people were." Veronica opened a case, considering the look if she left it that way. "People couldn't get enough of hearing him sing!"

Jillian blinked twice. "My dad?"

"No, Drew! The band turned out to be people he used to know, and they threw together a late set that just kept going. Where were you?"

"Work," Jillian said. "I went to Denver to use the library for some research."

"Too bad. It was great to see that side of Drew. So relaxed, like he was really being himself."

"Mmm." Jillian reached under her arm for the manila envelope and extended it toward Veronica. "Here's your dissertation. I made a copy, but I thought you should have the original back to decide what to do with it. Maybe a library or museum would be interested in it."

Veronica opened a second suitcase. "This is the case where it has lived for the last decade. I promise not to let it languish there another ten years."

"Thank you for letting me see it."

"Anything interesting?" Veronica picked up the tablecloth, and Jillian helped her spread and smooth it on the table.

"You mean like three Parisi brothers, one of whom moved to Denver?"

"No way!"

Jillian gave a quick summary of the three brothers and what the dissertation's writer posited about their connections to the Mafia wars of the era and her own letters.

"So do you think the Parisis only took a bad turn when they came to America," Veronica said, "or were they already trouble in Sicily?"

"Only in America, I think." Jillian smoothed the last wrinkle out of the tablecloth.

"Do you wonder sometimes what makes people change?"

"That's a good question. Survival. I don't think Luciano was bad at heart necessarily. He just had a family to look out for and did what he thought he had to do. Something specific must have happened to make Salvatore decide the moment had come to leave New Orleans, but the dissertation doesn't say, and neither do the letters from Luciano."

"It sounds like Luciano wanted to change."

"Agreed. Whether he did when he didn't get out of New Orleans, who knows?"

"And Geppetto?" Veronica asked. "Do you know who that is?"

Jillian shook her head. "My mother always seemed to think she didn't have any other branches of the family in Denver. Now I wonder. Though of course it was a long time ago. Anything could have happened to them."

The Inn's front door opened, and Kris Bryant came in.

"Look who's here," she said. "I thought I'd stop in and see if there's something more I can do to help your dad."

"He's grateful for space in your fridge," Jillian said. "Goodness knows every square inch at our house is in use."

"What's the word on the street?" Veronica asked.

"Sales were brisk yesterday," Kris said. "The fine weather means lots of people out—and in my case, selling lots of ice cream. Even Marilyn seems to be having a good time."

"Do I hear a band starting already?" Jillian said.

"Keep up with the schedule, girlfriend," Kris said. "Catch you later. I'm going to go find Nolan." She disappeared around a corner.

"I should go see if Dad needs help too," Jillian said.

"Don't leave yet." Veronica reached behind a chair where she'd stashed several bags of supplies. "I was going to give this to Nolan, but I suppose you'll know what to do with it just as well. It's the forensic accounting report from Luke's friend. He printed out the email."

Jillian scanned the sheet Veronica handed her and then raised her eyes to Veronica's. "Do me a favor, please. Let my dad know I decided to walk home. I want to do a couple of things before I get involved helping him in the kitchen."

Veronica pointed at the page. "This report changed your morning plans?"

"I need to check some things out. Just tell my dad, please."

In ten minutes she could be home comparing what this report confirmed with what the trial transcript revealed.

What makes people change, Veronica had asked a few minutes ago. Maybe she could figure out the answer to what made Lynnelle change in the way she did before she explained everything to Drew.

On top of the refrigerator, Jillian found a loaf of bread that was fair game for toast, and she made herself a second cup of creamless coffee before settling in to dissect the accountant's email alongside her notes from the trial transcript. For now she would have to do without her father's legal mind.

"In summary," the accountant wrote at the end of his message, "while it is clear that some prominent records are missing from the chronology these records present, a sly pattern is apparent in the timing of requests for funds allegedly for investment purposes, suggesting that these requests were made with increasing pressure that the client might miss out on unique opportunities for significant profit by demonstrating any hesitation in complying with the investment funding. At the same time, there is an alarming lack of accountability for the funds disbursed. The outgoing expense is not offset in an income column in the usual manner, but neither is it written off as an investment gone bad within a reasonable period of time, suggesting that the receiver of funds was continuing to make promises that the investments would yet pay off. In fact, similar yet gradually increasing amounts were disbursed, by a blend of wires and checks, to a shifting roster of investment opportunities that are most likely a coded arrangement for moving money between accounts in a way that would eventually create difficulties in tracking it and ultimately add up to fraud. However, without being able to do a full audit of the disbursing company's books and based on the explanation you provided of the reason for this inquiry, I would agree that the bearer of these documents was not complicit. To the contrary, she might well have been in grave danger if she trusted the wrong person. This would have been easy to do. The people who ran these confidence schemes were just as adept in their time as they are in our own."

CHAPTER TWENTY-NINE

Denver, Colorado
May 14, 1909

Dear Miss Bendeure,
    I am sure this will be our final correspondence before
your journey begins. The matters you have inquired about,
and the lines of investigation Pinkerton's has pursued on
your behalf, have revealed inconsistencies and irregularities that bear close scrutiny not only on your behalf but
on behalf of others who have been less vigilant than your
father or, in some cases, less determined to right injus-
tices once discovered. I do urge caution in all things upon
your arrival and look forward to speaking in person without
inhibition about all these details, realizing that since
our progress reports in the meantime cannot reach you, we
will simply hold them for your arrival.

Yours sincerely,
James McParland
Manager, Western Division
Pinkerton's National Detective Agency

Monday, May 24, 1909
Denver, Colorado

The next time a knock came, she said, "Who is it?"

"It's us." Willie's voice.

Lynnelle opened the door. "Where have you been all day?"

"We might ask the same question," Carey said.

So Geppetto's loyalty exceeded his instinct for self-protection. Lynnelle ignored the remark.

"Where are the papers?" Lynnelle said.

Willie unpinned Lynnelle's hat and shook her hair loose. "Everything went perfectly." She lifted the satchel over her shoulder and handed it to Lynnelle.

"They really believed you were me?"

"Right down to thinking I would go with them into the private offices of a bank and sign the authorization to move the accounts."

"But Clarice and Henry?"

"Just as we thought, they were smart enough not to be physically present," Carey said, "but our men were waiting for them as soon as their contact inside the bank tried to tamper with the accounts and shift funds to them."

"It really was them all along?"

Carey nodded. "They've been operating with half a dozen aliases in four states."

Lynnelle dropped into a chair. "A contact inside the bank is a frightening prospect."

"It was a chain of confidence schemes. I suspect your father's representative was legitimate at some point and fell prey to the temptation of greed promised by people like Clarice and Henry. He was integral in infiltrating the bank with his own promises of profit for a few moments of risk. The bank's president is horrified."

"So everyone has been arrested?" Lynnelle said.

"Right up the line."

"What a relief." Lynnelle exhaled and shook her head. "I didn't know what I was going to tell my father if you two had snookered me into a confidence scheme of your own."

"We were always the guys in white hats, Lynnelle." Carey's dimple was back.

"I have a telephone call of my own to make," Willie said. "Charles made me promise to call as soon as this was over."

"Charles?" Lynnelle said.

"Her beau." Carey winked. "Husband, if she would get around to saying yes."

Lynnelle looked from Willie to Carey. "But I thought—"

"The two of us?" Carey's dimple deepened. "Meet my twin sister. Everything I know about being sneaky, I learned from her."

"Your *sister?*"

"It was all part of the cover. You understand."

"I do now." Lynnelle feasted on those eyes and that dimple without guilt for the first time. "So I can call my father and then collect my trunk?"

The dimple disappeared.

"Carey," Lynnelle said. "My trunk. It's only been a day. Surely it's still at Union Station."

"I don't doubt it. But if you don't mind, we'd like you to let us handle the communication with your father. We're going to have to take you into hiding until the trial."

"What! We never discussed this."

"It seemed better to go one step at a time. We still need to keep you safe."

"But you said you arrested everyone right up the line, including Henry and Clarice."

"We have reason to believe they're not the absolute end of the line— or at least that they have nefarious contacts who would prefer that you do not testify at a trial."

"I haven't agreed to testify at a trial. And Pinkerton's is a private agency, not a branch of law enforcement."

"It's quite important that you do testify, Lynnelle. Bendeure & Company was not the only victim of these activities, but you were the one brave enough to become involved to the degree that you did, even when Mr. McParland tried to discourage it because he thought it might be unsafe."

"He never told me it might be unsafe, only that he thought my presence was not strictly necessary."

"But you did choose to come. Now your presence has become essential. The banks involved will be pressing charges. Your testimony is vital. We cannot risk having you seen at Union Station or have you exposed on a train anywhere else someone might expect to find you."

CHAPTER THIRTY

So glad you made it back." Nolan stood back from Nia's stove and let Drew make what was sure to be an exquisite glaze for the carrots soon to go in the ovens, cut and seasoned just the way Drew had suggested a few days ago.

"I wouldn't have missed this for the world." Drew lifted a spoon and sniffed his concoction.

"You're not going to taste it?"

"Don't need to," Drew said. "I've made this a hundred times. I'm sorry I had to leave you stranded yesterday, but I'm here today, and I'm all in."

Nolan probed. "Something came up at the ranch?"

"I had to run down there for a few hours, but everything's under control." Drew nodded toward rows of bacon and cabbage pies lining the counter. "I'm bummed I didn't get to see you put those together. I wanted to learn to make them from start to finish."

"Another time," Nolan said. "You know where to find me."

They'd been working together most of the day, readying everything that couldn't be prepared ahead and planning precise use of the oven space and stove burners. With only a couple of hours to go until the first seating, many items were out to bring them to room temperature before final roasting or warming.

"Jillian's working on the meat?" Drew said.

"I sliced it last night, and she volunteered to oversee warming it at our house."

"I could go check, as soon as the carrots are ready for the oven."

Nolan restrained his amusement. Jillian didn't need help warming pans of meat or preparing watercress and orange slices, the only other food not yet transported to the Inn.

"She might like some company," Nolan said. He'd text her as soon as he had his hands free. Something told him she would appreciate the warning.

Nia cruised into the kitchen.

"The place looks fabulous!" Nolan said.

"Let's hope it stays that way for a couple more hours," Nia said. "The wait staff and dishwashers should be here soon, so be thinking about whether there's anything you need to tell them about how to serve the food and clear up efficiently."

"Will do."

Nia peered at three sheets of paper taped to the refrigerator doors, outlining the schedule by fifteen-minute time segments. Drew had sufficient experience with banquets to be extraordinarily helpful mapping out the evening. The schedule and task list were printed in large type, and Nia's large kitchen clock would keep them both mindful of keeping things moving.

"We're on time," Nolan said.

"And you're confident you can keep to this?"

"Yes, ma'am."

"Don't ma'am me, Nolan," Nia said. "I used to babysit your kid."

"No, ma'am."

She scowled. "Can I do anything to be helpful?"

"You could slice bread," Nolan said. "Drew was just about to pop over and see if he can give Jillian a hand with the spiced beef."

Nia looked again at the list on the fridge. "Don't forget the watercress."

"No, ma'am." Drew ducked on his way out of the kitchen.

"You have corrupted a perfectly nice young man," Nia said.

Nolan shot off a text to Jillian and kept his singing to a minimum—humming, actually—while he and Nia worked their way down the tasks, adding the first batch of barley and wild rice casseroles to a low temperature oven to begin warming through, arranging the first vat of soup on the stove, where it would have to be watched carefully while it simmered, slicing bread, counting up how many vegetarian stuffed portobellos were reserved for the first seating.

He felt ready.

Forty minutes passed before Jillian arrived.

She came in through the front door, calling, "Hello!"

Nolan paced through the exquisitely appointed dining room and into the hall. His daughter looked spectacular in an emerald-green dress grazing the tops of her knees, her mother's pearls, and her black hair piled in waves on top of her head. He'd seen her speak before, and never had she presented herself with this degree of elegance. If she'd taken the extra effort because of Drew—well, it was about time she met someone who made her feel like doing it, even if it was just for an evening or two. Drew had found time to put on a clean, crisp white chef's shirt for the evening, one of his own he brought back from the ranch. He balanced three enormous containers of salad.

"He wouldn't let me carry anything," Jillian said.

"You're the featured speaker," Drew said. "We can't risk getting anything on your dress."

Nolan swallowed glee at the pair of them. "Here, let me take the salad. What have you done with the meat?"

"In my truck," Drew said. "In the insulated bags. I'll get them."

"You look very nice," Nolan said as Jillian followed him through the dining room.

"Nia and Veronica were afraid I might show up in jeans."

"Were you tempted?"

"I wouldn't do that to Marilyn," Jillian said.

Placating Marilyn would have taken far less effort than this stunning visage.

"I'm not sure you ought to come in the kitchen," Nolan said. "Things spatter and spill in there."

"Now you sound like Drew."

Nolan winked. "I like him. Don't you?"

Color rose in Jillian's cheeks. "Dad, stop."

Drew was coming through the front door again and caught up with them. "Nolan, I have to say this meat smells divine."

"Let's hope at some point in the evening we all get a chance to eat the fruit of our labors," Nolan said. "Time to start putting more things in the ovens."

Jillian dutifully remained beyond the boundary of any potential soiling of her ensemble, pulling a chair from the dining room table to a position where she could observe activity in the kitchen. Whenever Nolan glanced at his daughter, though, her eyes were not on him but on the movements of his assistant chef. Nia had withdrawn to her private quarters to get herself properly outfitted for hosting the evening. The clock ticked toward the arrival of the first guests. The entire day had gone precisely as planned.

The Inn's front door opened and thudded closed. The footsteps in the hall were measured but solid.

Nolan raised an eyebrow in Jillian's direction, and she got up off her chair to peer into the hall.

She scampered back. "Drew, you'd better come."

Startled, he dropped a ladle deep into the cucumber soup. Nolan grabbed a pair of tongs and fished it out.

"Drew!" Jillian hissed.

He ran his hands under some water at the sink, dried them, and paced—unenthusiastically—into the hall. Nolan followed his progress. Clearly, Drew had an inkling what he would find. Nolan turned off the burners and trailed behind.

Min stood in the hall examining one of Veronica's luggage arrangements, accompanied by a woman Nolan judged to be about his own age.

"Hello, Aunt Min," Drew said. "I thought you and Michelle were going straight back to the ranch today. Everything is ready. Fresh groceries. Made up the bed for Michelle. Animals all look great. Weeded the garden."

"Then all we need is you." Min glanced around. "I heard from your sister's husband that you'd been home, but then you drove all the way back up here for some wild reason."

"It's nice to see you, Drew," Michelle said. "We seem to have stumbled into an affair of some sort."

"Yes," Min said. "The place does look rather different than the last time I was here. But I can't imagine what any of this has to do with you. I'm certain I made my feelings quite clear when we were here together."

"Yes, you did," Drew said.

Nolan saw no sign of Drew's countenance shrinking in Min's presence this time even as concern vaulted into Jillian's features.

"I suppose your truck is around here somewhere," Min said, "but we can still caravan home."

"Not tonight, Aunt Min. I'll see you in a few days."

"I beg your pardon."

"Mom." Michelle touched Min's elbow. "Clearly there's a banquet tonight, and based on how Drew is dressed, I'd say he's cooking."

"They'll have to get along without him. I will not stand for this defiance."

Drew angled slightly toward Jillian, catching her eyes and then Nolan's before speaking again. "Aunt Min, I'm a grown man and a very good chef. I've made a commitment to help with this evening. It's important to my new friends. I'm staying."

"What about what is important to your family?"

"What difference can one evening make, or a couple of days, at this point? Michelle will be with you at home."

"Drew's right, Mom," Michelle said. "Why don't I just take you home as we planned?"

Min shirked off her daughter's touch. "If he's not leaving, then neither am I."

Dressed for the evening, Nia nudged her way past Nolan. "You're Drew's family. Can I help you?"

"Ah, the innkeeper." Min stroked her bobbed gray hair. "I suppose this shindig is your doing."

"It's a community effort," Nia said, "and we're grateful for Drew's help tonight. He's been a lifesaver."

"He has no business being here."

"We seem to be in the way," Michelle said. "We'll go sort ourselves out somewhere."

"We'll leave when Drew is ready to come with us," Min said.

Drew inhaled slowly through his nose. "Aunt Min, I love you dearly. You taught me everything I know about the ranch, a place I love with every fiber of my being. But I'm not going home tonight."

"Young man." Min's tone warned.

"I have soup on the stove that will be spoiled if I stand here and argue with you," Drew said, his posture erect as he pivoted and grazed Jillian's hand as he walked past.

Nolan wanted to whoop and cheer.

"Let's go, Mom," Michelle said.

"Nonsense," Nia said. "The first seating for dinner is not far off. We'll squeeze you in."

"The first seating?" Michelle echoed.

"That's right. Drew and Nolan are working their magic three times tonight. So you can see, we really can't lose him now. But you may as well enjoy the meal."

Flushed with embarrassment, Michelle fumbled for a response. "That sounds like it could be a late evening."

"It's no trouble," Nia said. "Since I knew I would be busy tonight, I purposely kept some of my rooms open so I wouldn't be too distracted with guests. If you don't mind fending for yourself, you're welcome to one of the rooms to freshen up. Stay the night if you like."

Michelle bypassed glancing at her mother this time. "That would be lovely. Late-night driving is not my favorite task."

Nia turned to Jillian. "Would you mind laying the extra places while I show our guests to a room?"

"Of course," Jillian said.

Nolan smiled and rubbed his palms together. "We have plenty of food, and Drew has been making it better and better."

"When things are quieter," Jillian said, "I think you'll be interested to hear about our time with Drew these last few days. It's been so nice having him here."

Min's brow furrowed in suspicion.

"This way," Nia said. "I hope the stairs are not a problem."

Nia led the travelers upstairs, and Nolan and Jillian withdrew into the dining room.

"With so many tables set, I don't have a clue where any extra dishes are." Jillian clamped a hand over her mouth, but Nolan saw her green eyes dancing in amusement.

"The evening certainly has taken a turn," Nolan said. "But our Drew did well. We just have to get him through the evening."

Our Drew.

"I've got this, Dad. I've been wanting to talk to you and Drew, but everything's been too busy. But it's going to be all right."

Nolan exhaled. "I'm sorry I've put off hearing what you found."

"Try to come out of the kitchen when I give my talk," she said. "And bring Drew."

CHAPTER THIRTY-ONE

April 2, 1910
Outside Pueblo, Colorado

The elk looked familiar. A few pounds heavier, perhaps, but that was to be expected coming out of the winter and the herd migrating to summer ranges. As food became plentiful, all the animals would grow more robust. When he lifted his head from the ground, he swept his neck in a distinctive arc she'd come to recognize. And if Ela was not mistaken, the bull's antlers were not as firmly fixed as the last time she watched him forage in the scrub oak and forbs of the ranch. Perhaps the next time she walked the property, companioned only by her introspection, she would find shed antlers on the path, and his doleful eyes would stare at her across wide yardage above his shoulders in a new unencumbered stance. Seeing the elk, and others like him, united with the herd would bring her some comfort. The ranch was not home for transitory elk or mule deer or antelope. Stately and wondrous, they would pass through for a few weeks as they had in the fall in the opposite direction.

With a hefty mortgage, the ranch was only beginning to support cattle—its true purpose—and might not be profitable for years. A handful of calves would birth in the next few weeks, but buying open land and turning it into a working ranch was a slow proposition. Chicken coops. Milking barns. Corrals. Outbuildings. They had a long way to go.

But the land.

The sheer lustrous wonderment.

The Wet Mountains in one direction and the San Isabels in another.

The chattering birds and skittering wildlife.

The creek beds to catch and hold water in the spring runoff, which had already begun even though the locals assured her they were not yet clear of the season's last potential for blizzard.

At least they had the house. The winter had given them enough mild days—and they'd been stubborn enough to use even the days that weren't—to make steady progress toward finishing the remodeling of the ragged structure and make it more than livable. Now it was a cozy white house with green shutters and trim and a porch sheltering two green wicker chairs. She could manage in the kitchen better than she'd ever expected, and a fire took the chill off the main room in the evening as they read and dreamed. Two bedrooms would be enough for now, though she hoped they'd want more later.

Wearying of the palette that greeted her eyes every morning and soothed her spirit each evening was unimaginable. The constant cerulean expanse beyond inspiration. Jumbled russets and golds and browns of fall, frosted alabaster of winter, shimmering spring greens bursting out of the ground in unfathomable shades.

She hooked one foot on the lowest rail of the slip board wooden fence, leaned both elbows on the top rail, and sighed forward.

Staring. Absorbing. Longing.

"Hello, Mrs. Kyp."

She turned toward the sound of her husband's voice. "Hello yourself, Mr. Kyp."

He put an arm around her shoulders and joined the staring.

"It's so beautiful," she said. "And so far away."

"Do you miss her—Lynnelle?"

She angled her head up at him. "I'd feel better if she could see her father. He should have been at the wedding."

"Maybe in a few more months."

"I know. After the trial."

"There *will* be a trial. It's on the docket now. It has to be safe for everyone. But it's okay for you to miss her, Ela. To wish she could see him."

She nodded. He would give her a different answer if he could.

"What's the news from Helmi?" She leaned into him, notching her shoulder under his.

"You can read her letters, you know."

"I do know. But I think you ought to read them first."

"They'll be here on next Saturday's train."

"Oh good!"

"They might stay this time."

"What do you mean, stay?"

"He's ready to consider settling in Colorado."

"I thought he couldn't imagine living anywhere but San Francisco."

He kissed the top of her head. "You never thought you'd live here either."

"That's different."

"Is it?"

He had a point. Circumstances dictated her initial stay. But marrying Carrick Kyp sealed her future.

"It would be nice to have them close," she said.

"The ranch is large enough to support two families—or it can be. We could build another house, or add on to ours for the time being."

Ela chuckled. "I've only met Charles a couple of times, but he doesn't strike me as a rancher."

"He could still keep his hand in with Pinkerton's if he wants to. Even in San Francisco he's part of the Western region."

"Then we shall have to do our very best to be persuasive."

"I thought I might see if Geppetto and Caterina might like to explore ranch life." Carrick tilted a questioning head.

"Geppetto? Here?"

"He's a good man. If he doesn't like the ranch, he could always open a hotel in Pueblo."

"The Parisis are counting on him for Aldo's future, you know."

"Geppetto has trained him well. He could stay at the hotel if he wants to. Personally I think the boy should go to school."

"I guess we could talk to them," Ela said, "if you really think we could afford to pay someone, and fix up an outbuilding for them to live."

"It's something to think about." He reached into a pocket. "I picked up today's mail when I went into town. This came for you."

Ela took the envelope, thick cream stationery with a return address showing a law office in Ohio.

Mrs. Carrick M. Kyp.

She met her husband's gray eyes. "I don't understand. Who would...?"

"I'm not sure. Let's just read it."

Ela sucked in her lips, ran a finger under the flap of the envelope, and tugged out a sheet of paper matching the color of the envelope.

"Dear Mrs. Kyp," she read. "This is to inform you of a bequest left to you upon the death of Mr. Warren Bendeure of Cleveland, Ohio."

Her spine lost its shape, and only the arms of the man she trusted caught her before she met the earth.

"Ela, I'm so sorry."

Her chest heaved, and she gulped for air. "My greatest fear. My greatest fear."

He gathered her in his arms, as she keened, her wail as wild and fiercely lonesome as the land around them.

At last she pushed off his chest, swiped at the torrent of tears streaming from her eyes, and returned to the correspondence. The typed letters resisted a straight, focused line, instead waving in the sea of her flooded vision.

"I can't see the words." She handed the letter to him.

He cleared his throat. "Although it was unexpected, and I have not before this matter served as Mr. Bendeure's personal attorney, he came to me some months ago to write a new will, in which he named you as a beneficiary with the additional unusual instruction that I also include the explanation that because he has no surviving children, the bulk of his estate, including Mr. Bendeure's majority holdings in Bendeure & Company, will go to his grandsons to be held in trust until the time they come of age. This inheritance will hold even under the circumstances of their mother's recent remarriage, as was our client's express wish. We prepared, and Mr. Bendeure executed, the new will as required under the laws of the State of Ohio.

"The matter of your bequest is being handled by the firm that has arranged the business proceedings of Bendeure & Company for some years now. My only responsibility is to inform you of the bequest Mr. Bendeure made on your behalf, which I believe you will find generous. The enclosed document outlines the particulars, which will be administered by the executor of the estate and come to you in due time after the estate is settled and all fees and liabilities have been accounted for.

"If I can be of further service, please do not hesitate to contact me.

"Yours sincerely,

"Franklin Z. Hendricks, Esquire

"Attorney at Law."

A rabbit scampered past them on the other side of the fence, its rustle the only sound other than Carrick scratching the letter back into the envelope.

"No surviving children," Ela said. "Is that really what he told people? What he felt?"

"I guess we don't know what he told people—other than Mr. Hendricks," Carrick said, "but he made provision for you the best he could."

"Under the circumstances." Ela choked on the words. "I came to Colorado because he was not well enough to come himself. It's not fair that I never got to see him again."

"No, it's not."

"I thought Pinkerton's agreed he would tell people I fell in love with the West or some such thing."

"We didn't specify what he *must* say so much as what he must *not* say." Carrick stroked her cheek. "We did our best to take your letters back and forth safely, carried by Pinkerton operatives."

"But he was never allowed to keep them, was he?"

Carrick shook his head.

"I know. Not safe."

"Not for your father. No one wanted to put him in danger. If anyone found evidence he knew where you were—"

"You don't have to say it." Ela held up her hands. "And under the circumstances, he could hardly leave the bulk of his estate or any interest at all in the company to a woman whose name no one recognizes or whose relationship he could not explain. That would be asking for the will to be contested. Perhaps even this bequest will find objection."

Carrick said nothing.

"He never even got to meet you." Ela's voice hitched.

"At least he knew *about* me. He knew you were happy." He dropped his head to search her eyes. "You are happy, aren't you? With me?"

Ela met his gaze. "Very. But I will always feel cheated of a moment that now can never be, when the loop would have been closed and what I got on that train to do was accomplished and Papa's peace of mind was fully restored and we could be together again. Who knows, in time maybe even my brother's widow would have found her way out of her grief and back to us. Now I don't suppose I'll ever have reason to go back to Ohio. I don't even have the photographs of my brother's boys. There's no telling what will have happened to the trunk by the time the trial is resolved."

The truth, the weight of stones pushing uphill, hung between them.

"Must I really face them, Carrick?" She searched his face. "What have I to gain now? They've taken it all." Some days the thought of Clarice Hollis's blue eyes in a courtroom, sure to be icy more than friendly now, woke Ela in the night.

"I will be there," Carrick said. "We will face them together, with the evidence and law on our side."

She said nothing. She did have one more secret to protect, to keep safe.

"When we get this behind us," Carrick said, "would you like to have your name back?"

Ela tapped her fingers against the lawyer's envelope as she considered the suggestion. With today's mail, she'd already lost the final vestige of her past that mattered to Lynnelle. *Under the circumstances.* By the time she could reclaim her name, she couldn't even go back to choose a treasured belonging that had been her father's. The house would be gone, everything liquidated. She'd have no way to know what had become of his personal possessions. Even her nephews would have a new father, and she doubted their mother would speak of her brother to them more than necessary.

She could only pray that even now she was making the right decision to follow through on the wheels of earthly justice and leave heavenly judgment in the hands of a merciful God. With a deep inhale, she recalled the psalmist's words. *"Justice and judgment are the habitation of thy throne: mercy and truth shall go before thy face."* May God have mercy on the generations to come.

"After all the trouble we went through to lose Lynnelle?" Ela turned back to the scrub oak–spattered pasture. The elk had moved on, but in the distance was a muley, with its big ears. "No. You've left Pinkerton's, and there's nothing for me at Bendeure & Company or in Ohio. I'm a Colorado rancher's wife now. Mr. Hendricks is right. The bequest is quite generous. Think of everything we'll be able to do for the ranch. Papa was always one to look to the future."

"Then that's what we'll do."

Ela tangled her arm around his. "If the baby is a girl, I want to call her after your sister."

"Excuse me? Baby?"

"But not Helmi. That name should just be for your sister."

"Baby?" Carrick repeated.

"And I know Willie was just a name the two of you used during your detective escapades. But we could still name her Wilhelmina and call her Mina for short."

Carrick spun her around and put his hands on her shoulders. That dimple.

"Are we talking about a theoretical future baby?"

"It's a good thing you've given up Pinkerton's, because I think you've lost your touch for detecting." Ela beamed. "So Wilhelmina's name, but I'm very much hoping for your dimple."

CHAPTER THIRTY-TWO

The chairs were turned toward the small landing where Jillian stood, including the ones repositioned from spaces without clear views of her small podium during the meal. The tables were cleared, and an army of high schoolers, many no doubt earning community service credit for one project or another, were behind the closed kitchen door cleaning dishes while Jillian spoke so tables could be rapidly reset according to the diagram and photos Nia provided.

Jillian blocked out the scraping chairs and clinking dishes in the background. She'd spent the last hour sequestered in Nia's office behind the main parlor outlining a new talk. Having Min in the audience changed everything. The talk was not meant to be long. Twenty minutes. Not a minute more. Marilyn had been emphatic about that, and Nia and Veronica had left no doubt that the time required to clear the Inn and reset sixty-five place settings, even with a battalion of volunteers, left little flexibility. She scribbled out one point, underlined another, and raised her eyes to get her bearings with the crowd.

Min and Michelle hadn't moved from the corner of the dining room where Jillian had made sure to seat them over objections that they weren't dressed up enough to be so conspicuous. She wanted them where she could make eye contact.

And where she could look over their heads and see Drew when he came out of the kitchen.

Where was he? *Come on, Dad. Get him out here.*

"Good evening." Jillian smiled at the sated crowd, which a few moments ago had been buzzing about the elegant culinary offerings. Complicated as it was, Nolan's menu was a dazzling success. "As your program indicates, my topic tonight is 'Your Family's Then and Your Now: Knotting the Threads Together.' I'm sure you've noticed the wonderful decor Veronica O'Reilly has created with the cases and trunks in the various rooms. You might enjoy visiting some of the rooms other than the one you dined in to soak up even more of the ambiance of the evening. I want to tell you the story of one particular steamer trunk. I was not able to have it here with me tonight, but it could just as well have been any one of a number of the steamers you see around the Inn."

For now she avoided Min's eyes. It was Drew's dark gray eyes she wanted to soak up, to see the spark in at the story she was about to share. She imagined Nolan and Drew putting the next round of casserole dishes and roasting pans in the ovens. Or was Nolan having trouble convincing Drew to leave the kitchen as long as his great-aunt was on the premises?

"This steamer trunk," Jillian continued, "took a long journey not on the ocean but on several branches of the complex web of passenger railroads that sprang up, merged, and reshaped over several decades in the nineteenth century and early twentieth."

The kitchen door eased open. There was Nolan. And then Drew.

Jillian relaxed and settled her eyes on Min for a moment. Min crossed her arms.

"The trunk traveled from Cleveland, Ohio, in 1909. The stickers on it tell us it came via the New York Central and the Union Pacific Railroads, arriving at Denver's Union Station in the historic days when the iconic Welcome Arch was just a few years old. Most of you have probably seen pictures of the arch. This trunk, of course, did not travel alone. It belonged to a young woman, Lynnelle Bendeure.

"And here the plot thickens, because Lynnelle Bendeure of Cleveland, Ohio, never claimed her trunk when she arrived in Denver, Colorado. Now, more than a hundred and ten years later, her trunk has surfaced in pristine condition—and with Lynnelle's secrets still locked inside.

"But what became of Lynnelle? I certainly wondered. Don't you?" Jillian settled her eyes once again on Min. "Perhaps you've heard bits and pieces of your own family's history and wondered what became of Great-Great-Grandma Betty or your mother's cousin Fred. I'm here with you today, as Canyon Mines celebrates our heritage and history, because I am a genealogist and I have a passion for uncovering heritage and history. I believe that the mysteries of the past often answer the questions of the present. Sometimes we find the answers to questions we've been curious about, and sometimes we finally put to rest questions we were afraid to hear the answers to."

She paused to catch Drew's eyes for a few seconds before letting her gaze roam the assembly. "Lynnelle's trunk didn't arrive in Denver locked and empty. It arrived locked and full of clues that can help us know her, her desires, her challenges, who her family was a hundred years ago, and also—I believe—who her family is today. So let me tell you the story that Lynnelle's trunk has told me over the last couple of weeks."

Min's gray eyes zoned in on Jillian now. Jillian didn't have to glance at her notes to continue and instead spoke directly to Drew's great-aunt and hoped he was listening as intently as Min seemed to be.

"It's not unusual for families to have items that have come down through the generations. Your mother's china. Your grandmother's hand-made quilt. A pipe that once belonged to your great-grandfather. An army blanket that reminds you of a loved one's service when it seemed the whole nation was touched by a war in some way. Books you keep because they were your father's when he was little and you hope someday your own grandchild will find them interesting." Jillian took a breath and glanced at Nolan, who nodded encouragement. "A traditional white lace christening gown. An old wool overcoat your mother used to play dress-up in that had belonged to her grandfather. Old maps and correspondence and photos that still somehow make you feel connected to your family tree, even if you can't name the people in the photos or read the language the letters are written in. The trunks around us tonight remind us we all come from somewhere, and our stories often are handed down in the physical items that have survived the journeys of the generations that have come before us.

"So what did Lynnelle's trunk, and its journey from Ohio, tell me about her story? I learned she was a determined, trustworthy person on an important mission safeguarding the welfare of her family and their company. She was organized, thorough, businesslike, and prepared. But she also traveled with items that must have meant the world to her sentimentally—photos of her loved ones and the family Bible. Even the trunk had another person's initials on it and perhaps first belonged to someone she wanted to feel close to. I believe our friend Lynnelle intended to accomplish her purpose and return to the bosom of her family, and something very unexpected happened in the course of her travels between Cleveland

and Denver. But what?"

Jillian swept the intertwining dining room, wide hall, and parlor with her eyes before again settling on the last-minute guests who had caused the rushed alterations to her talk.

"Where did Lynnelle disappear to? Did she meet foul play on the Union Pacific? Did she mean to abandon her steamer trunk, with its precious personal belongings? Lynnelle's trunk contained valuable tools for a genealogist to work with. I mentioned the family Bible. This one contained many entries of births, marriages, and deaths. It seems that someone had fallen behind on updating entries. We all know what that's like! Yet it was a treasure trove of names going back many generations. The trunk also contained business records suggesting the nature of the challenge Lynnelle faced and the risks she may have faced aboard the trains. Finally, we have correspondence with the manager of the western region of the famous Pinkerton's National Detective Agency, whose assistance Lynnelle had sought on behalf of her father's business interests.

"In the earliest years of the twentieth century, Pinkerton's was well known for assisting the American Bankers Association with minimizing financial fraud and identifying individuals running confidence schemes under a variety of false identities. They often had name variants that might have some thread that knotted them together or something less obvious, such as a ring of partners in various cities or even on the railroad lines themselves. A bit of flirting and flattery. Gaining trust. A promise of a quick return on an investment. A limited opportunity requiring a moment's decision. Signing some papers. Moving money between banks. Then on to a fresh identity and a new con in a new place."

Drew had tilted his head to one side, as if he couldn't quite believe what he was hearing. But he made no move to withdraw to the kitchen. Min had uncrossed her arms and leaned forward. Michelle looked lost, but Jillian could tell not all of this was new to Min.

"I hunt for people from the past," Jillian said. "It's what I do for a living, and let's face it, I do it for a hobby as well. I wanted to know what happened to Lynnelle. At first, I thought she'd been the victim of foul play and identity theft. Even before Social Security numbers, the internet, and online shopping, people were stealing identities! If someone on the train had discerned that Lynnelle's business connections were considerable, there would be substantial motivation to simply become Lynnelle Bendeure long enough to sign some papers, get access to the Bendeure & Company holdings in Denver, and move on to a new identity with a new name and a nicely padded bank account. And Lynnelle's family would never know what happened to her. I'm afraid I made rather a fool of myself chasing down that theory! Thankfully, I came to my senses.

"I did get a couple of things right, though—a new name and a financial scam. Lynnelle helped to intercept an ongoing financial scheme that was bigger than just her own family's company, and for her own safety, until the trial to bring the perpetrators to justice, she had to stay under the radar. Lynnelle lived a long time before what we think of as the witness protection program, but she did have the help of Pinkerton's, who very much wanted to see the case they helped to crack successfully prosecuted. In fact, she had the help of one particular Pinkerton's detective who developed a personal interest—the man she married! They moved to a lovely ranch outside Pueblo, Colorado, where some of their descendants still live today. Lynnelle likely chose to peacefully live out her life under her new name, and for reasons I don't know—yet—likely never returned to Ohio."

Jillian shifted her eyes back to Drew. "Yet in this fabulous age of the internet and DNA and spitting in tubes, one of her descendants has discovered distant cousins in Ohio. And who knows? Perhaps we'll still be able to reunite branches of the family tree for the first time in over a century and honor a heroic ancestor who made a great personal sacrifice to help not only her own family but many others who might have come to financial ruin if not for her actions.

"We will draw to a close soon, but I again invite you to have a look around at the trunks and cases and think about the journeys of your own family's 'then' and how it connects to your own 'now.' When you go home, reconsider the heirlooms handed down in your family. They may tell you more of the story than you ever thought. Thank you."

Jillian picked up her notes and stepped away from the podium on the landing as the applause began. No matter what kind of talk she gave, there were always listeners who wanted to speak with her afterward, and this was no different. She would have to be polite—and she knew Drew had to return to the kitchen. The food schedule awaited, the volunteer staff would be chafing to begin resetting the tables, and before she knew it, diners for the next seating of the meal would begin arriving. Across the dining room, Drew lifted one arm and waved a couple of fingers at her. Nolan gave a small nod, a grin sloping up one side of his face, before following Drew into the kitchen. She'd have to catch them later.

Min and Michelle hung back until finally the gathering thinned and Jillian had shaken as many hands as necessary.

"May we talk?" Michelle asked.

"Of course." Jillian glanced into Nia's office off the parlor, certain it would be all right to borrow a quiet corner there.

"Well, you've gone and done it anyway," Min said. But the fury Jillian had heard in every interaction before now was gone. "I never knew her name."

"But you knew it wasn't Ela, didn't you?" Jillian's question was quiet.

Min nodded. "Once, when I was a little girl, I had a school project to do a family tree. I got marked off for not including my grandmother's maiden name. It seems a small thing now, but I never did know it. She just said Ela Kyp was the only name that mattered."

"I read the trial transcripts," Jillian said. "After all she went through, I suppose it was."

"Those cousins Drew found," Min said. "My grandmother said her brother had died and his widow kept his children from her, which grieved her greatly. That's all I knew. I figured somehow that was why she thought the old name didn't matter. You're right. If he has descendants, it would honor her to find them and reconnect the branches of the family tree. Surely whatever grudge happened is ancient history. Who would be alive to even know what it was? Please, finish your work."

Jillian swallowed the knot in her throat. "Drew did the most important part. We'll work on it together."

CHAPTER THIRTY-THREE

T his is Wilhelmina?" Jillian looked up from a black-and-white photo of a woman in her midsixties with a child in her lap. "With you?"

Min nodded. "I was seven or eight. I remember the day. My mother told me I was getting too big to sit in Aunt Willie's lap. That was probably the last time I ever did."

The girl in the photo had gangly limbs and a satisfied grin uninhibited by the permanent teeth that had not quite grown into proper position. In Jillian's mind, Willie was a young woman, and Min was the older one. The photo, preserved with its corners held in place against a black page in a maroon vinyl-covered album for decades, flipped the time line. Underneath it, clear lettering said *Helmi and Min.*

"Who kept the album?" Nolan asked.

"My mother." Min met Jillian's eyes freely in her own living room at the big house on the ranch. "Ela's—Lynnelle's—daughter, Dottie. She didn't leave a lot of details, and her albums are not in very good chronological order, but she tried to at least write down who was in some of the photos."

Jillian flipped a page. "This one says Mina, but it can't be you or Willie. It's not the right age."

"It's not. It's my mother's older sister, the eldest sibling. She was named for Wilhelmina, but she died as a child in the Spanish influenza epidemic in 1918."

"So you're named for her and for Willie?" Jillian asked.

Min nodded. "I've always been proud to bear the name."

"As you should be," Nolan said.

Min leaned forward from her chair and turned a couple of pages. A photo stared up at Jillian, labeled *Carrick, Ela, and Helmi.*

"Wow." Jillian ran her finger across the ragged edge of the old photo. "There they are. Brought together by events they didn't know were going to change their lives."

"I wish I'd known more about what my aunt and grandparents did back in 1909," Min said. "As far as anyone knew, they were ranchers and that's all there was to the story. They just told people they met on a train, which was true, I guess, but hardly the whole story. I knew Grandpa and his sister could be a goofy pair. I remember they had a way of looking at each other when the shenanigans were about to start, and that's when he would call her Willie instead of Helmi."

Around the room, heads bent forward, listening intently. Jillian could tell the family was hearing a more straightforward narrative than ever before. Michelle had stayed through the week, anticipating this visit from Jillian and Nolan, and Drew was there. His sister and her husband, Josie and Jake, had come for the afternoon from Pueblo proper with their two small children. His parents, Carol and Jason, were present as well. Jillian's mind's eye placed faces in the family tree where she had only seen names. From Carrick and Ela to Josie and Jake's children were six generations.

"Why didn't they ever tell anyone?" Drew asked. "The danger had passed. It would have been like talking about an old job, that's all."

"That's impossible to say." Jillian wished she had a better answer. "If it's any help, it's not uncommon in my work to discover that children and especially grandchildren don't know much about family members' lives when they were younger. We tend to identify them in the roles that we know them in as we grow up ourselves. And perhaps they felt that the ranch and the family were more significant than anything that came before."

Min took the album from Jillian and stroked the open page.

"Mom?" Michelle said.

"There's more to it." Min flipped back to the photo of herself as a leggy child on her aunt Helmi's lap. "Something else happened that day. It frightened me. I suppose I've been frightened all these years."

"Mom, what was it?" Michelle said.

"An argument. I didn't like what my mother said about being too old to sit in Aunt Helmi's lap. She scolded me for doing it, as if I should have known better because Helmi was getting older and I was being rambunctious. So I stomped off and went to play in the little red house. It's always been red. Aunt Helmi and Uncle Charles were the first ones to live there, and she always liked red. So we've always kept it that way. They moved off the ranch when they had their own family. But by this time their children were grown, and Charles was ill, and Helmi wanted to come back to the ranch. They were staying in the main house until the cabin was ready for them again, but some of their things were there, and I got into a shoebox of papers."

"Aunt Min," Drew said, "what did you find?"

"I'm not sure. I was a child—and a late reader, so I didn't understand everything. Documents. My grandmother came looking for me to say supper was ready and saw the papers. She snatched them and stormed back to the main house to find Helmi. I was afraid I was in trouble for getting into Helmi's things, but Aunt Helmi had never scolded me a day in my life. I wasn't supposed to be listening, but I did. Grandma said that those papers should have been destroyed forty years ago, and Helmi had no right to keep them all this time, not after what they'd all been through. Not after what she—Grandma—had sacrificed, and did Helmi really not understand what it had cost her? How could she have kept evidence all those years that could have put her and Grandpa at risk?"

"Wow," Drew said softly.

"Mom," Michelle said, "you never told me."

"My mother grabbed me then and dragged me away. Grandma and Aunt Helmi came to the supper table a few minutes later and didn't say anything more about it. When I tried to ask my mother, she hushed me. But no one really called her Willie again after that except in family stories. Not even Grandpa. The games were over." Min looked at Jillian. "And then you turned up at the ranch with some cockamamie story about foul play and how the family got the ranch and asking questions about that photo."

Nolan cleared his throat. "I can see how that would upset you. You never got answers about what frightened you as a child—and what you thought frightened your grandmother. And you probably felt responsible in some way."

"I did." Gravel in Min's voice cluttered her tone. "Whatever the documents were, I'm sure my grandmother destroyed them, and they carried on from there. Helmi and Charles moved back into the little red house and lived there until they both passed."

"I'm so sorry you've carried that around all your life." Jillian reached into the bag she'd brought with her on this excursion. "I have some papers that might answer some of the questions you never got to ask when you were a child. Before we get to the trunk, maybe you'd like to see them."

"Of course," Min said.

"I made copies of the parts of the trial transcript that were most illuminating of events," Jillian said. "You can actually read the words spoken by Carrick and Ela and Helmi when they testified. I've also made a list of all the names I found in the Pinkerton's archives referring to operatives working undercover on cases like this one that I think are actually pseudonyms for Carrick and Helmi."

Nolan chuckled. "I have a feeling this list will be similar to what was on your office walls a couple of weeks ago."

Jillian's lips turned up on one side as she passed the list to Min.

Carey Meade. Will Meade. William Meade. Caroline Meade. Liam Carey. Willie Meade. William Meade. Carey Willis. Kip Willis. Kiplan Carey. Kip Meade. Caroline Wills. Caroline Willis. Carey Kipling. C. W. Krispin. C. M. Kaplan. Cara Willis. Cara Williams. Carolyne Mead. Cara Charles. William Charles.

Drew stood reading over his aunt's shoulder. "They really did borrow each other's names. My grandmother had that part right! The transformation from Wilhelmina to William to Liam is particularly inventive."

Jillian nodded. Inventive, yet still in the realm of playfully nodding to each other as the twins must have done when they were children.

"If I may ask," Jillian said, "what were their full legal names?"

"Carrick Meade Kyp," Min said, "and Wilhelmina Caroline Kyp—then Lewis, after she married Uncle Charles."

"But what about Ela?" Michelle asked. "Mom, you always said she was always just Ela Kyp. She never even used a middle initial, but now we know she was Lynnelle Bendeure."

"Dad," Jillian said, "it's time for the Bible."

Nolan got up and carefully opened Lynnelle's steamer trunk, which stood in Min's living room. Once Jillian had established a connection to Lynnelle's descendants, the museum curator in Denver had been happy to cede possession to the rightful heirs. Nolan handed the Bible to Jillian, who gingerly opened it to the pages of family births and deaths and turned the volume for the others to see.

"Lynnelle was born Lynnelle Elaine Bendeure. When I first started looking for name variants that might surface, I explored variations of her unusual first name—dropping an *l*, Lynne E., Lynn with no middle initial, changing Lynnelle to Lynnette, and so on."

"Another long list on your whiteboard," Nolan said.

Jillian nodded.

"But the one you circled was Ela Bends," Nolan said.

"She shortened Elaine," Michelle said, "and simplified her last name."

"And I found a marriage record for Ela Bends and C. M. Kyp," Jillian said. "Carrick Meade Kyp, I now know. That's what led to my very rude intrusion onto your peaceful and stunning ranch a few weeks ago, when I thought someone had taken over her identity and used it for illegal gain to buy a large piece of land shortly after Lynnelle Bendeure disappeared. Then I saw that photo on Drew's mantel and realized I might have the whole thing wrong. This ending to the story may still have mystery, but it's so much happier."

She caught Drew's eye. His cheek dimpled.

"In the trial transcript," Jillian said, "someone asked Lynnelle why she changed her name. They were trying to establish the need for keeping her safe until she testified, I think. In the course of the back-and-forth, they asked how she chose the name she did. She said she'd never particularly liked her whole middle name, but it had come from her mother's family, so she chose to preserve a piece of it that she did like the sound of."

Min wiped the corner of one eye, and Michelle handed her a tissue.

"Would you like to see what else is in the trunk?" Nolan asked.

Heads bobbed, and he dragged the small rug on which it sat toward the center of the room.

"I've seen it," Drew said. "It's remarkable. Josie—our great-great-grandmother's clothes. It's like a time capsule."

Someday, Jillian wondered, would she have the chance to tell Drew about the time capsule of her own trunk?

"Go ahead," Jillian said, "open the drawers." There was no need for the white gloves now. The trunk was home. She could suggest the gloves later if the family wanted to take particular care, but in this moment, they should touch and feel the past however they wished.

"Mom," Michelle said, "you should go first."

As everyone who encountered the steamer seemed to do, Min stroked its canvas fibers before reaching into the shelf above the hanging clothes.

"The brush set," Min said.

"You know it?" Jillian asked.

"Not directly. My grandmother told me about it a couple of times. When I was little, she used to braid my hair and we talked." Min lifted the brush and hand mirror. "This is remarkable. This is exactly what she said it looked like, right down to the way the brush and the mirror had the same shape, just in different sizes, and the same trim on the back. She said she wished she still had it, because she would love to give it to me."

"What a sweet memory." Jillian had held the items in the trunk looking for clues, never shifting to the possibility that someone related to Lynnelle might have sentimental connections to belongings they'd never seen.

"That was over seventy years ago," Min said. "I haven't thought about it in decades. My sister and I used to play with an old wicker case she had for our dress-up clothes. I don't know what became of it. We wore it out."

"You did get her brooch," Michelle said, "the one you gave me on my wedding day."

Min nodded. "And now this. Her Bible. Her clothes. Her things."

"And photos," Jillian said. "Look in the next drawer."

Josie extracted the photos that had been sheltered from light for more than a century, flipping through them before handing them to Min.

"You said your grandmother said her brother had died," Jillian said, "and her widow had separated from the family. There they are."

The family passed the photos around in reverent awe.

"Did you figure out what happened?" Min asked.

Jillian glanced at Drew. "Do you want to tell her?"

He nodded. "Using the names from the DNA site, I tracked down some of the distant cousins it said I had on Facebook and Twitter and reached out. I got some responses—and answers."

"Well, out with it," Min said.

"When Ela's brother's widow remarried, her husband adopted her sons and changed their last name. But they still inherited the Bendeure company when they were older. Their biological grandfather made sure they knew who they were. The distant cousins that showed up when I spit in a tube really are related to Ela—and all of us—through these little boys."

"The missing nephews," Min whispered.

"Like most American families, the descendants are scattered over multiple states," Jillian said, "but a couple of them have been really friendly and curious—and very helpful in filling in the family tree. So I have one more surprise for you."

Drew helped clear off the coffee table, and Nolan took one end of the roll Jillian had prepared and unfurled it while she held down the other end. A family tree beginning with Lynnelle Bendeure, a.k.a. Ela Bends, and Carrick Meade Kyp unwound, running to the sixth generation. Beneath it, in parallel fashion, were the descendants of Lynnelle's brother and his wife through their two sons.

"I'm sure it's not complete," Jillian said. "Six generations is a lot to fill in, and most people don't even know all the names of their cousins' kids if they're from large families, much less their cousins' grandchildren. But it's only been a week, and with some time, I'm sure we'll fill in the rest. What Lynnelle lost will be found again."

Min no longer tried to wipe the moisture overflowing her tear ducts. "I'll have to call Ronald—my little brother. He'll want to know about this. I wish your grandmother were still alive, Drew."

Nolan stood with his hands in his pockets. "I'm so pleased that the steamer has come to where it belongs at last. I hope your family enjoys it for generations to come."

"Actually," Drew said, "I have a thought about that."

Jillian blinked, confused.

"This is my proposal," Drew said. "We keep many of the things in the trunk—the photos, the Bible, the hairbrush, the Bendeure business papers, the Pinkerton's correspondence. But we let the steamer trunk and clothes live in Canyon Mines, at the Heritage Society, where it can remind other families not to let anything get in the way of what matters most. It can be on indefinite loan with a small plaque that tells our story."

Jillian's throat thickened. The room went silent.

"It's a lovely idea." Min's voice rasped. "We can visit it any time we like when we go through Canyon Mines, which I'm sure will be often now. Particularly Drew."

Heat climbed across Jillian's neck. Drew snatched her glance with his own.

CHAPTER THIRTY-FOUR

Three boxes ought to be enough. The time capsule would never fit in a box anyway, with its awkward tubular shape. The heavy wool coat would need its own box. She'd taken the items she wanted and placed them downstairs already. The remaining items were most of the dishes and the heirloom christening gown. For now, Jillian would leave the boxes in the attic until she decided where in the house to incorporate the belongings. The immediate concern was to transport the trunk itself down the steep steps and then another flight to the main floor. For as long as she'd lived in this house, since she was two years old, the trunk had been in the attic. When she was little and explored its contents under her mother's supervision, it had been in the attic. She had no memory of move-in day and how the trunk had gotten up to the attic, but today she would sort out how to get it down.

Jillian folded the flaps of the last box and tucked them into each other.

"Dad!" she called down the stairs.

"What is it, Jilly?"

"I need your help up here."

Nolan's footsteps came up the steps. Jillian was already dragging the trunk on a blanket across the rough attic floor.

"What are we doing, Silly Jilly?" Nolan asked.

"Drew had a great idea." Jillian gave the blanket another tug. "I already talked to Marilyn. She's thrilled with the idea of having both trunks."

Nolan put his hand on the trunk. "Are you sure about this?"

"Absolutely. But I can't get it down the stairs by myself."

"You're sure you're not avoiding something by giving the trunk away?"

"I'm sorry, Dad. I should have asked you how you would feel about this. It was Mom's trunk." Jillian sat down and hung her elbows over her knees.

Nolan shook his head. "That's not it. She always wanted you to have the trunk, so it's yours now. It's you I want to be sure about."

"You can be sure, Dad. The trunk would be on loan. I could have it back anytime I want. If I want to put any of the items on display with it, I can—and then have them back if I want them. This is not one of those decisions that has to be forever."

"You've thought about this."

"All night."

"Discussed it with Drew?"

She looked away. "Might have."

"Your two trunks together in the same exhibit."

"Dad. Don't read more into it than is there." Jillian stood again and started dragging. "Are you going to help me or what?"

"Of course."

The task took negotiating, false starts, trying again, and stopping on the upstairs landing to catch their breath, but they got the trunk down to the first floor. At the foot of the stairs they paused again, and Nolan wiped his brow with his handkerchief.

"I see you added some new photos to the piano," he said.

Jillian nodded. "I found the silver frames at Veronica's shop. They seemed fitting."

"I think your mother would have been pleased."

"I made sure to digitize the images too. If anything happens to the originals, they are in the cloud. I always want to know they're safe."

"She'd like that too. The plate and cup are a nice touch from Grandma Marta's side."

"I'm going to get Marilyn's advice about the christening gown. Maybe there's a way to preserve it for posterity that's better than a musty attic."

Nolan nodded. "I'm sure she'll know."

"I made one last decision," Jillian said.

"Please don't tell me you want to take this trunk back up two flights of stairs. I'm not as young as I was the first time I did it twenty-six years ago."

"Nope. I'm going to spit."

His eyebrows went up. "In a tube?"

"Yep. I'm a genealogist. It's inexcusable that I've never done it before now."

"That may be a little harsh."

"I read other people's results all the time," Jillian said, "but I've never done my own."

"You know plenty about the Duffy side of your genes," Nolan said.

"That's true. And I don't have any first cousins on the Parisi side. Neither did Grandpa Steve. But I bet if I spit in a tube I'll find fourth and fifth cousins, just like Drew did, and maybe they'll have answers to questions I thought I missed my chance to ask."

"Maybe."

"A genealogist should have done this a long time ago."

"Then let the story continue."

AUTHOR'S NOTE

On my mantel are several family photos of people whose names I don't know. The full story is those photos come from my husband's side of the family, and we came into possession when we went through a box of his mother's things. The photos are unlabeled, and my husband is just not certain anymore. In one photo, the family includes a little girl. Another photo of a young woman looks like it might be the same little girl grown up.

I'm not sure. I'm not very good at looking at old photos and saying definitively it's the same person.

But based on the wardrobe and hairstyles—and mustache style on the man—I know the images are quite old. And I know my husband is related to them, which means my children are too. I don't know if I'll ever know their names.

Also from my mother-in-law we have a large book about the Holy Land that her aunt was awarded in 1910, around the time of this story, as third prize in a Sunday school competition, the pipe my mother-in-law's father smoked, a tiny, tiny child's ring still in a cardboard jeweler's box, and baby shoes my husband wore nearly seventy years ago.

And of course I have other items that have come from my side of the family. Some of my favorites are the passports my parents traveled back and forth with when my dad first immigrated to the US, then they decided to return and live in Brazil after they married, then they decided to settle permanently in the US, now with a toddler in tow. The last passport in the stack is the last one my father used the final time he traveled to visit his family a few years before his death. Last year one of my brothers unearthed a copy of my father's citizenship naturalization record. I remember the day my dad came home, having taken the oath that made him an American citizen. I was six and went running out of the house to congratulate him. Those documents tell a story of our family.

What do you have around your house that tells your family's story but lose some of the details with each generation? My hope with a story like *When I Meet You* is that you will value those items, ask the questions of people who know the answers while you still can, and add to the flow of the narrative with your own items and the reasons they are meaningful for the next generation.

Writing historical fiction always means taking some liberties. *Pinkerton's Great Detective: The Amazing Life and Times of James McParland* by Beau Riffenburg is a thorough telling of the colorful career of James McParland and the high-profile cases he investigated—not always without bias—particularly in the mining industry in western states. My story is set in the waning years of his career, but at its height, he was a powerful figure, and the western region he oversaw for Pinkerton's was essentially half the country. Archives at the University of Boulder include trial transcripts for high-profile cases McParland was involved with. To his consternation, they did not always turn out his way. I borrowed the idea of transcripts and placed them at the Denver Public Library, where they do not exist. The particular case and the trial I write about are completely fictitious.

The American Bankers Association's reliance on Pinkerton's for many years to track with their operatives the swindlers and fraud operations between banks around the country is true. That became a substantial inspiration for placing most of the historical thread of this story on trains, where it was not uncommon for confidence schemes to occur as seemingly harmless fellow passengers struck up friendly conversations. The pattern of con men (and women) to operate under strings of false identities also influenced developing story threads around sorting out what might have been foul play over a hundred years ago—or other less nefarious reasons for name changes. (Even James McParland's surname spelling morphed for reasons no one is sure of.) The reports Pinkerton's made annually to the American Bankers Association detailed who they investigated, what names the individuals had operated under, which banks they had used to transact fraudulent business through spurious accounts, and so on.

The Italian wave of immigration that brought many Italian families to New Orleans in the late 1880s is based in fact, including the descriptions of the two primary Mafia crime families seeking dominance and the death of the police chief that spurred a new wave of violence. I simply placed Jillian's fictitious Parisi ancestors in the midst of the socioeconomic patterns known to be true of the time. While occasional groups of Italian immigrants came to Denver in the very early twentieth century, for the most part the Italian Mafia's stronghold in Denver came much later than the timing of my historical story. Thus I have used the arrival of a fictitious Parisi in Denver as a way to escape true events going on in New Orleans and created the playful intersection of Jillian's ancestry with the very mysterious person she is trying to discover.

I know there's a lot of food in this story! Maybe in the next story, Nolan will be too busy to cook. (But I sort of hope not.) Communal meals nourish the body, but they also gather us around tables and memories and remind us that we are better together than on our own. Feel free to gather friends and family with food of your own and share the Duffy blessing.

May you always find nourishment for your body at the table.
May sustenance for your spirit rise and fill you with each dawn.
And may life always feed you with the light of joy along the way.

Olivia Newport
2020

Coming November 2020

WHAT YOU SAID TO ME
Book 4

Enjoy the following preview chapter.

CHAPTER ONE

While slightly on the monochromatic end of the culinary spectrum, the dish would pass for edible—more than edible in most family kitchens that wouldn't have Jillian Parisi-Duffy's father due to come through the door before it came out of the oven. Every food he prepared was better than everything she made, but she tried to hold up her end of the household balance of chores. Nolan had been coming home late more and more evenings recently with a bulging briefcase, reminiscent of her childhood when it was her mother who fed the family and her father either missed the evening meal or ate hastily so he could work again in his home office.

That was before Nolan discovered his inner chef self because circumstances thrust upon him the responsibility to feed a motherless child.

Jillian was fairly certain she had no inner chef self waiting for discovery. She just plodded along following recipes the way most people did.

This one had been successful enough to repeat every now and then. The casserole dish held cubed chicken with peas, carrots, celery, and onions covered in a roux. Jillian stabbed at a lump in the sauce with a fork and sighed, wondering how many other clots had gotten past her effort this time. In a mixing bowl, she had dough ready to drop biscuits over the top. A cheater's chicken pot pie, she called it. No real crust, which she would have failed at miserably, but plenty of hearty satisfaction, reasonable nutrition, and leftovers for easy lunches.

Jillian had a year and a few days before her thirtieth birthday. Maybe if she didn't share a home with a widowed father who had become such an enthusiast in the kitchen, she would be more impressive herself by now.

Doubtful. She was one of those people who enjoyed eating interesting meals but found less pleasure in creating them.

She turned on the oven to preheat and dropped rounds of biscuits at carefully calculated intervals. The refrigerator held arugula, avocado, and plum tomatoes for a salad she could throw together at the last minute.

While she waited for her dad, Jillian cleaned up after herself, rinsing the pans and utensils she'd used before loading the dishwasher and wiping down the gray-speckled granite counter and breakfast bar. By then the oven was just about ready. Nolan's pickup rumbled into the driveway, and a couple of minutes later he ambled through the back door.

"You cooked?" Nolan dropped his keys in the copper bowl on the counter.

"I sent a text telling you I would."

He plopped his briefcase on the breakfast bar and dug for his phone in a pocket. "I see that now. Sorry. It's been a hairy day."

"The mediation isn't going well?"

"I can't seem to get the parties in the same library, much less reading the same book or on the same page."

"You'll do it, Dad. I know you can."

"Thanks for the vote of confidence, Jilly. And for dinner." He inspected her offering. "I don't see enough little black flecks."

Jillian rolled her eyes. "Pepper is your department. Just don't overdo it, all right?"

"I don't conceive that as a possibility in the existing universe."

"Your taste buds live on steroids." Jillian tossed her sponge in the sink. "Do you want to make the dressing for the arugula?"

"Happy to." Nolan sprinkled pepper on the main dish and put it in the oven. "I arranged some help for you today."

Jillian cocked her head. "I wasn't aware I needed any help."

Nolan spun her around by the shoulders and marched her into the dining room. "Has it occurred to you that we have been unable to dine in this room for quite some time? That in fact it is becoming increasingly difficult even to traverse safely through on the way to the living room?"

"You can always go by way of the hall. I have it under control, Dad."

"I beg to differ."

Jillian scowled. Usually she kept her work contained to her office, which was right off the kitchen on the ground floor. Overflow files might temporarily occupy the two side chairs across from her desk, but not often for long. Many of her genealogical research projects required no physical files at all.

The St. Louis project was different. It involved hundreds of physical papers from the client dating back long before the internet was in everyone's house. It would take time to sort through what she had to work with and find credible starting points for all the genealogical trails the work involved. Files from decades ago rambled over the dining table and on half the chairs. Several stacks on the floor converged in a trail leading into the living room. But she knew generally what everything was and what she intended to do with it. Eventually.

"I have a system," she said. "I know how to do my job. This contract is just larger than most."

"Monstrously," Nolan said. "I know you plan to subcontract some of it out to other genealogists once you get a better grasp of what all is here, but don't you think you could use a teeny bit of administrative help on the front end?"

"Maybe." She wasn't persuaded. "I don't even know how I'd figure out what to pay someone. I'm still getting my head around the project."

"The beauty of my plan," Nolan said, "is you don't have to pay a penny."

"Oh no."

"What does that mean?"

"It means—*Dad!*"

"Aren't you getting a little old to use that suspicious tone?"

Jillian cleared her throat. "Would you like to explain?"

The doorbell rang.

"No time." Nolan headed for the front door. "She's here."

"Who's here?"

"Just give her a chance."

"Dad!"

He wagged a finger at her.

Nolan opened the door on one side of the spacious Victorian home that served as its main entrance. Jillian hung back, but she could see the figure on the porch.

A waif of a teenage girl, with bright pink hair, ripped cut-off shorts, and twigs for legs met Nolan's exuberant greeting with the deadpan expression of a comedic straight man.

This was help?

Surely she had a crate at her feet and was about to launch into a canned speech about how buying candy or magazine subscriptions would help underprivileged youth such as herself go to camp to develop leadership skills. Someone else would come to the door in response to Nolan's arrangement.

Instead, Nolan opened the door and welcomed the girl in.

No crate of items to sell.

"Jillian, this is Tisha Crowder."

"Hello." Jillian knew who she was—at least by sight—and who her mother was. Jenna Crowder was three years ahead of Jillian in school. Everyone knew her. She'd always been popular. Then the rumors started flying that she was pregnant even though she'd never had a steady boyfriend in Canyon Mines—that anyone knew about—and she was tight-lipped about who the baby's father was. But Jillian was a freshman and Jenna a senior, or would have been, when the baby was born. She'd dropped out. The rumors shifted to saying that she never told a single person who the child's father was. Not her mother. Not her best friend. Not her doctor. No one. Jillian didn't care. By the time Jenna had her baby, Jillian was mourning her mother. Speculating about another student she barely knew was the last thing on her mind.

Jenna kept the baby and continued living with her mother and grandmother. Over the years, the three women rotated through working in one Main Street shop or another, so their faces were familiar to everyone. Jillian always tried to ignore the gossip about why there were never any men in that family. Tisha's hair had been blue and then green before this summer's pink. Once it had even been half and half. Then there was the year she'd cut the hair on two sides of her head two different lengths.

It would be hard not to notice Tisha Crowder.

Jillian eyed Nolan. It was true her father could strike up a conversation with every stranger he met, but even for him it seemed a stretch to propose Tisha as an answer to Jillian's need for help.

Help she did not actually need and hadn't asked for and didn't want.

"Tisha is in a bit of a pickle," Nolan said. "She needs to do some volunteer hours between now and when school starts again in a few weeks."

"Oh?" Jillian looked from her father to the girl. "A school project of some sort?"

"No." Tisha blew a bubble with her gum and popped it, staring at Jillian all the while. It was as if she was reading off a script about how to fail a job interview.

Look like a punk. Check.

Wear inappropriate clothes. Check.

Seem uninterested. Check.

Display annoying habits. Check.

"Not school," Nolan said. "A legal matter."

Jillian returned her gaze to Nolan, feeling her eyebrows lift involuntarily.

"Why don't we sit down?" Nolan cleared a stack of yellow file folders from the purple chair where Jillian liked to sit. While she settled in, he sat beside Tisha on the navy sofa.

"Tisha pleaded guilty to shoplifting at a downtown Denver department store," Nolan said.

Tisha shrugged and muttered, "They had me on camera."

Undeterred, Nolan proceeded. "It was her first time in court, and the value of the item was low enough that she qualified for alternative sentencing. No one is interested in ruining a young person's life over one overpriced silk scarf."

Jillian tried to picture a silk scarf from a department store around the neck of Tisha Crowder. The mental image lacked coherence. Wouldn't a designer shirt or even a handbag make more sense? Or electronics?

"Her lawyer was someone whose services her mother once used, a long time ago."

"I see."

"I know him from family court connections. It's pro bono all around. When he saw Tisha had a legal address in Canyon Mines," Nolan said, "he reached out to me to see if I would be willing to supervise something."

"I'm sorry, I don't follow," Jillian said. "Supervise?"

"Tisha needs some sort of structured community service or volunteer work experience over the summer to meet the terms of her alternative sentencing. Doing it in Denver isn't practical. We're already past the fourth of July. Half the summer is gone. The rest will go fast. If she completes her hours successfully and stays out of more serious trouble for the next twelve months, the incident will go off her record. Happily I knew somebody who could use an extra pair of eyes and hands for a few weeks."

Oh Dad oh Dad oh Dad. You've got to be kidding.

"Tisha," Jillian said, "do you have any work experience?"

"Nah." She smacked her gum and crossed her bare legs, letting a yellow flip-flop dangle from one big toe.

"Tisha just turned fifteen," Nolan said, "so she would have needed a work permit. But I had quite a lengthy conversation with her case worker, and she is confident of Tisha's abilities."

And what abilities are those?

In response to a buzz, Tisha pulled an iPhone several models newer than Jillian's from her back pocket and began texting. Where did she get the money for that? Or had she bypassed cash in the manner in which she acquired it?

Monosyllabic responses. Check.

No prior experience. Check.

Text during interview. Check.

"What kinds of things are you interested in?" Jillian asked. "Do you like history?"

"History?" Tisha didn't look up from her phone. "Not really."

"Do you have computer skills?"

"Duh. Internet native generation."

Jillian glared at Nolan. Tisha didn't look up.

"Are you good at sorting information into files?"

"Don't know. Never tried."

"Tisha needs about fifteen hours a week for the rest of the summer," Nolan said. "That sounds right, doesn't it, Tisha?"

"I guess." Tisha finally shoved her phone back in her pocket.

"We can make up some kind of a time sheet. It doesn't have to be the same three hours a day, as long as it comes out to fifteen every week. And this week we need to make up for missing today."

"So you're thinking we'd start tomorrow? Tuesday?" Jillian said.

"Can you think why not?"

"Kris might need some extra help down at the ice cream shop. She hires teenagers," Jillian said. "And summer housekeeping is always busy for Nia at the Inn. She takes on extra people for the season. We could check around for something we're sure is the best fit for Tisha's skills."

"Every plan should always be open to adjustments, of course," Nolan said, "but I'd like to see us give this a chance before we reevaluate. You could really use some help in an immediate way."

He pointed toward the dining room, and Jillian's gaze followed his finger.

So you brought me a juvenile delinquent who clearly doesn't want to be here?

ABOUT THE AUTHOR

Olivia Newport's novels blend the truths of where we find ourselves now with insights into what carried us in the past. Enjoying life with her husband and nearby grown children, she chases joy in stunning Colorado at the foot of Pikes Peak.